FOR WANT OF A HORSE

TWENTY-THREE TALES OF
SUPERNATURAL STALLIONS,
MAGICAL MARES AND
PARANORMAL PONIES

EDITED BY
EVEY BRETT

LETHE PRESS
MAPLE SHADE, NEW JERSEY

Published by LETHE PRESS
118 Heritage Ave, Maple Shade, NJ 08052
lethepressbooks.com

Full short story publishing history
continued at the rear of the book.

ISBN 9781590215623

Cover and Interior design
by INKSPIRAL DESIGN

CONTENTS

DEDICATION

To my girl Carrma, Lipizzan mare extraordinare

And to all my horse teachers:

Ichobod, Sport, Junior, Ms. Bianca, Ginger,

Gus, Frosty, Capria, Khepera, Pooka,

Pandora, Camilla, Ephiny, Tia and Gabriella.

And in loving memory of Gary.

The dude abides.

INTRODUCTION
EVEY
BRETT

WHEN I THINK OF SUPERNATURAL HORSES, THE FIRST IMAGE THAT COMES to mind is the ghostly mare in Disney's *Darby O'Gill and the Little People* who whickers in apparent glee as she pushes Darby down the well into the realm of the Leprechauns. Later, a spectral horse-drawn carriage comes to whisk Darby away. In real life, however, I found a different sort of magic with horses.

I didn't grow up a horse girl, craving a pony in the backyard or showing a horse in the arena. The only time I rode was on a patient old gelding nicknamed Frog one year at summer camp. Then, when I was thirty, I met Carrma, a Lipizzan brood mare who'd been a mother, grandmother and auntie to a number of babies. I saw her, and just knew we were meant for each other.

Carrma has fantastical forebears going back for generations. She comes from a line that narrowly escaped the ravages of World War Two thanks to General Patton's rescue. Her sire, the noted Maestoso Africa, survived a deadly flood by swimming to safety, and at the famed Spanish Riding School, her cousins can almost fly when they perform the Airs Above the Ground. Ask anyone who knows Carrma, and they'll tell you that she has a habit of arranging the universe to her liking, even if it means making a certain gullible human move from one state to another to serve her every whim.

Many of the stories in this volume feature horses performing equally fantastic feats either alone or with their human companions. Some equines are helpful, like James Baldwin's tales of Griffen, Pegasus, Sleipnir, and Al Borak, who take their riders on wondrous journeys, while in D. H. Lawrence's "The Rocking Horse Winner," a boy goes on one desperate ride after another in an attempt to save his family.

Other horses are constructed as things of wonder, such as the title character in "The Horse of Brass" and the creation of a girl who dreams of bringing horses to Mars in Beth Cato's "Red Dust and Dancing Horses"

There are light-hearted tales, such as L. Frank Baum's "Jack Pumpkinhead and the Sawhorse," and the Grimm brothers' "The Fox and the Horse." Men fear the unexplainable in spectral tales like Washington Irving's "The Devil and Tom Walker" and Ambrose Bierce's "Horseman in the Sky," while the horse becomes a thing to terrify in both "The Goblin Pony" and Renee Carter Hall's "Horseman."

"Ivan and the Chestnut Horse" involves a boy seeking his true love. "The Black Horse, Dapplegrim" and "The Magician's Horse" also feature young men who enlist the aid of a talking steed that guides him through one quest or another to get the girl, though in "The Goose Girl," it's a displaced princess who aided by her loyal horse, Falada.

Man's tampering with a horse's nature leads to disastrous consequences in Cynthia Seelhammer's "Gentle Horses." A little kindness earns great rewards in both "The Dun Pony" and my own original story, "Rafael," in which a priest learns to accept his gifts with the aid of his equine companions. Some horses are merely being true to themselves, as in Kate Chopin's "Ti Démon" and Deborah J. Ross's "Hero of Abarxia," in which an aged king discovers the true hero at the end of the war has four legs instead of two.

The stories included here come from all over the world, including Russia, France, Germany, Greece, Native America and beyond. Some are fairy and folk tales, others are classics, one is original to this volume and four are reprints from within the last sixteen years. It was quite an adventure searching for and collecting these diverse tales.

As for Carrma, well, she's retired and quite happy to hang out in the barn and chat with her horse friends when she's not dragging her human around from one patch of grass to another. But if she could talk (and who says she can't?) I'm sure she'd tell you to hang on tight and enjoy the ride.

Evey Brett
Tucson, Arizona

GENTLE HORSES
CYNTHIA SEELHAMMER

DIANE SLOWED THE ELECTRIC CAR AND EXAMINED THE CALM YEARLINGS grazing in the paddocks that bordered the drive leading to Equigenics stable. Most were bays or chestnuts, clean-lined and healthy looking, if a little eerie in their stillness. She was impressed and a bit surprised to find that this relatively new genetic engineering operation included nearly a hundred acres of irrigated fields and pastures as well as the modern stable and arenas.

Her first job interview, by vidphone, had left her with the impression that Equigenics was little more than a start-up business, just a riding academy with maybe an old barn, a lab in the garage and a handful of horses. The director, Len Malcolm, had emphasized the need for someone willing to do "hands-on dirty work." He needed someone to run the stable and manage riding lessons, but he wanted someone who knew the science as well. It sounded exactly like what she needed: way too much work and responsibility, enough to absorb her completely and force her to forget everything else. And, better yet, it would be a return to the world of horses. It seemed that most the recent wrong turns in her life had started when she left that world for university research. That turn in the road of life, like her marriage, had led to a deadend. So now, after three months of unemployment, Diane was determined to get this job.

She parked the car, stepped out onto the gravel lot and squinted in the sharp sunlight. She shaded her eyes and watched an impatient looking woman urge two little girls wearing riding clothes into the back seat of an expensive propane sedan. The sight made her smile a little wryly, it was so familiar. How many hundreds of times had her mother shuttled her to riding lessons? For a time it had seemed as if she might follow her mother's example and be the one doing the shuttling. But not anymore.

As the sedan drove away, Diane followed it with her eyes, watching it disappear behind the low, rolling hills where the road curved back toward the wealthier suburbs of the city. The green of the fenced fields and the tan of the distant hills, calmed her. She took a deep breath and headed for the office.

Len Malcolm in person was as abrupt and no-nonsense as he had been on the vidphone. He was clean shaven and his dark hair was trimmed short. He wore very plain clothes. He shook her hand with precisely the appropriate amount of pressure; this was a man used to control. She felt her own emotions rise a notch in response and had to squelch the desire to say something outrageous. She doubted that this man had any sense of humor.

Len did not look at her when he spoke. Instead, he seemed to talk just past her head, never making eye contact. He acted as if her were irritated by her very presence. Diane tried to ignore it. After some brief, uncomfortable small talk came a tour of the facility. They would continue the interview when they returned to the office, Len said.

In the arena, two of the advanced students were practicing jumps. They rode grays with identical programming -- and it showed in the way the horses approached each jump. Diane recognized the physical type of the horses from some of the cataloging she had done at the university: a common Irish hunter line. The source of the viral programming was not familiar to her. But then that was the specialty of Equigenics -- tailoring programming of knowledge with viruses.

She and Len leaned against the arena rail and watched the grays canter, each hoof kicking up a puff of dust, the horses grunting when they jumped. One of the riders was less skilled than the other; when she sat too fast, she threw off the balance of her horse and there was a loud thunk as the left rear hoof knocked off the top rail.

On the walk back, Diane saw grooms distribute alfalfa cubes to the box stalls of the breeding stock. Three stalls were empty, the horses turned out into paddocks while their stalls were cleaned. The smells of the feed and manure brought back memories. It smelled like home.

Len narrated the tour in abrupt announcements of fact. He pointed out things that anyone who had spent any time at all in a stable would know. Diane nodded politely.

"Arion is the center of the current research," Len said as they turned the corner toward the most isolated of the box stalls. For the first time, his stony face showed some expression: a combination of pride and something else, something like lust. When he noticed her watching him, the expression vanished. But she had seen it and it reminded her of her exhusband when he used to speak about the mindgames he played on those who competed with him for research dollars.

Diane followed his gaze. The stall had reinforced bars and an industrial strength door. At first she could not see into the gloom behind the bars. Something moved in that dark, something breathed, but she could not make out a shape until her eyes adjusted.

The stallion was taller than was usual, at least eighteen hands. He stood in the far corner and watched them, crunching the hay cubes, his finely boned head tilted to one side so he could watch them with one too-intelligent eye, both sharp-pointed ears straining forward to catch Len's voice.

Arion was black. Very black. Not dark bay, not a coat that faded to gray or seal brown or that would fade in the sun, but so black that the light reflected from his coat looked blue; a fantasy color that immediately identified him as a designed horse. The horse snorted and took the few steps to the door, lifting his nose to the grate. Diane moved forward, pressing her palm on the other side and gently blew into the horse's nose, trading breath. The stallion snorted and backed up. Diane turned and looked at Len. "Nice."

Len narrowed his eyes. "You have no idea." He walked back toward the office.

Diane felt a stab of embarrassment, quickly squelched by anger. "So tell me," she said, walking fast to catch up with him. "I can't appreciate what I don't know."

"He is not just some pretty genetic package. He is programmed at championship level," Len said, slowing down slightly.

"Okay. So where's he competed?"

"He hasn't -- yet. I plan to start him in the fall. When I find the right rider." He stopped and turned toward her. "Listen, I think you've seen enough. I'll call you if I want to talk to you again."

Diane felt as if she had been dismissed. She stopped walking. "Wait just a minute," she said. "That's it? That's the interview?" She felt herself grow tense with rage. "What kind of a..."

A crash interrupted her, then a horse's scream. "Arion," Len shouted and ran back toward the stall, Diane one step behind him.

The stallion stood trembling at the back of the stall, one rear leg still in the air, ready to kick. There was a gouge in the wall from an earlier kick. He shook his head and bared his teeth, crashing both rear hooves at the stall wall, the impact so severe it shook the wall.

A groom ran to Len with a med kit and a palm-sized trank gun. Len shoved him out of the way, yanked open the big latch on the stall door and shouldered his way in. Arion paced in tight circles, pawing straw and striking the wall with rear hooves. Len slid the heavy door closed behind him.

Diane watched through the door's metal screen as Len whispered to the horse. The stallion was backed into a corner now, head high, nostrils flared, white foam of sweat along his arched neck and wide chest. The groom cursed in Spanish behind her. He called Arion a devil horse.

Whatever Len was doing seemed to be working; Arion lowered his head and calmed his breathing.

"Diane." Len spoke in the same calming tone, but he gestured slowly toward her without turning his head. She slid the door open enough to squeeze into the stall and walked up behind Len. Arion snorted and jerked his head up; she froze.

"Talk to him," Len said. "He's the most important part of this operation. He's going to be your responsibility, if you're good enough."

"I'm good enough," she said. "I have years of experience in training, stable management and I just left a research position...." Arion snorted again, rolled an eye, and began to shift his weight.

"Shut up," Len said in the same soothing voice he'd been using on the horse. "Just shut the fuck up and talk to the horse. Tell him what a beauty he is, what a technological wonder, how you will ride him, how he is going to make us all famous. He doesn't give a shit about your degrees or experience."

Diane felt herself blush, a heat that crawled up her neck to her face. She was about to turn and leave when Len added "...or aren't you good enough, after all?"

She took another step forward and began to prattle in a calm tone, words from lullabies, sound that ran from her toward the stallion. She reached to touch the horse and he let her caress his neck. She felt something like electricity between them; it flowed up her arm and she knew she had the stallion's complete attention. He stretched his big head toward her and sniffed loudly. She blew into the wide nostrils. He was a beautiful animal and all her thoughts focused on his large, dark eyes. She forgot about Len except to notice he was no longer in the stall. She talked to the stallion until he was completely calm and his head leaned against her shoulder. By then it was dark outside.

That should show the bastard, she thought as she slipped out of the stall.

She moved into the empty apartment above the stable the next day. And she got the pay she asked for.

THE NEXT WEEK, THE NIGHT THAT THE TWO NEW BREEDING MARES arrived, Arion had another episode. The mares were in the box stalls as far from Arion as possible. But that night the stallion could smell them, hear them nicker to him, feel their heat, sense their raised tails and winking vulvas. When he started to kick the walls, the crashing woke Diane. She ran out of her apartment in her night-clothes to find Len was already at Arion's stall.

Len moved the mares one at a time to pens just outside the barn, disappearing into the night as soon as he stepped outside. Diane stood in the stall next to Arion's, talking soothing nonsense in the gloom, fingers hooked into the steel screening. The stallion's frustration came in waves, an invisible heat flashing across her skin. Then Len walked up behind her and she could sense him, just as Arion had sensed the mares. She heard the crisp sound of crushed new straw as he approached. Arion was suddenly still. She didn't turn toward Len, didn't even think; he put one hand over hers on the screen, the other around her waist. She felt his weight, heavy as the silence, and his breath on the tender skin between her collar and hairline. She pressed into Len, all of her back and hips curved against him. Len pushed his face to her neck, nipping her with soft lips. She turned toward him and lifted her arms. He held her and rocked gently back and forth. She twined a leg around him and he lowered her to the deep straw, lay beside her and lowered his head to her breasts. She ran her fingers through his hair in short, hard motions.

The rest of the horses were oblivious to their movements in the straw, but Arion breathed in harsh, nervous gasps. A small voice in Diane's mind objected, but she was so filled with longing that she only gasped, matching the sound of the stallion. She fumbled with the snaps of Len's shirt and felt him tense and pull away from her. He pushed himself to his feet and walked from the stall fast, his boots clicking on the flooring of the alley. Diane sat up and wondered what the hell had happened.

Her mother called too early that morning, awake and cheerful in another time zone. What had happened in the night with Len came back to Diane with a rush. He had all but run away from her.

"You sound tired," her mother said.

"It's four a.m.," Diane growled.

"Is it? I always forget how that works. Your father's in Rio with his latest `friend.' He says hello and congratulations on your first real job, but he wishes you would have let him find you something better. He could have helped you get something permanent at the university, you know. How are things?"

"I don't know yet," Diane said, thinking how she would never again put up with the politics at the university, politics she had failed at. And she hoped she would never have to ask her father to pull strings for her. But what could she tell her mother about this place, or about Len? Not a thing.

"It's really busy here, Mom," she said. "Everyone wants foals born just after the first of the year, so all the mares are being implanted now. And we still have to run all the riding lessons."

"Are you sure this is the right kind of job? I know you feel you need to prove something after the trouble at school, but..."

"Mom. You promised."

"Well, I can't help it. You had every advantage here and you just... Divorce is not the worst thing in the world, you know. And the loss of that research project was not your fault, you were just the one easiest to blame. None of that matters. But you sound sad. I can't believe you don't have a vidphone. What kind of place is that?"

Diane thought about what she could possibly say that would reassure her mother. "It's a start-up, Mom. My boss is...brilliant. But I don't really know him at all."

"What's his name?"

"Len Malcolm."

"Malcolm? I don't know any Malcolms. It's not like he owns the place, is it? Your father said it's a corporate operation."

"It's not corporate -- yet. This is just a little place with a couple of investors. But Len's got some corporation interested. He owns the stud that's going to be used as a source. He helped design him. If this new line makes it, he'll be able to have his own place. It's a big risk."

"Then he should be careful. I always told your father to be careful. He never listened to me though. If this Malcolm succeeds, he won't need you anymore, right? Maybe you can come home then, and settle down."

"I'm not moving back there, Mom. And if he succeeds, maybe I'll be part of the success." If I can stick it out, Diane thought. If I don't go crazy.

THAT NIGHT, AFTER A LONG DAY OF WORK WITH GROOMS AND TEACHING staff and watching the progress of little girls in pigtails, Diane stopped in the office to look through the e-mail. She half hoped Len would stop by so they could talk, but he stayed in his lab, as usual. Later, on the way to her apartment, she was drawn to the stall of each of the motionless brood mares. She touched their velvet muzzles, the prickle of whiskers like the stubble of an unshaved lover. She pushed forelocks from deep brown eyes, scratched around ears, and whispered into the long, smooth necks, inhaling the smell of spring grasses, salt, and autumn straw.

Len found her with the mare nearest Arion. He stood behind Diane and reached over her shoulder to run his hand down the mare's smooth withers and across the intricate whorl of hair along a flank. With his other hand he stroked the back of Diane's head, the arch of her neck, and brushed salty fingers gently across her lips. She wondered, just faintly and for a fleeting moment, why she was doing this, why Len, why they had not spoken of it. Arion snorted and pawed with a forefoot, sharp punctuation to his ragged breathing. Then all her conscious thoughts vanished, replaced with longing, desire, need.

The next morning, except for the bruises on her hips and the fragment of straw in her hair, Diane would have thought she had dreamed it.

"WHILE I'M GONE, STICK TO THE SCHEDULE."

Len was packing his briefcase for a shuttle to Dallas to judge a week-long dressage competition. There was talk that one of the contenders was worth considering for sourcing. Len wanted to check him out and compare him to Arion. "Make no changes, got it? And keep an eye on that Cunningham kid."

Diane had been called into the office for this briefing. It was the first time they had talked face to face since the interview. He usually just left her e-mail and locked himself in his lab with orders not to be disturbed.

And when they met at night, there was no talk.

"That kid could be trouble," Len said. "She's on some kind of scholarship and the other students don't like her."

"I thought she was doing okay, that we had all the right horses and right programs for all the riders."

"She's riding fine, but keep her away from Arion. I caught her at his stall this morning when I went to exercise him. I told her to stay away, that he could be dangerous. He's not like the mares she rides."

"Maybe she's just curious."

Len looked up from the briefcase for a second, eyes a startling and angry flash of blue, then back down. He pushed a handful of folders into a side pocket. "I'm serious. I don't want her, or any of the others, near him. Only you."

"She's dropped off here really early and she stays all day. If the other students don't like her she probably gets bored. Why are you so touchy?"

Len shrugged. He zipped the briefcase shut.

Diane wanted to scream Why won't you look at me? Talk to me? Instead she took a deep breath and said softly: "Is it this trip? What's wrong?"

"No, this trip is important. The Texas breeders are important. It's the timing of it. Keeping everything constant is essential. You're sure you're ready for the viral transfers?"

"All I do is run the programs, right? It's not a big deal. Don't worry."

"I always worry," he said. "That's one of the secrets to success in this business."

FIVE HORSES WALKED NOSE TO TAIL ALONG THE RAIL OF THE INDOOR arena, moving in and out of dusty pools of light cast by spots hidden in the high ceiling. Little girls, backs very straight, hands held low, sat atop them. The horses moved at a regular, patient gait, gazing straight ahead. Two were bays, one with a cropped mane; one gray; one chestnut with white pasterns and a blaze; and the last was spotted, a black-and-white paint. Except for the rhythmic motion of legs and bobbing heads, the horses and small riders could have been from an old-fashioned carousel, spinning in slow motion with no music.

Beginner classes require patience, Diane thought as she watched the students and their teacher. Not patience on the part of these pampered girls in their jewel- and pastel-colored clothes, sitting so high up the backs of such immense animals. The teacher, standing in the center of the ring, turning to watch the riders, needed the patience. There was no possibility of any unexpected action. The mares were walking wombs, nothing more: perfect practice mounts, so placid there was sometimes a risk that health problems would be overlooked. Making sure nothing was overlooked was part of Diane's job.

Diane's thoughts drifted. What did these students feel? Diane tried to remember from her early lessons but she realized it didn't compare.

Confident. That's how they would feel. Confident that they looked good and would soon learn enough to try one of the horses programmed with a more complex riding program. In a couple of years they would own their own top-of-the-line mounts, bring home ribbons and trophies enough to fill fireplace mantels, and fulfill parental expectations and financial investments. Then they would move on, train in dressage or jumping, or lose interest in riding and study etiquette or gymnastics, prepare for the cotillion, the grand tour, the next season's coming-out event.

The monied class was grasping at past symbols of privilege, staying "pure," as if doing so would stop changes in the world. The families of these girls guarded them every bit as much as they did their homes with their interactive security systems and their walled, guarded communities. After these lessons, and other rites of passage, these girls would make the financially correct marriage, conceive the appropriate number of heirs, and nurture the next generation of monied little girls to take riding lessons. Diane realized that the girls might not be that different from the very gentle mares they were riding. After all, they were bred and programmed for one purpose, weren't they? Maybe that was unfair. The same thing could have been said about her.

The difference was that she had managed to escape and build her own life. Or at least she was trying to, even if it meant a false start or two.

Besides, her history was not quite the same as that of the little girls'. Yes, she came from the same class and background. But the horses Diane learned to ride hadn't been programmed at all. How had she felt when she rode? Excited. Knowing that the thousand-kilo animal she was learning to control had a mind of its own and could choose to obey or not, to throw her off and run away, or to execute the turn she was trying for, making her look as if she were the one in charge.

The teacher clapped her hands and the five horses stopped and stood still, not even an ear twitching. The girls dismounted, four from tiny English saddles, slithering off as if from a playground slide. The fifth, on the paint, swung her right leg over the back of the horse and dropped from a western saddle. She was much taller than the others and wore creamy buckskin chaps, a fringed shirt and bolero. The other four girls wore brilliant jodhpurs with silk tops, soft black knee-high boots and velvet-covered hard hats. Two carried riding crops.

Once they stood in the sand of the ring floor, these four began to chatter among themselves; they took the reins and led their horses out of the ring into the main part of the barn. Two of the girls were so small they could almost walk right underneath the horses. Their voices were chirps in the immense arena, distorted and lost in the soft sand and high, dark ceilings. The horses followed the girls with careful, patient steps.

Diane watched the four who rode English. The girl in the chaps trailed behind. She was Vita Cunningham, but Diane could never remember which of the other four girls was which. She thought of them by the horses they rode, using the mares' code names or file numbers from their lip tattoos. The horses' histories, bloodlines, tailoring and programming she knew in exact detail. They were the purest of traditional strains, no cross-genre or constructs here.

The two bays were Beta 8 and 9, genetically identical, a combination of the Dublin and Kodaka lines, considered state-of-the-art six years ago, now rumored to be susceptible to colic or founder toward end of term. Diane had notes to watch them closely when the time came. The gray Cosmo came from a knock-off Arabian splicer and she was old, but had a good record. The chestnut Gusto 24 was carrying her first foal and had no record, but others with similar combinations had good reports. The paint was Navajo, some kind of personal preference of Len's, Kodaka genes wrapped in Indian pony coloring. A horse from his northern Arizona ranch childhood or something. He never explained anything. All five were programmed for maximum stability, basic brood mare traits, and beginner riding lessons.

Diane followed the black-and-white paint down the immaculate alley and turned right, toward the box stalls, to do a visual check. One mare stood in a corner of its stall, chewing hay cubes from a feeder. The others hung their heads over the stall door into the alley, the flutter of eyelashes and breath from nostrils their only movement, eyes black and motionless. The girls groomed their beginner mares, each horse cross-tied in front of its stall. Diane stopped to watch the girls as they stretched and ducked, using soft brushes and hard currycombs to groom their horses.

"You have to finish intermediate, then you can ride a jumper," Diane heard the girl from the gray say. She was brushing a foreleg. "It took my sister two years."

"Some people go faster," Vita said. She stood near the paint's head, fiddling with the bit on the bridle. Her hair hung down to hide her face. Her hands were large, nails chewed short. "If you have the right program and the right horse, you can learn faster."

"That's stupid. You still have to learn all the levels. And as you advance, you change horses to one with more advanced programming."

"Yeah, and if you want to compete, you have to prove you did them all," said the girl from the chestnut.

"I heard that it used to be if you rode the same horse all the time, you got so good you could read each other's mind."

"That's stupid, too. If you rode the same horse all the time then both you and the horse would have to learn everything and it would take twice as long." She looked around at Diane. "Right, Ms. Newton?"

Diane thought about how she learned. "It used to take a long time," she said. "People lost interest, it took so long. It was dangerous too."

"But that's the way you learned." Vita tilted her head so her hair fell across one eye. "With just one horse."

"Yes. A thoroughbred gelding." She remembered the sense of victory when she'd finally gained control of him, making him do just what she wanted when she wanted.

"Could you read his mind?" There was longing in Vita's voice.

"No." Not really, no matter how much she had wished for it. "But when you ride well, it looks that way." Felt that way, too.

"Staying with one horse would be boring anyway," said the girl with the gray.

Diane left them and went to Arion's stall.

The stallion was near the door, looking through his screen which was closed so he couldn't put his head out. Couldn't risk having some student getting bitten, after all. The barred window on the far wall painted a square of morning sunlight onto the golden straw and black lacquer of Arion's chest and forelegs.

When he saw Diane, the horse shook his head, black mane tumbling from one side of his long neck to the other, and took a step back out of the sunlight. For a second she felt a flash of fear. Any stallion was unpredictable. Arion stretched his neck toward the screen, nostrils wide, breathing with a huffing sound. She thought of Len, a quick stab of heat in her belly. She pressed her palm against the screen. "Hey, boy, it's okay, shhh." Arion's nose nearly touched her hand, a fine soft gray blending to black. There would be parties in Dallas, and trade shows with corporate breeders. What would Len be doing tonight? Arion jerked his head back. He pawed the straw. Why did she care? Diane walked off toward the office.

THAT EVENING DIANE SPENT A FRUSTRATING HALF-HOUR IN HER

apartment trying to reason on the phone with the mother of one of the riding students, a woman who was convinced that her daughter was a genius and should progress faster than the others. The call had interrupted dinner. The stir-fry cooled and her appetite sank as her anger rose. When she hung up the phone, after agreeing to meet with the woman later in the week, she accidently kicked the saddle stand, tripped, and fell onto the couch. She pounded her fists on the couch cushion in frustration.

Crashing sounds from the stable interrupted her fit of temper. She raced down the stairs, headed straight for Arion. As she neared the stall, her heart pounding, the screen above the door flew open with the sound of shrieking metal. Arion continued to kick, using both back feet, making strangled noises of rage. Diane thought about using the intercom to call some of the grooms from their trailers. Someone would get hurt if she did, she knew it. She scuttled along the alley as far from Arion as possible and went to the lab for the trank gun.

LEN WOKE HER EARLY IN THE MORNING, CALLING FROM DALLAS, HIS VOICE lost in the noise of a party.

"How is everything?"

"What?" Dreams of flight still clouded her mind, images of deserts, skies the color of flame. Her legs tangled in the sheets. She had slept so soundly she had trouble waking.

"How is Arion acting?"

"Fine, everything is fine." She yawned and tried to remember what she had meant to tell him.

She heard laughter and shouting. Music blared loud and faded again. "...revolution," someone said. A woman's shrill voice said, "They'd pay millions!" Len said nothing.

"Where are you? It sounds like a party." Diane asked.

"It is, sort of. It's the investors. I have to go but I wanted to make sure everything was okay. We might have some important visitors when I get back."

"Everything's fine," Diane said. "Good luck."

The conversation ended. She realized as she hung up that he'd said nothing to her, not really. He'd just been checking in with the office.

At dawn, when she got up despite a foggy headache, she realized she had forgotten to tell him about Arion and the smashed stall door. She pulled on jeans and a soft, warm shirt, and walked down the stairs to the stable, through the tender sounds of the mares sleeping, their dreams as blank as their eyes.

In the lab she made a cup of very strong coffee and looked through the latest readouts. Test results showed an anomaly in the hormone levels of the two Beta bays. She checked the file cabinet for copies of their levels from last year, but she couldn't find them. She wondered if Len had them in his lab. As she headed in that direction she felt a stab of guilt. She ignored it. After all, he had never exactly ordered her not to go into the lab.

The place was smaller than she remembered from the brief tour. A computer console and a row of file cabinets lined one wall. The rest of the space was taken up by the thermo-cycler on a table in the center, the walk-in refrigerator and shelves of carefully labeled beakers, flasks and milk bottles. She headed for the file cabinet. All the drawers were locked.

She was about to leave when she noticed the row of bound printouts stacked next to the console screen. The corner of a file folder stuck out beside one of them. She slid it out and found it filled with clippings and hardcopies about the stable.

She looked through the clips, reading things she already knew about the operation. Others were about Len Malcolm: his scholarships and research awards when he was young, his work with Kodaka on the Falk hunter. One clipping from a small town paper in Arizona described his graduate degrees. She read that with interest. One early thesis was titled Exploration of Recessive Nature of Sensitive Traits Among Highly Trained Performance Horses. Another was Field Observations of Stallion Dominance in Wild Mustang Herds. Another was Marketing Progressive Lessons Through the Use of Incremental Program Changes.

She closed the file and started to slide it back where she had found it. She paused and pulled open one of the bound printouts.

Records of some experiments, she noted. Careful descriptions of the effect of various dosages on test subjects. The dates were recent and it looked as if a new subjects had been added. She knew some horses required drugs to be made susceptible to programming with viruses. She could not tell which horses were the subjects of these tests; the names were in some kind of code.

Diane sighed, put the book back and left the lab. She made a note to herself to talk to Len about the mare's hormone levels -- and about these tests. If one of the brood mares was being drugged, she needed to know it.

ARION WAS QUIET WHEN DIANE CHECKED HIM, AN HOUR BEFORE THE beginner class. Vita was peering over the stall door at him, but she disappeared around a corner as soon as she saw Diane approach. The stallion stood in the center of his stall, legs braced outward and head hanging toward the straw. He reminded Diane of the brood mares. She ordered the door repaired and reduced his feed. That might help keep him calm.

LEN RETURNED WITH CONTRACTS SECURED FOR MOST OF THE UNBORN foals. He had arranged preliminary distribution rights with the new dressage source. He should have been jubilant, but he was distant. Diane had reports on fetal development and hormone levels waiting for him, but he didn't even look at them.

"How is Arion?" was his first question.

"He was almost unmanageable a couple times, but he's fine now. I changed his feed."

"What?" His face hardened and he stared at her with narrowed eyes.

"I reduced the calories. There's no need for him to be hyped up all the time now."

"I told you -- no changes while I was gone. Change it back. Kodaka is sending a team here to look at him. They're bringing a mare too. I want him like he was before I left, right on the edge, ready for breeding. This is important."

"Why?"

"Just do it."

THE KODAKA MARE ARRIVED IN THE NIGHT; LEN TOOK CARE OF SETTLING her into a stall himself. This visit had to be kept very quiet, Len told Dianer; too many students were around and information traveled way too fast. Diane never saw the people who brought the mare, but when they left, Len went with them.

That night Diane dreamed of roaring sounds, twisting motions, burning flames, and woke to find herself visiting the mares again. She'd been asleep but now she stood barefoot in the straw. She could hear Arion squealing. She longed for something, fought desire, felt waves of heat. She forced herself back to the stairs and up to her apartment. She sat on the floor, back against the door, knees curled to her chest, waiting for daylight. She could not define the turmoil she felt, did not know what she needed. She suffered passion soaring and falling. But there was fear most of all.

AT DAWN DIANE DRESSED SLOWLY, HER HANDS SHAKING AS SHE PULLED on her boots. She went down the stairs to the stallion's stall, her steps loud in the quiet.

Vita stood in front of the stall door, on tiptoes, fingers curled into the screen. Arion faced her, making low, rough sounds. The girl did not move.

There was a sound from the stall across from Arion and Diane saw the new mare, black as cinders, circling, rubbing up against the door and screen of her stall. No placid brood mare, she snorted and struck out, turning fast. Vita turned too, first to one side, then the other, pressing herself against the stall door. The mare pawed the straw. Vita moaned.

Diane felt the heat from all the nights, frustration and longing filling her mind, stretching into her soul. She took a step forward. The stallion rumbled. The mare squealed. Vita echoed the sound, thin and sharp.

No, no, this is wrong, Diane thought. I am in control, you obey me. She remembered the gelding she first learned to ride, his sly movements, testing her. She remembered the feel of Len pressed against her, the feel of the sharp blades of straw against her back. The mare squealed again, turning to kick at the stall door. Vita cried out.

Diane realized she was panting. She wrapped her hands around the handle of the nearest stall door, her nails digging into the wood.

Len had done this. This was the secret, the horse to replace all the programmed steps, the horse that would change the industry. One horse, not just programmed, but linked to its rider. So closely linked that when Arion was tranquilized, she had felt tranquilized too. But who would be in control?

He had experimented on her, testing Arion's abilities, observing them just like he'd watched the wild mustangs, noting dominance and control. She took deep breaths, focused on her anger. Arion whirled in his stall, facing her. The window glowed behind him, soft light silhouetting his head and neck. He shouted a challenge, head up, leaping a stiff step forward.

She felt her anger grow, her legs relax. She sidled past the stalls, step by step, headed for the lab. The trank gun was there, and the other things she would need. She would be in control.

Arion shrieked another challenge behind her. She felt her anger grow and used it to fire her determination. She began to count loudly inside her mind, blocking out all emotion. One, two, three... She carried the gun back to the mare, pushing Vita aside as she did so. The girl stumbled and fell.

Diane set the gun to the highest level, aimed through the grill, and shot the mare three time. She kept counting in her mind, four, five, six... The mare grunted, then grew still, and collapsed like a string puppet into the straw. Diane felt the tension fall, as if a window had closed. Then she sensed fear from Arion, then rage.

There was a choking sound from Vita. The girl was scrambling to her feet, growling in fury, seven, eight, nine... Diane set the gun to it's lowest level and shot Vita, the dart hitting the girl in the front of her thigh. Vita stumbled, leaned against the stall door and slid to the floor, ten, eleven, twelve...

Diane stood and looked at the stallion. He was so enraged that he shuddered as he stood. This was no horse, this was a mind-controlling evil. This animal had no right to exist, to dominate the minds of people around it. He was the pinnacle of Len's research, but he was wrong, all wrong. All the breeding and programming, it was a mistake. It had to be ended.

She tucked the trank gun into the oversized pocket of her jacket. But still, all that programming, all the pain she had been through... Would it all be wasted? No. She headed for the tack room to collect bridle and saddle. Before Arion was destroyed, she would ride him.

She grew calm with the certainty. She visualized herself saddling a calm horse and concentrated on the image. She carried the tack toward the now silent stall where the stallion stood waiting for her.

She opened the stall door and left it open, stepping into the straw. She avoided looking at the horse's head. I have no emotions but calm, she thought as she mechanically lifted the saddle onto the stallion's back. He flinched, but did not step away. I have no emotions, just steady progress, she thought to herself and began to again count in her mind, one, two, three... She reached under his belly for the cinch and pulled it tight in one swift movement, four, five, six... Then she took the bridle from her shoulder and, without making eye contact, slide the bit into Arion's mouth and the leather over his ears, buckling the strap under his jaw, seven, eight, nine...

She put her hands onto his withers and with one jump, she was on her stomach across his back, ten, eleven, twelve... She swung her right leg over and searched for the stirrups with her feet as she ducked her head and directed the horse out of the stall. She felt Arion tremble beneath her, sensed his confusion. She visualized the paddock in front of the stable. She concentrated hard and turned the horse toward the door, one, two, three...

The door opened and Len stepped inside. Arion stopped dead. Diane forgot what number came next.

"What the hell are you doing?" Len shouted.

Arion began to tremble violently. He tried to turn his head but Diane corrected him with a jerk of the rein.

"Get out of my way," Diane said, suddenly more angry than afraid, feeling her emotion begin to mix with that of Arion.

Len ran a few steps toward them. The horse took a fast step back and hopped to the side. Len grabbed for the rein, but the horse shied away.

"Get off! Right now, get off!" He grabbed again for the rein, but Arion took two fast steps backwards. Diane had sensed the move and was able to keep her balance. She felt the horse as if he were an extension of her own body.

For a second she imagined herself with Len, at night in the stall. She viewed the scene, and herself, from above and behind. She sensed the control that Len has used on her, feeding his lust to the stallion. And hadn't she been full of desire? But it had not been real. It had not been her choice. She looked down at Len, red faced and shouting as he again reached for the rein.

Still watching from above, she saw herself shift her weight and she felt the strength of the stallion as he reared. She sensed the feel of the kick, the stretch of the full extension as the horse lashed out at Len, hitting him full in the chest and knocking him back against the wall. She felt the perfection of the controlled spin as the horse pirouetted 180 degrees, then bucked, hitting Len again with both back hooves. She watched herself and the horse sidestep, then two more strikes with the forefeet, before a leap toward the door. She did not turn to look at the crumpled and bloody body as she lunged into the dawn.

As she galloped onto the gravel she felt herself expand, to move higher, to watch from farther above. She sensed a fury from the stallion, a desire to flee, to escape the fight. It matched her own emotions. She loosened her control, both physical and emotional. She focused her thoughts on the trank gun tucked in her pants, and the horse slowed, hesitating for a fraction of second before extending his stride and racing faster. She could feel his heart pumping, hear the rush of his breathing. Her mind was filled with the steady motion of the horse, the feel of the wind. Arion surged forward, stretching to a faster gallop, down the road and toward the dusty hills.

GRIFFEN THE HIGH FLYER
JAMES BALDWIN

I. THE WIZARD OF THE PYRENEES

OLD ATLANTES, THE WIZARD OF THE PYRENEES, HAD BUILT A TOWER FOR his laboratory on the topmost peak of a gray mountain. There was no magic about the tower at first — only solid walls of masonry with one narrow door and, at the top, a dome of glass, where the sage could sit and gaze at the stars. But the wise wizard hoped that by the exercise of his art he would be able to bring magic out of the place by-and-by. And so, if you could have looked in upon him on any fair night or rainy day, you would have seen him surrounded by retorts and alembics, and pots and vials, and wands, and magic circles and books, and signs of the zodiac, and the thousand and one things necessary to the wizard's trade. Scattered about the room, in no very orderly manner, were bundles of all kinds of herbs, ingots of gold and silver, thin sheets of tin and copper and zinc, curiously-shaped bits of colored glass, rolls of wire, and many a strange instrument and tool, the uses of which were known only to Atlantes himself. Sometimes the people in the valley below saw thick clouds of black smoke coming out of the chimney of the wizard's den, as they called it; and belated travelers, groping along the highway on dark nights, reported that they had seen sheets of flame and balls of red fire shooting from the high tower.

Atlantes had not been long in his lofty perch before he was the terror of all the country round about. When he ventured down into the valley, the poor folk who saw him would cross themselves and mutter prayers to the Virgin and look at his feet to see whether they were not hoofed. Men would go miles out of their way rather than venture along the highroad that ran directly beneath his aery; and strange tales were told of children and knights and ladies that had been spirited away by his enchantments and held in captivity by him. But old Atlantes cared little for what people said about him, so long as they did not disturb him in his studies and experiments.

Like other alchemists, he hoped that his experiments would someday lead him to the discovery of the philosopher's stone, which would transmute all the baser metals into gold, and hence the most of his studies were directed to that end. He thought that, if he could only get the smallest vialful of the fluid called lightning, and mix it with some other ingredients which he had at hand, the secret would be within his grasp. But how to obtain the lightning-fluid was the puzzle — and having obtained it, how could he control it until the mixture should be effected?

One night, when a great storm was raging in the mountains, and the thunder was rolling from peak to peak, and flashes of lightning filled the air with terror, he tried a very odd experiment which he had been thinking of for a long time. He understood very well the terrible nature of the lightning-fluid in its free state, and hence he was wise enough not to risk bringing it into his laboratory until it was properly confined. He had arranged, therefore, for trying the experiment at some distance from his tower. There he had hewn a deep cavity in the rock, within which he now placed a huge jar and several pots containing some objects the names of which he would never disclose. I think that among them there were several strips of copper and zinc, a solution of potash, a bar of soft iron bent into the shape of a horseshoe, and possibly some other things now well known to electricians. At any rate, he arranged them very carefully, and having laid a slab of marble over the cavity, went back to his tower to await what might happen.

In the morning the storm had cleared away, the sky was cloudless, and the wizard, as he stepped from his door, could hear the peasants singing in the harvest-fields far over the hills. When he called to mind the experiment of the night before, he smiled at his ludicrous folly, as it now seemed to him. And yet, curious to know what the storm might have done with his magic mixture, he went out and lifted the marble slab. Had a flash of lightning really issued from the cavity, he could not have been more astounded.

For, from the urn wherein he had placed, as I suppose, the zinc and the copper, and the potash solution, there sprang a white horse with great wings, from which the sunlight reflected all the colors of the rainbow.

Any other man would have been much more astounded than Atlantes. But you must know that he was acquainted with all the lore of the ancients and he recognized the horse at once as the modern descendant of Pegasus the carrier of the thunderbolts of mighty Zeus. He was happier than if he had really discovered the philosopher's stone. He called the horse Griffen, and the airy creature submitted itself at once to his mastership.

II. THE CASTLE IN SPAIN

AND NOW THE WIZARD, WITH THE AID OF HIS WINGED STEED, BEGAN TO build a marvelous castle of magic among the mountains of Spain. The structure was finished in a day and a night, and, viewed from the plains below, it appeared to be as beautiful as a dream and as delicate and ethereal as the white clouds of a midsummer day.

The country people were not more surprised to see the shining walls and lofty turrets looming up from the hitherto barren summit of the mountains than they were astounded at the unwonted sight of a horse winging its way in mid-air with the white-bearded wizard seated on its back. Knights and soldiers riding through the country wondered what feudal lord had built his stronghold so high above the plain; but, search as they would, they could find no road nor even so much as a pathway by which any one could ascend to it. Nobody would have been surprised to see the castle disappear as suddenly as it had come into being; but there it stood day after day, its roof and battlements gleaming in the sunlight, and the blue smoke rising from its tall chimneys. It seemed to have come to stay.

But what was the use of a noble castle without any noble men or fair women to live in it? If Atlantes had been less wise, this question would have given him some concern; but he had built the palace for inhabitants, and he understood exactly how to encourage immigration into his territories. He might have filled his halls with phantoms bred of his own fanciful dreams and as unsubstantial as the castle itself; but he was too much of a realist for that. He was himself a creature of flesh and blood, of brawn and brains, and he felt that only men and women of the same persuasion were fit to enjoy the delights of his airy palace. To obtain the kind of guests which he preferred, therefore, he had recourse to a cunning stratagem.

Early every morning, with his great spectacles astride his nose and a big book in his hands, he would mount his winged horse and soar out over the country to some spot where a noble cavalier or a fair, high-born dame would be likely to pass during the day. There he would wait until his unsuspecting victim drew near, when the horse would suddenly alight and block up the road. Then the wizard, still sitting in his saddle, would begin to read aloud from the book. At the sound of the very first word, the knight or fair lady would forget everything that had ever happened before, would forget home, friends, and name, and think only of the honey-sweet tones that issued from the magician's lips. When the last words were pronounced the victim would come meekly forward, and, being lifted upon the pillion behind Atlantes, would be firmly strapped to the saddle. Then the good horse would spread his rainbow wings, and carry his double burden to the great air-castle on the Spanish mountain.

Thus the wizard filled his halls with the nobility of France and Spain. Nobody who once entered the golden gateway cared to go out again : each one lived in utter forgetfulness of his past life, thinking only of the delights of each passing hour. He could not even recall his own name, and he never thought of asking for the names of others.

Everything was done that could be done for the comfort and amusement of the wizard's guests. In the great courtyard was a fountain playing in a huge marble basin supported by crouching lions. Beyond it were pleasure gardens filled with flowers and fruits. The interior of the palace was in keeping with its marvelous exterior. The floors were of marble or were covered with the softest carpets, the walls were hung with the finest tapestry, the ceilings glittered with many a gem. Soft couches invited everyone to rest. The sweetest music floated on the perfumed air. The tables in the dining-hall were loaded with delicacies. Servants moved hither and thither, attentive to every call. What mortal would wish to awaken from such dreams of enchantment, to return again to the world of war and bloodshed and toil and trouble?

III. THE FOILED ENCHANTER

IT IS ALTOGETHER POSSIBLE THAT ATLANTES WOULD HAVE ROBBED ALL Europe of its chivalry and beauty, had not something occurred to put an end to his schemes. But as it often happens to mice and men, so also did it happen to the wizard. The fact is that he had grown tired of sallying out every day on Griffen's back in search of new guests, and so he had planned another way of entrapping unwary cavaliers into his prison-house. After much labor and thought he cleared away a narrow bridle-path from the highroad at the foot of the mountain to the gates of his castle at the summit. The lower end of this pathway was hidden in a thicket close by a gushing spring of water, and so cunningly was the whole thing constructed that nobody, looking up from below, would notice the smallest sign of a path ; and yet if knight or footman once entered the hidden road, he could follow it with the greatest ease to the end.

Old Atlantes, like a spider in his den, sat in his high towers and kept a sharp lookout for his prey. Whenever he saw any knight riding along the highroad who appeared to be worthy of becoming his guest, he devised some means of enticing him to enter the bridle-path. After that, of course, it was very easy to persuade him to ascend until he had safely entered the great trap that had been set for him at the top. This new scheme seemed to succeed wonderfully well, and in a short time there was scarcely a horseman of any note in all Spain who had not fallen into the snare.

It so happened one warm day in summer that a famous English traveler named Astolpho stopped at the spring to rest and to bathe his hot face in the flowing stream. He rode a beautiful black horse named Rabican, which the King of Cathay had lately given him as a token of his esteem. This horse he left in the shade of some trees at a little distance from the road, while he returned to the spring to quench his thirst. He laid his spear and shield down upon the ground, and by them placed the heavy helmet that he had lifted from his head. Then, on hands and knees, he leaned over to drink. But scarcely had his lips touched the water, when a noise caused him to look around.

A gawky countryman had loosened Rabican and was in the act of leaping upon his back. Astolpho quickly seized his spear and ran to save his horse and take the thief. But the rogue was not so easily captured. He entered the bridle- path and urged the horse up the steep ascent. Astolpho followed, always upon the point of laying hold of the horse, but always just a little too far behind. Soon he was surprised to find himself at the top of the mountain and at the very entrance to the great white castle whose towers he had seen and admired from below. The gate was open, as if beckoning him to enter, and Rabican and his rider had already disappeared within. Astolpho, not minded to lose so good a steed, ran boldly onward into the courtyard.

Some knights were there, pitching horseshoes, but they were so busy with their game that they did not notice his entrance. He looked into the banquet hall. A number of lords and ladies were seated about the table, feasting and making merry. He ran into the garden. There was no Rabican there. He peeped into the cellars. Hogsheads of wine and barrels of beef and pork were ranged about the walls, and red-faced kitchen servants were running here and there; but there were no signs of either the horse or the thief. He asked a lubberly boy to show him the way to the stables, but the fellow merely stared at him and made no answer. As he went into the courtyard again, an old man with long, flowing beard came out with a book in his hand and began to read.

But Astolpho, too, had a book — a book which a prince of India had given him, and which he always carried with him — and he was proof against all enchantments of that kind. He knew at once that he had been entrapped in a magic castle, and without heeding the wizard in the least, he turned to his own book to learn from it how he might escape. It was a kind of guidebook to all the houses of enchantment in the world, and he soon found the chapter that was devoted to the air-castles of Spain. The directions were very plain:

"How To Foil the Enchanter and Set his Prisoners Free. Raise the white stone slab that lies beneath the doorway. The spirit that is pent beneath will escape, and the palace will go up in smoke."

It was all very simple, certainly. Astolpho had no trouble in finding the white stone, and he began prying it up with his spear. Atlantes, greatly alarmed, cried out to the watchman to open the gate and let the intruder go ; and in order to drive him out he tried all the new enchantments that he could think of. The guests, hearing the unwonted uproar, came crowding out to see what new thing had been invented for their amusement. All wore curious colored glasses that the wizard had given them, and to each of them Astolpho appeared in a different form. To one he seemed a giant ; to another a dragon ; to a third an ugly dwarf; and to still another a savage beast. All with one purpose rushed upon him with swords and sticks and stones, anxious to drive him away from their palace of pleasure.

It would have gone hard with Astolpho, had he not thought of a magic horn which he wore suspended by a gold chain about his neck. It was the gift of a famous enchantress, and was worth a thousand swords. He put it to his lips and blew a single blast. The sound was so fearful that Atlantes and all his guests and servitors took to their heels, and hastened to hide themselves in the inner chambers of the palace. It was then but the work of a few moments for Astolpho to raise the white stone. It revealed the entrance to a spacious chamber in which were a thousand curious things — burning lamps, magic circles, golden bridles, and the like — and at the farther end, tethered by a golden cord, was our old friend Griffen, fully caparisoned with saddle and bridle, ready for a flight among the clouds. What was Rabican compared to such a steed as this? Astolpho lost no time in leading him from the chamber. At the very moment that Griffen emerged from the underground chamber, a clap of thunder rent the air, and lo! the wonderful palace of enchantment disappeared. Not one sign of the beautiful structure was left to show where it had stood. The barren rock, which formed the summit of the mountain, was as smooth and clean as if it had been swept by the winds and polished by the hail. And there were the knights and fair ladies who had so lately been the guests of Atlantes, standing bewildered and frightened and cold on the very edge of the dizzy cliff. Soon, as if by instinct, they turned about and filed sadly and silently down the narrow bridle-way to the plain. Once safely on the highroad, they betook themselves their several ways, but neither their memory nor their proper senses came back to them until each had reached his own home.

As for old Atlantes, he skulked down the mountain, and made his way on foot across the country to the high-built tower in the Pyrenees, where he was when we first met him. And there, I have been told, he was content to stay for the rest of his life, busy among his retorts and alembics and herbs and minerals and signs of the zodiac.

IV. THE FLIGHT TO THE MOON

AND GRIFFEN? YOU SHOULD HAVE SEEN HOW PROUDLY HE SOARED into the sky with brave Astolpho on his back. He and his master became famous as the greatest travelers of their time. Distances were nothing to them. Mountains and seas and broad rivers were no barriers to hinder them. At one time they journeyed northward above the vineyards and fields of fair France, and stopped for an hour in Paris, where Charlemagne was then reigning in the height of his power. There Astolpho learned that Orlando, the noblest of the men of his time, had lost his senses and had wandered away to

Africa, or somewhere else, in search of them.

Astolpho set off at once to find him, resolved that he would never rest until he had brought the lost hero back to France. And so the gallant Griffen winged his way back toward Spain; he hovered for a few minutes above the wizard's high-built tower, while his rider consulted with Atlantes about the direction he should take; he turned eastward and skirted the vine-clad hills of Provence ; he floated high above the snow-clad Alps, and neighed shrilly as he passed over Genoa, nestled between the mountains and the sea; he dropped one of his quills in Florence, and whinnied with delight as he saw the City of Seven Hills sleeping beneath him; and, all the time, Astolpho sat astride of him, with pen in hand, inditing wonderful stories of his adventures in foreign lands.

They alighted only when they were hungry, for the horse never tired, and Astolpho had only to look at a city to know all about its history, its people and their customs, its public buildings and its laws, and whether any demented knight was wandering about its streets. Leaving Italy, they passed over the Mediterranean, flinging down another quill at Malta, and throwing side glances toward Athens and Constantinople. Speeding over old Egypt, from north to south, Astolpho read the history of thirty centuries in the Pyramids, and wise Griffen solved the mystery of the Sphinx. Finally, after topping the Abyssinian mountains, they alighted in the mythical land of Prester John, and Astolpho at once introduced himself to that wise monarch, and stated the business which had brought him thus to the very ends of the earth.

"Great king," he said, "we had in our country a knight, noble, and brave, and kind, who in an unlucky moment had the misfortune to lose the greater part of his senses. I have searched for them in every nook and corner of the known world, but, alas, I cannot find them. The unfortunate knight himself is at this moment somewhere in the Dark Continent, useless alike to himself and his country. As a last resort I have come to you, knowing how wise you are, to ask whether there are not some superfluous senses lying about, unclaimed, in your kingdom."

"That is a fine horse that you ride," said the king. "He must be a swift traveler."

"He is very fleet, indeed," answered Astolpho. "Why, sir, he can girdle the earth in forty minutes."

"Then, how long would it take him to fly to the moon?"

"He has never been there, but I suppose it would not require very long — say, not more than twenty minutes — half as long as to go round the earth."

"Then, if you are willing to make the journey," said Prester John, "I doubt not but you will find there the thing that you are looking for. For the moon, you must know, is the attic chamber of the world, and everything that is lost finds its way there sooner or later. Lost pins, lost stitches, lost opportunities, lost sheep, lost time, lost causes, lost money, lost senses — they all go to the moon, where the three weird Sisters bottle them up and label them, and lay them on the shelf till called for. There is only one thing that is never given back again, no matter how loudly its owner demands it."

"What is that?"

"Lost time," said old Prester, solemnly; "and I would advise you to lose none of it if you would go to the moon to recover your friend's senses."

Astolpho, taking the hint, threw himself astride of Griffen, and the horse soared aloft toward the full moon, which had just risen, round and bright, above the eastern hills.

But why should I weary you with the story of that marvelous flight? And why need I tell you how the brave Astolpho found Orlando's senses just as the wise king had said he would? Neither would you care to hear how Griffen winged his flight back to the earth again; nor how his master searched through darkest Africa until he had found his demented friend; nor how Orlando took his recovered senses as a child takes nauseous medicine; nor how good Griffen, with proud Astolpho on his back, finally wended his way over the sea and land to the noble island of Britain. I will not tell you of any of these things, nor of any of the later journeys of the two famous travelers. For you will find the whole story truthfully narrated in the books which Astolpho wrote with a pen plucked from the gallant Griffen's wing.

THE BLACK HORSE
CELTIC FAIRY TALE

ONCE THERE WAS A KING AND HE HAD THREE SONS, AND WHEN THE KING died, they did not give a shade of anything to the youngest son, but an old white limping garron.

"If I get but this," quoth he, "it seems that I had best go with this same."

He was going with it right before him, sometimes walking, sometimes riding. When he had been riding a good while he thought that the garron would need a while of eating, so he came down to earth, and what should he see coming out of the heart of the western air towards him but a rider riding high, well, and right well.

"All hail, my lad," said he.

"Hail, king's son," said the other.

"What's your news?" said the king's son.

"I have got that," said the lad who came. "I am after breaking my heart riding this ass of a horse; but will you give me the limping white garron for him?"

"No," said the prince; "it would be a bad business for me."

"You need not fear," said the man that came, "there is no saying but that you might make better use of him than I. He has one value, there is no single place that you can think of in the four parts of the wheel of the world that the black horse will not take you there."

So the king's son got the black horse, and he gave the limping white garron.

Where should he think of being when he mounted but in the Realm Underwaves. He went, and before sunrise on the morrow he was there. What should he find when he got there but the son of the King Underwaves holding a Court, and the people of the realm gathered to see if there was anyone who would undertake to go to seek the daughter of the King of the Greeks to be the prince's wife. No one came forward, when who should come up but the rider of the black horse.

"You, rider of the black horse," said the prince, "I lay you under crosses and under spells to have the daughter of the King of the Greeks here before the sun rises to-morrow."

He went out and he reached the black horse and leaned his elbow on his mane, and he heaved a sigh.

"Sigh of a king's son under spells!" said the horse; "but have no care; we shall do the thing that was set before you." And so off they went.

"Now," said the horse, "when we get near the great town of the Greeks, you will notice that the four feet of a horse never went to the town before. The king's daughter will see me from the top of the castle looking out of a window, and she will not be content without a turn of a ride upon me. Say that she may have that, but the horse will suffer no man but you to ride before a woman on him."

They came near the big town, and he fell to horsemanship; and the princess was looking out of the windows, and noticed the horse. The horsemanship pleased her, and she came out just as the horse had come.

"Give me a ride on the horse," said she.

"You shall have that," said he, "but the horse will let no man ride him before a woman but me."

"I have a horseman of my own," said she.

"If so, set him in front," said he.

Before the horseman mounted at all, when he tried to get up, the horse lifted his legs and kicked him off.

"Come then yourself and mount before me," said she; "I won't leave the matter so."

He mounted the horse and she behind him, and before she glanced from her she was nearer sky than earth. He was in Realm Underwaves with her before sunrise.

"You are come," said Prince Underwaves.

"I am come," said he.

"There you are, my hero," said the prince. "You are the son of a king, but I am a son of success. Anyhow, we shall have no delay or neglect now, but a wedding."

"Just gently," said the princess; "your wedding is not so short a way off as you suppose. Till I get the silver cup that my grandmother had at her wedding, and that my mother had as well, I will not marry, for I need to have it at my own wedding."

"You, rider of the black horse," said the Prince Underwaves, "I set you under spells and under crosses unless the silver cup is here before dawn to-morrow."

Out he went and reached the horse and leaned his elbow on his mane, and he heaved a sigh.

"Sigh of a king's son under spells!" said the horse; "mount and you shall get the silver cup. The people of the realm are gathered about the king to-night, for he has missed his daughter, and when you get to the palace go in and leave me without; they will have the cup there going round the company. Go in and sit in their midst. Say nothing, and seem to be as one of the people of the place. But when the cup comes round to you, take it under your oxter, and come out to me with it, and we'll go."

Away they went and they got to Greece, and he went in to the palace and did as the black horse bade. He took the cup and came out and mounted, and before sunrise he was in the Realm Underwaves.

"You are come," said Prince Underwaves.

"I am come," said he.

"We had better get married now," said the prince to the Greek princess.

"Slowly and softly," said she. "I will not marry till I get the silver ring that my grandmother and my mother wore when they were wedded."

"You, rider of the black horse," said the Prince Underwaves, "do that. Let's have that ring here to-morrow at sunrise."

The lad went to the black horse and put his elbow on his crest and told him how it was.

"There never was a matter set before me harder than this matter which has now been set in front of me," said the horse, "but there is no help for it at any rate. Mount me. There is a snow mountain and an ice mountain and a mountain of fire between us and the winning of that ring. It is right hard for us to pass them."

Thus they went as they were, and about a mile from the snow mountain they were in a bad case with cold. As they came near it he struck the horse, and with the bound he gave the black horse was on the top of the snow mountain; at the next bound he was on the top of the ice mountain; at the third bound he went through the mountain of fire. When he had passed the mountains he was dragging at the horse's neck, as though he were about to lose himself. He went on before him down to a town below.

"Go down," said the black horse, "to a smithy; make an iron spike for every bone end in me."

Down he went as the horse desired, and he got the spikes made, and back he came with them.

"Stick them into me," said the horse, "every spike of them in every bone end that I have."

That he did; he stuck the spikes into the horse.

"There is a loch here," said the horse, "four miles long and four miles wide, and when I go out into it the loch will take fire and blaze. If you see the Loch of Fire going out before the sun rises, expect me, and if not, go your way."

Out went the black horse into the lake, and the lake became flame. Long was he stretched about the lake, beating his palms and roaring. Day came, and the loch did not go out.

But at the hour when the sun was rising out of the water the lake went out.

And the black horse rose in the middle of the water with one single spike in him, and the ring upon its end.

He came on shore, and down he fell beside the loch.

Then down went the rider. He got the ring, and he dragged the horse down to the side of a hill. He fell to sheltering him with his arms about him, and as the sun was rising he got better and better, till about midday, when he rose on his feet.

"Mount," said the horse, "and let us begone."

He mounted on the black horse, and away they went.

He reached the mountains, and he leaped the horse at the fire mountain and was on the top. From the mountain of fire he leaped to the mountain of ice, and from the mountain of ice to the mountain of snow. He put the mountains past him, and by morning he was in realm under the waves.

"You are come," said the prince.

"I am," said he.

"That's true," said Prince Underwaves. "A king's son are you, but a son of success am I. We shall have no more mistakes and delays, but a wedding this time."

"Go easy," said the Princess of the Greeks. "Your wedding is not so near as you think yet. Till you make a castle, I won't marry you. Not to your father's castle nor to your mother's will I go to dwell; but make me a castle for which your father's castle will not make washing water."

"You, rider of the black horse, make that," said Prince Underwaves, "before the morrow's sun rises."

The lad went out to the horse and leaned his elbow on his neck and sighed, thinking that this castle never could be made for ever.

"There never came a turn in my road yet that is easier for me to pass than this," said the black horse.

Glance that the lad gave from him he saw all that there were, and ever so many wrights and stone masons at work, and the castle was ready before the sun rose.

He shouted at the Prince Underwaves, and he saw the castle. He tried to pluck out his eye, thinking that it was a false sight.

"Son of King Underwaves," said the rider of the black horse, "don't think that you have a false sight; this is a true sight."

"That's true," said the prince. "You are a son of success, but I am a son of success too. There will be no more mistakes and delays, but a wedding now."

"No," said she. "The time is come. Should we not go to look at the castle? There's time enough to get married before the night comes."

They went to the castle and the castle was without a "but"——

"I see one," said the prince. "One want at least to be made good. A well to be made inside, so that water may not be far to fetch when there is a feast or a wedding in the castle."

"That won't be long undone," said the rider of the black horse.

The well was made, and it was seven fathoms deep and two or three fathoms wide, and they looked at the well on the way to the wedding.

"It is very well made," said she, "but for one little fault yonder."

"Where is it?" said Prince Underwaves.

"There," said she.

He bent him down to look. She came out, and she put her two hands at his back, and cast him in.

"Be thou there," said she. "If I go to be married, thou art not the man; but the man who did each exploit that has been done, and, if he chooses, him will I have."

Away she went with the rider of the little black horse to the wedding.

And at the end of three years after that so it was that he first remembered the black horse or where he left him.

He got up and went out, and he was very sorry for his neglect of the black horse. He found him just where he left him.

"Good luck to you, gentleman," said the horse. "You seem as if you had got something that you like better than me."

"I have not got that, and I won't; but it came over me to forget you," said he.

"I don't mind," said the horse, "it will make no difference. Raise your sword and smite off my head."

"Fortune will now allow that I should do that," said he.

"Do it instantly, or I will do it to you," said the horse.

So the lad drew his sword and smote off the horse's head; then he lifted his two palms and uttered a doleful cry.

What should he hear behind him but "All hail, my brother-in-law."

He looked behind him, and there was the finest man he ever set eyes upon.

"What set you weeping for the black horse?" said he.

"This," said the lad, "that there never was born of man or beast a creature in this world that I was fonder of."

"Would you take me for him?" said the stranger.

"If I could think you the horse, I would; but if not, I would rather the horse," said the rider.

"I am the black horse," said the lad, "and if I were not, how should you have all these things that you went to seek in my father's house. Since I went under spells, many a man have I ran at before you met me. They had but one word amongst them: they could not keep me, nor manage me, and they never kept me a couple of days. But when I fell in with you, you kept me till the time ran out that was to come from the spells. And now you shall go home with me, and we will make a wedding in my father's house."

THE ROCKING HORSE WINNER
DH LAWRENCE

THERE WAS A WOMAN WHO WAS BEAUTIFUL, WHO STARTED WITH ALL the advantages, yet she had no luck. She married for love, and the love turned to dust. She had bonny children, yet she felt they had been thrust upon her, and she could not love them. They looked at her coldly, as if they were finding fault with her. And hurriedly she felt she must cover up some fault in herself. Yet what it was that she must cover up she never knew. Nevertheless, when her children were present, she always felt the centre of her heart go hard. This troubled her, and in her manner she was all the more gentle and anxious for her children, as if she loved them very much. Only she herself knew that at the centre of her heart was a hard little place that could not feel love, no, not for anybody. Everybody else said of her: "She is such a good mother. She adores her children." Only she herself, and her children themselves, knew it was not so. They read it in each other's eyes.

There were a boy and two little girls. They lived in a pleasant house, with a garden, and they had discreet servants, and felt themselves superior to anyone in the neighbourhood.

Although they lived in style, they felt always an anxiety in the house. There was never enough money. The mother had a small income, and the father had a small income, but not nearly enough for the social position which they had to keep up. The father went into town to some office. But though he had good prospects, these prospects never materialised. There was always the grinding sense of the shortage of money, though the style was always kept up.

At last the mother said: "I will see if I can't make something." But she did not know where to begin. She racked her brains, and tried this thing and the other, but could not find anything successful. The failure made deep lines come into her face. Her children were growing up, they would have to go to school. There must be more money, there must be more money. The father, who was always very handsome and expensive in his tastes, seemed as if he never would be able to do anything worth doing. And the mother, who had a great belief in herself, did not succeed any better, and her tastes were just as expensive.

And so the house came to be haunted by the unspoken phrase: There must be more money! There must be more money! The children could hear it all the time though nobody said it aloud. They heard it at Christmas, when the expensive and splendid toys filled the nursery. Behind the shining modern rocking-horse, behind the smart doll's house, a voice would start whispering: "There must be more money! There must be more money!" And the children would stop playing, to listen for a moment. They would look into each other's eyes, to see if they had all heard. And each one saw in the eyes of the other two that they too had heard. "There must be more money! There must be more money!"

It came whispering from the springs of the still-swaying rocking-horse, and even the horse, bending his wooden, champing head, heard it. The big doll, sitting so pink and smirking in her new pram, could hear it quite plainly, and seemed to be smirking all the more self-consciously because of it. The foolish puppy, too, that took the place of the teddy-bear, he was looking so extraordinarily foolish for no other reason but that he heard the secret whisper all over the house: "There must be more money!"

Yet nobody ever said it aloud. The whisper was everywhere,

and therefore no one spoke it. Just as no one ever says: "We are breathing!" in spite of the fact that breath is coming and going all the time.

"Mother," said the boy Paul one day, "why don't we keep a car of our own? Why do we always use uncle's, or else a taxi?"

"Because we're the poor members of the family," said the mother.

"But why are we, mother?"

"Well - I suppose," she said slowly and bitterly, "it's because your father has no luck."

The boy was silent for some time.

"Is luck money, mother?" he asked, rather timidly.

"No, Paul. Not quite. It's what causes you to have money."

"Oh!" said Paul vaguely. "I thought when Uncle Oscar said filthy lucker, it meant money."

"Filthy lucre does mean money," said the mother. "But it's lucre, not luck."

"Oh!" said the boy. "Then what is luck, mother?"

"It's what causes you to have money. If you're lucky you have money. That's why it's better to be born lucky than rich. If you're rich, you may lose your money. But if you're lucky, you will always get more money."

"Oh! Will you? And is father not lucky?"

"Very unlucky, I should say," she said bitterly.

The boy watched her with unsure eyes.

"Why?" he asked.

"I don't know. Nobody ever knows why one person is lucky and another unlucky."

"Don't they? Nobody at all? Does nobody know?"

"Perhaps God. But He never tells."

"He ought to, then. And aren't you lucky either, mother?"

"I can't be, it I married an unlucky husband."

"But by yourself, aren't you?"

"I used to think I was, before I married. Now I think I am very unlucky indeed."

"Why?"

"Well - never mind! Perhaps I'm not really," she said.

The child looked at her to see if she meant it. But he saw, by the lines of her mouth, that she was only trying to hide something from him.

"Well, anyhow," he said stoutly, "I'm a lucky person."

"Why?" said his mother, with a sudden laugh.

He stared at her. He didn't even know why he had said it.

"God told me," he asserted, brazening it out.

"I hope He did, dear!", she said, again with a laugh, but rather bitter.

"He did, mother!"

"Excellent!" said the mother, using one of her husband's exclamations.

The boy saw she did not believe him; or rather, that she paid no attention to his assertion. This angered him somewhere, and made him want to compel her attention.

He went off by himself, vaguely, in a childish way, seeking for the clue to 'luck'. Absorbed, taking no heed of other people, he went about with a sort of stealth, seeking inwardly for luck. He wanted luck, he wanted it, he wanted it. When the two girls were playing dolls in the nursery, he would sit on his big rocking-horse, charging madly into space, with a frenzy that made the little girls peer at him uneasily. Wildly the horse careered, the waving dark hair of the boy tossed, his eyes had a strange glare in them. The little girls dared not speak to him.

When he had ridden to the end of his mad little journey, he climbed down and stood in front of his rocking-horse, staring fixedly into its lowered face. Its red mouth was slightly open, its big eye was wide and glassy-bright.

"Now!" he would silently command the snorting steed. "Now take me to where there is luck! Now take me!"

And he would slash the horse on the neck with the little whip he had asked Uncle Oscar for. He knew the horse could take him to where there was luck, if only he forced it. So he would mount again and start on his furious ride, hoping at last to get there.

"You'll break your horse, Paul!" said the nurse.

"He's always riding like that! I wish he'd leave off!" said his elder sister Joan.

But he only glared down on them in silence. Nurse gave him up. She could make nothing of him. Anyhow, he was growing beyond her.

One day his mother and his Uncle Oscar came in when he was on one of his furious rides. He did not speak to them.

"Hallo, you young jockey! Riding a winner?" said his uncle.

"Aren't you growing too big for a rocking-horse? You're not a very little boy any longer, you know," said his mother.

But Paul only gave a blue glare from his big, rather close-set eyes. He would speak to nobody when he was in full tilt. His mother watched him with an anxious expression on her face.

At last he suddenly stopped forcing his horse into the mechanical gallop and slid down.

"Well, I got there!" he announced fiercely, his blue eyes still flaring, and his sturdy long legs straddling apart.

"Where did you get to?" asked his mother.

"Where I wanted to go," he flared back at her.

"That's right, son!" said Uncle Oscar. "Don't you stop till you get there. What's the horse's name?"

"He doesn't have a name," said the boy.

"Gets on without all right?" asked the uncle.

"Well, he has different names. He was called Sansovino last week."

"Sansovino, eh? Won the Ascot. How did you know this name?"

"He always talks about horse-races with Bassett," said Joan.

The uncle was delighted to find that his small nephew was posted with all the racing news. Bassett, the young gardener, who had been wounded in the left foot in the war and had got his present job through Oscar Cresswell, whose batman he had been, was a perfect blade of the 'turf'. He lived in the racing events, and the small boy lived with him.

Oscar Cresswell got it all from Bassett.

"Master Paul comes and asks me, so I can't do more than tell him, sir," said Bassett, his face terribly serious, as if he were speaking of religious matters.

"And does he ever put anything on a horse he fancies?"

"Well - I don't want to give him away - he's a young sport, a fine sport, sir. Would you mind asking him himself? He sort of takes a pleasure in it, and perhaps he'd feel I was giving him away, sir, if you don't mind."

Bassett was serious as a church.

The uncle went back to his nephew and took him off for a ride in the car.

"Say, Paul, old man, do you ever put anything on a horse?" the uncle asked.

The boy watched the handsome man closely.

"Why, do you think I oughtn't to?" he parried.

"Not a bit of it! I thought perhaps you might give me a tip for the Lincoln."

The car sped on into the country, going down to Uncle Oscar's place in Hampshire.

"Honour bright?" said the nephew.

"Honour bright, son!" said the uncle.

"Well, then, Daffodil."

"Daffodil! I doubt it, sonny. What about Mirza?"

"I only know the winner," said the boy. "That's Daffodil."

"Daffodil, eh?"

There was a pause. Daffodil was an obscure horse comparatively.

"Uncle!"

"Yes, son?"

"You won't let it go any further, will you? I promised Bassett."

"Bassett be damned, old man! What's he got to do with it?"

"We're partners. We've been partners from the first. Uncle, he lent me my first five shillings, which I lost. I promised him, honour bright, it was only between me and him; only you gave me that ten-shilling note I started winning with, so I thought you were lucky. You won't let it go any further, will you?"

The boy gazed at his uncle from those big, hot, blue eyes, set rather close together. The uncle stirred and laughed uneasily.

"Right you are, son! I'll keep your tip private. How much are you putting on him?"

"All except twenty pounds," said the boy. "I keep that in reserve."

The uncle thought it a good joke.

"You keep twenty pounds in reserve, do you, you young romancer? What are you betting, then?"

"I'm betting three hundred," said the boy gravely. "But it's between you and me, Uncle Oscar! Honour bright?"

"It's between you and me all right, you young Nat Gould," he said, laughing. "But where's your three hundred?"

"Bassett keeps it for me. We're partners."

"You are, are you! And what is Bassett putting on Daffodil?"

"He won't go quite as high as I do, I expect. Perhaps he'll go a hundred and fifty."

"What, pennies?" laughed the uncle.

"Pounds," said the child, with a surprised look at his uncle. "Bassett keeps a bigger reserve than I do."

Between wonder and amusement Uncle Oscar was silent. He pursued the matter no further, but he determined to take his nephew with him to the Lincoln races.

"Now, son," he said, "I'm putting twenty on Mirza, and I'll put five on for you on any horse you fancy. What's your pick?"

"Daffodil, uncle."

"No, not the fiver on Daffodil!"

"I should if it was my own fiver," said the child.

"Good! Good! Right you are! A fiver for me and a fiver for you on Daffodil."

The child had never been to a race-meeting before, and his eyes were blue fire. He pursed his mouth tight and watched. A Frenchman just in front had put his money on Lancelot. Wild with excitement, he flayed his arms up and down, yelling "Lancelot!, Lancelot!" in his French accent.

Daffodil came in first, Lancelot second, Mirza third. The child, flushed and with eyes blazing, was curiously serene. His uncle brought him four five-pound notes, four to one.

"What am I to do with these?" he cried, waving them before the boys eyes.

"I suppose we'll talk to Bassett," said the boy. "I expect I have fifteen hundred now; and twenty in reserve; and this twenty."

His uncle studied him for some moments.

"Look here, son!" he said. "You're not serious about Bassett and that fifteen hundred, are you?"

"Yes, I am. But it's between you and me, uncle. Honour bright?"

"Honour bright all right, son! But I must talk to Bassett."

"If you'd like to be a partner, uncle, with Bassett and me, we could all be partners. Only, you'd have to promise, honour bright, uncle, not to let it go beyond us three. Bassett and I are lucky, and you must be lucky, because it was your ten shillings I started winning with ..."

Uncle Oscar took both Bassett and Paul into Richmond Park for an afternoon, and there they talked.

"It's like this, you see, sir," Bassett said. "Master Paul would get me talking about racing events, spinning yarns, you know, sir. And he was always keen on knowing if I'd made or if I'd lost. It's about a year since, now, that I put five shillings on Blush of Dawn for him: and we lost. Then the luck turned, with that ten shillings he had from you: that we put on Singhalese. And since that time, it's been pretty steady, all things considering. What do you say, Master Paul?"

"We're all right when we're sure," said Paul. "It's when we're not quite sure that we go down."

"Oh, but we're careful then," said Bassett.

"But when are you sure?" smiled Uncle Oscar.

"It's Master Paul, sir," said Bassett in a secret, religious voice. "It's as if he had it from heaven. Like Daffodil, now, for the Lincoln. That was as sure as eggs."

"Did you put anything on Daffodil?" asked Oscar Cresswell.

"Yes, sir, I made my bit."

"And my nephew?"

Bassett was obstinately silent, looking at Paul.

"I made twelve hundred, didn't I, Bassett? I told uncle I was putting three hundred on Daffodil."

"That's right," said Bassett, nodding.

"But where's the money?" asked the uncle.

"I keep it safe locked up, sir. Master Paul he can have it any minute he likes to ask for it."

"What, fifteen hundred pounds?"

"And twenty! And forty, that is, with the twenty he made on the course."

"It's amazing!" said the uncle.

"If Master Paul offers you to be partners, sir, I would, if I were you: if you'll excuse me," said Bassett.

Oscar Cresswell thought about it.

"I'll see the money," he said.

They drove home again, and, sure enough, Bassett came round to the garden-house with fifteen hundred pounds in notes. The twenty pounds reserve was left with Joe Glee, in the Turf Commission deposit.

"You see, it's all right, uncle, when I'm sure! Then we go strong, for all we're worth, don't we, Bassett?"

"We do that, Master Paul."

"And when are you sure?" said the uncle, laughing.

"Oh, well, sometimes I'm absolutely sure, like about Daffodil," said the boy; "and sometimes I have an idea; and sometimes I haven't even an idea, have I, Bassett? Then we're careful, because we mostly go down."

"You do, do you! And when you're sure, like about Daffodil, what makes you sure, sonny?"

"Oh, well, I don't know," said the boy uneasily. "I'm sure, you know, uncle; that's all."

"It's as if he had it from heaven, sir," Bassett reiterated.

"I should say so!" said the uncle.

But he became a partner. And when the Leger was coming on Paul was 'sure' about Lively Spark, which was a quite inconsiderable horse. The boy insisted on putting a thousand on the horse, Bassett went for five hundred, and Oscar Cresswell two hundred. Lively Spark came in first, and the betting had been ten to one against him. Paul had made ten thousand.

"You see," he said. "I was absolutely sure of him."

Even Oscar Cresswell had cleared two thousand.

"Look here, son," he said, "this sort of thing makes me nervous."

"It needn't, uncle! Perhaps I shan't be sure again for a long time."

"But what are you going to do with your money?" asked the uncle.

"Of course," said the boy, "I started it for mother. She said she had no luck, because father is unlucky, so I thought if I was lucky, it might stop whispering."

"What might stop whispering?"

"Our house. I hate our house for whispering."

"What does it whisper?"

"Why - why" - the boy fidgeted - "why, I don't know. But it's always short of money, you know, uncle."

"I know it, son, I know it."

"You know people send mother writs, don't you, uncle?"

"I'm afraid I do," said the uncle.

"And then the house whispers, like people laughing at you behind your back. It's awful, that is! I thought if I was lucky -"

"You might stop it," added the uncle.

The boy watched him with big blue eyes, that had an uncanny cold fire in them, and he said never a word.

"Well, then!" said the uncle. "What are we doing?"

"I shouldn't like mother to know I was lucky," said the boy.

"Why not, son?"

"She'd stop me."

"I don't think she would."

"Oh!" - and the boy writhed in an odd way - "I don't want her to know, uncle."

"All right, son! We'll manage it without her knowing."

They managed it very easily. Paul, at the other's suggestion, handed over five thousand pounds to his uncle, who deposited it with the family lawyer, who was then to inform Paul's mother that a relative had put five thousand pounds into his hands, which sum was to be paid out a thousand pounds at a time, on the mother's birthday, for the next five years.

"So she'll have a birthday present of a thousand pounds for five successive years," said Uncle Oscar. "I hope it won't make it all the harder for her later."

Paul's mother had her birthday in November. The house had been 'whispering' worse than ever lately, and, even in spite of his luck, Paul could not bear up against it. He was very anxious to see the effect of the birthday letter, telling his mother about the thousand pounds.

When there were no visitors, Paul now took his meals with his parents, as he was beyond the nursery control. His mother went into town nearly every day. She had discovered that she had an odd knack of sketching furs and dress materials, so she worked secretly in the studio of a friend who was the chief 'artist' for the leading drapers. She drew the figures of ladies in furs and ladies in silk and sequins for the newspaper advertisements. This young woman artist earned several thousand pounds a year, but Paul's mother only made several hundreds, and she was again dissatisfied. She so wanted to be first in something, and she did not succeed, even in making sketches for drapery advertisements.

She was down to breakfast on the morning of her birthday. Paul watched her face as she read her letters. He knew the lawyer's letter. As his mother read it, her face hardened and became more expressionless. Then a cold, determined look came on her mouth. She hid the letter under the pile of others, and said not a word about it.

"Didn't you have anything nice in the post for your birthday, mother?" said Paul.

"Quite moderately nice," she said, her voice cold and hard and absent.

She went away to town without saying more.

But in the afternoon Uncle Oscar appeared. He said Paul's mother had had a long interview with the lawyer, asking if the whole five thousand could not be advanced at once, as she was in debt.

"What do you think, uncle?" said the boy.

"I leave it to you, son."

"Oh, let her have it, then! We can get some more with the other," said the boy.

"A bird in the hand is worth two in the bush, laddie!" said Uncle Oscar.

"But I'm sure to know for the Grand National; or the Lincolnshire; or else the Derby. I'm sure to know for one of them," said Paul.

So Uncle Oscar signed the agreement, and Paul's mother touched the whole five thousand. Then something very curious happened. The voices in the house suddenly went mad, like a chorus of frogs on a spring evening. There were certain new furnishings, and Paul had a tutor. He was really going to Eton, his father's school, in the following autumn. There were flowers in the winter, and a blossoming of the luxury Paul's mother had been used to. And yet the voices in the house, behind the sprays of mimosa and almond-blossom, and from under the piles of iridescent cushions, simply trilled and screamed in a sort of ecstasy: "There must be more money! Oh-h-h; there must be more money. Oh, now, now-w! Now-w-w - there must be more money! - more than ever! More than ever!"

It frightened Paul terribly. He studied away at his Latin and Greek with his tutor. But his intense hours were spent with Bassett. The Grand National had gone by: he had not 'known', and had lost a hundred pounds. Summer was at hand. He was in agony for the Lincoln. But even for the Lincoln he didn't 'know', and he lost fifty pounds. He became wild-eyed and strange, as if something were going to explode in him.

"Let it alone, son! Don't you bother about it!" urged Uncle Oscar. But it was as if the boy couldn't really hear what his uncle was saying.

"I've got to know for the Derby! I've got to know for the Derby!" the child reiterated, his big blue eyes blazing with a sort of madness.

His mother noticed how overwrought he was.

"You'd better go to the seaside. Wouldn't you like to go now to the seaside, instead of waiting? I think you'd better," she said, looking down at him anxiously, her heart curiously heavy because of him.

But the child lifted his uncanny blue eyes.

"I couldn't possibly go before the Derby, mother!" he said. "I couldn't possibly!"

"Why not?" she said, her voice becoming heavy when she was opposed. "Why not? You can still go from the seaside to see the Derby with your Uncle Oscar, if that that's what you wish. No need for you to wait here. Besides, I think you care too much about these races. It's a bad sign. My family has been a gambling family, and you won't know till you grow up how much damage it has done. But it has done damage. I shall have to send Bassett away, and ask Uncle Oscar not to talk racing to you, unless you promise to be reasonable about it: go away to the seaside and forget it. You're all nerves!"

"I'll do what you like, mother, so long as you don't send me away till after the Derby," the boy said.

"Send you away from where? Just from this house?"

"Yes," he said, gazing at her.

"Why, you curious child, what makes you care about this house so much, suddenly? I never knew you loved it."

He gazed at her without speaking. He had a secret within a secret, something he had not divulged, even to Bassett or to his Uncle Oscar.

But his mother, after standing undecided and a little bit sullen for some moments, said: "Very well, then! Don't go to the seaside till after the Derby, if you don't wish it. But promise me you won't think so much about horse-racing and events as you call them!"

"Oh no," said the boy casually. "I won't think much about them, mother. You needn't worry. I wouldn't worry, mother, if I were you."

"If you were me and I were you," said his mother, "I wonder what we should do!"

"But you know you needn't worry, mother, don't you?" the boy repeated.

"I should be awfully glad to know it," she said wearily.

"Oh, well, you can, you know. I mean, you ought to know you needn't worry," he insisted.

"Ought I? Then I'll see about it," she said.

Paul's secret of secrets was his wooden horse, that which had no name. Since he was emancipated from a nurse and a nursery-governess, he had had his rocking-horse removed to his own bedroom at the top of the house.

"Surely you're too big for a rocking-horse!" his mother had remonstrated.

"Well, you see, mother, till I can have a real horse, I like to have some sort of animal about," had been his quaint answer.

"Do you feel he keeps you company?" she laughed.

"Oh yes! He's very good, he always keeps me company, when I'm there," said Paul.

So the horse, rather shabby, stood in an arrested prance in the boy's bedroom.

The Derby was drawing near, and the boy grew more and more tense. He hardly heard what was spoken to him, he was very frail, and his eyes were really uncanny. His mother had sudden strange seizures of uneasiness about him. Sometimes, for half an hour, she would feel a sudden anxiety about him that was almost anguish. She wanted to rush to him at once, and know he was safe.

Two nights before the Derby, she was at a big party in town, when one of her rushes of anxiety about her boy, her first-born, gripped her heart till she could hardly speak. She fought with the feeling, might and main, for she believed in common sense. But it was too strong. She had to leave the dance and go downstairs to telephone to the country. The children's nursery-governess was terribly surprised and startled at being rung up in the night.

"Are the children all right, Miss Wilmot?"

"Oh yes, they are quite all right."

"Master Paul? Is he all right?"

"He went to bed as right as a trivet. Shall I run up and look at him?"

"No," said Paul's mother reluctantly. "No! Don't trouble. It's all right. Don't sit up. We shall be home fairly soon." She did not want her son's privacy intruded upon.

"Very good," said the governess.

It was about one o'clock when Paul's mother and father drove up to their house. All was still. Paul's mother went to her room and slipped off her white fur cloak. She had told her maid not to wait up for her. She heard her husband downstairs, mixing a whisky and soda.

And then, because of the strange anxiety at her heart, she stole upstairs to her son's room. Noiselessly she went along the upper corridor. Was there a faint noise? What was it?

She stood, with arrested muscles, outside his door, listening. There was a strange, heavy, and yet not loud noise. Her heart stood still. It was a soundless noise, yet rushing and powerful. Something huge, in violent, hushed motion. What was it? What in God's name was it? She ought to know. She felt that she knew the noise. She knew what it was.

Yet she could not place it. She couldn't say what it was. And on and on it went, like a madness.

Softly, frozen with anxiety and fear, she turned the door-handle.

The room was dark. Yet in the space near the window, she heard and saw something plunging to and fro. She gazed in fear and amazement.

Then suddenly she switched on the light, and saw her son, in his green pyjamas, madly surging on the rocking-horse. The blaze of light suddenly lit him up, as he urged the wooden horse, and lit her up, as she stood, blonde, in her dress of pale green and crystal, in the doorway.

"Paul!" she cried. "Whatever are you doing?"

"It's Malabar!" he screamed in a powerful, strange voice. "It's Malabar!"

His eyes blazed at her for one strange and senseless second, as he ceased urging his wooden horse. Then he fell with a crash to the ground, and she, all her tormented motherhood flooding upon her, rushed to gather him up.

But he was unconscious, and unconscious he remained, with some brain-fever. He talked and tossed, and his mother sat stonily by his side.

"Malabar! It's Malabar! Bassett, Bassett, I know! It's Malabar!"

So the child cried, trying to get up and urge the rocking-horse that gave him his inspiration.

"What does he mean by Malabar?" asked the heart-frozen mother.

"I don't know," said the father stonily.

"What does he mean by Malabar?" she asked her brother Oscar.

"It's one of the horses running for the Derby," was the answer.

And, in spite of himself, Oscar Cresswell spoke to Bassett, and himself put a thousand on Malabar: at fourteen to one.

The third day of the illness was critical: they were waiting for a change. The boy, with his rather long, curly hair, was tossing ceaselessly on the pillow. He neither slept nor regained consciousness, and his eyes were like blue stones. His mother sat, feeling her heart had gone, turned actually into a stone.

In the evening Oscar Cresswell did not come, but Bassett sent a message, saying could he come up for one moment, just one moment? Paul's mother was very angry at the intrusion, but on second thoughts she agreed. The boy was the same. Perhaps Bassett might bring him to consciousness.

The gardener, a shortish fellow with a little brown moustache and sharp little brown eyes, tiptoed into the room, touched his imaginary cap to Paul's mother, and stole to the bedside, staring with glittering, smallish eyes at the tossing, dying child.

"Master Paul!" he whispered. "Master Paul! Malabar came in first all right, a clean win. I did as you told me. You've made over seventy thousand pounds, you have; you've got over eighty thousand. Malabar came in all right, Master Paul."

"Malabar! Malabar! Did I say Malabar, mother? Did I say Malabar? Do you think I'm lucky, mother? I knew Malabar, didn't I? Over eighty thousand pounds! I call that lucky, don't you, mother? Over eighty thousand pounds! I knew, didn't I know I knew? Malabar came in all right. If I ride my horse till I'm sure, then I tell you, Bassett, you can go as high as you like. Did you go for all you were worth, Bassett?"

"I went a thousand on it, Master Paul."

"I never told you, mother, that if I can ride my horse, and get there, then I'm absolutely sure - oh, absolutely! Mother, did I ever tell you? I am lucky!"

"No, you never did," said his mother.

But the boy died in the night.

And even as he lay dead, his mother heard her brother's voice saying to her, "My God, Hester, you're eighty-odd thousand to the good, and a poor devil of a son to the bad. But, poor devil, poor devil, he's best gone out of a life where he rides his rocking-horse to find a winner."

THE HORSE OF BRASS
JAMES BALDWIN

CAMBUSCAN WAS THE NOBLEST RULER IN ALL THE EAST. ON THE DAY upon which he completed the twentieth year of his reign, he held a great feast in his palace, to which all the princes of his realm were invited. The royal dining-hall was a marvel of beauty and magnificence, and the table was the finest that the world has even seen. At the head of the board sat the king, with his wife Elfeta, his two sons, Algarsif and Camballo, and his daughter Canace. On either side were ranged, in the order of their rank, the noblest lords and the most beautiful ladies of the land. The minstrels played sweet music, and the hearts of the king and his guests were filled with joy. In the midst of the festivity there came into the hall, without invitation or announcement, a strange knight mounted upon a steed of brass, and holding in his hand a broad, bright mirror. By his side hung a jewel-hilted sword, and on his thumb was a ring of dazzling beauty. Everybody was So astonished that the hall became suddenly silent; the laughter ceased, the minstrels forgot their music, and the guests turned about in their places to gaze at the unexpected sight. The horse walked straight toward the dais where the king sat, and when he was within speaking distance paused. Then the knight saluted the king and queen and lords with a grace and courtesy which none of them had ever seen excelled, and with a manly voice delivered his message.

"The king of Araby and of Ind, whose servant I am," said he," sends salutations to you. He has also sent to you, O king, in honor of your anniversary, this horse of brass, which can in the space of four and twenty hours bear you without danger into whatsoever part of the world you may wish to go. Or if you choose to soar aloft as an eagle, and look down from the mountain-tops, he will carry you thither. The whole thing is as simple as turning a pin. This sword is also a present to you from my king. It has an edge so keen and sharp that it will cut through the heaviest armor, and no metal can withstand its stroke. And yet it has another property that makes it even more valuable; for, should any man be wounded with it, you can immediately heal him by passing the flat part of it over the wound. This mirror and the ring are for your daughter, fair Canace. In the mirror she can see everything that is going on in your kingdom, and can even read the thoughts of her lover. And while wearing the ring she will understand the language of all the birds, and be able to answer them in their own manner of speaking."

Then the knight, having delivered his message, turned his steed around and rode out into the courtyard. Having dismounted, he was conducted, by the king's command, back into the banquet-hall, where a place was made for him at the feast. But the horse of brass stood in its place immovable, the center of a gaping, wondering crowd. It was as tall and well-proportioned as the famous steeds of Lombardy, and as handsome and light of limb as the finest horses of Polish breed. Some said that it was such a steed as the fairies ride; others that it was Pegasus, the winged steed of Grecian story; still others declared that it looked like the great horse which Epeus contrived for the destruction of the Trojan people; and they feared that armed men might somehow be hidden within it. But the greater number were agreed that it was the skilful work of the Arabic magicians, and hence would better not be tampered with by ignorant hands.

Cambuscan, when he had done feasting, went out into the

courtyard, with all his lords and ladies, to look at the wonderful gift which the king of Araby had sent him.

"I pray you," said he to the knight who had brought it, "tell us how to manage this strange creature."

"There is but little to tell," said the knight, laying his hand upon the horse, which began to skip and prance in the strangest manner possible. "When you wish to ride anywhere you have simply to remove this peg which you see between his ears, mount him, and name the place. He will carry you thither by the shortest route, and without ever missing his way. When you wish him to stop, or to descend to the ground, turn this wooden pin half way round, and he will do your bidding. Or, if you wish him to leave you for a time, turn this iron pin, and he will vanish out of sight, and come to you again when he is called by name. Ride when and where you please, he will always be ready to obey."

The king was wonderfully pleased, and resolved that on the morrow he would ride out to see the world. Then he ordered the groom of the bedchamber to take off the horse's jeweled bridle and carry it into the strong room of the palace, where it should be locked up among his costliest treasures. This being done, he gave a sudden turn to the iron pin, as he had been directed, and the horse vanished from sight. The knight, too, had disappeared from the palace, and King Cambuscan remembered when it was too late that he had not told him how or by what name to call the magic steed.

If anyone will go to Sarra in Tartary — wherever that may be — and shout the right name of the horse of brass, I doubt not but that he is still waiting to appear. And what more wonderful piece of mechanism could anyone wish to own?

GOOSE GIRL
JACOB AND WILHELM GRIMM

THERE ONCE LIVED AN OLD QUEEN WHOSE HUSBAND HAD BEEN DEAD FOR many years, and she had a beautiful daughter. When the princess grew up she was promised in marriage to a prince who lived far away. When the time came for her to be married, and she had to depart for the distant kingdom, the old queen packed up for her many costly vessels and utensils of silver and gold, and trinkets also of gold and silver, and cups and jewels, in short, everything that belonged to a royal dowry, for she loved her child with all her heart.

She likewise assigned to her a chambermaid, who was to ride with her, and deliver her into the hands of the bridegroom. Each received a horse for the journey. The princess's horse was called Falada, and could speak. When the hour of departure had come, the old mother went into her bedroom, took a small knife and cut her fingers with it until they bled. Then she held out a small white cloth and let three drops of blood fall into it. She gave them to her daughter, saying, "Take good care of these. They will be of service to you on your way."

Thus they sorrowfully took leave of one another. The princess put the cloth into her bosom, mounted her horse, and set forth for her bridegroom. After they had ridden for a while she felt a burning thirst, and said to her chambermaid, "Dismount, and take my cup which you have brought with you for me, and get me some water from the brook, for I would like a drink."

"If you are thirsty," said the chambermaid, "get off your horse yourself, and lie down near the water and drink. I won't be your servant."

So in her great thirst the princess dismounted, bent down over the water in the brook and drank; and she was not allowed to drink out of the golden cup. Then she said, "Oh, Lord," and the three drops of blood answered, "If your mother knew this, her heart would break in two."

But the king's daughter was humble. She said nothing and mounted her horse again. They rode some miles further. The day was warm, the sun beat down, and she again grew thirsty. When they came to a stream of water, she again called to her chambermaid, "Dismount, and give me some water in my golden cup," for she had long ago forgotten the girl's evil words.

But the chambermaid said still more haughtily, "If you want a drink, get it yourself. I won't be your servant."

Then in her great thirst the king's daughter dismounted, bent over the flowing water, wept, and said, "Oh, Lord," and the drops of blood again replied, "If your mother knew this, her heart would break in two."

As she was thus drinking, leaning over the stream, the cloth with the three drops of blood fell from her bosom and floated away with the water, without her taking notice of it, so great were her concerns. However, the chambermaid what happened, and she rejoiced to think that she now had power over the bride, for by losing the drops of blood, the princess had become weak and powerless.

When she wanted to mount her horse again, the one that was called Falada, the chambermaid said, "I belong on Falada. You belong on my nag," and the princess had to accept it.

Then with many harsh words the chambermaid ordered the princess to take off her own royal clothing and put on the chambermaid's shabby clothes. And in the end the princess had to swear under the open heaven that she would not say one word of this to anyone at the royal court. If she had not taken this oath, she would have been killed on the spot. Falada saw everything, and remembered it well.

The chambermaid now climbed onto Falada, and the true bride onto the bad horse, and thus they traveled onwards, until finally they arrived at the royal palace. There was great rejoicing over their arrival, and the prince ran ahead to meet them, then lifted the chambermaid from her horse, thinking she was his bride.

She was led upstairs, while the real princess was left standing below. Then the old king looked out of the window and saw her waiting in the courtyard, and noticed how fine and delicate and beautiful she was, so at once he went to the royal apartment, and asked the bride about the girl she had with her who was standing down below in the courtyard, and who she was.

"I picked her up on my way for a companion. Give the girl some work to do, so she won't stand idly by."

However, the old king had no work for her, and knew of nothing else to say but, "I have a little boy who tends the geese. She can help him." The boy was called Kürdchen (Little Conrad), and the true bride had to help him tend geese.

Soon afterwards the false bride said to the young king, "Dearest husband, I beg you to do me a favor."

He answered, "I will do so gladly."

"Then send for the knacker, and have the head of the horse which I rode here cut off, for it angered me on the way." In truth, she was afraid that the horse might tell how she had behaved toward the king's daughter.

Thus it happened that faithful Falada had to die. The real princess heard about this, and she secretly promised to pay the knacker a piece of gold if he would perform a small service for her. In the town there was a large dark gateway, through which she had to pass with the geese each morning and evening. Would he be so good as to nail Falada's head beneath the gateway, so that she might see him again and again?

The knacker's helper promised to do that, and cut off the head, and nailed it securely beneath the dark gateway.

Early in the morning, when she and Conrad drove out their flock beneath this gateway, she said in passing, "Alas, Falada, hanging there!"

Then the head answered:

Alas, young queen, passing by,

If this your mother knew,

Her heart would break in two. Then they went still further out of the town, driving their geese into the country. And when they came to the meadow, she sat down and unbound her hair which was of pure gold. Conrad saw it, was delighted how it glistened, and wanted to pluck out a few hairs. Then she said:

Blow, wind, blow,

Take Conrad's hat,

And make him chase it,

Until I have braided my hair,

And tied it up again. Then such a strong wind came up that it blew Conrad's hat across the fields, and he had to run after it. When he came back, she was already finished combing and putting up her hair, so he could not get even one strand. So Conrad became angry, and would not speak to her, and thus they tended the geese until evening, and then they went home.

The next morning when they were driving the geese out through the dark gateway, the maiden said, "Alas, Falada, hanging there!"

Falada answered:

Alas, young queen, passing by,

If this your mother knew,

Her heart would break in two. She sat down again in the field and began combing out her hair. When Conrad ran up and tried to take hold of some, she quickly said:

Blow, wind, blow,

Take Conrad's hat,

And make him chase it,

Until I have braided my hair,

And tied it up again. Then the wind blew, taking the hat off his head and far away. Conrad had to run after it, and when he came back, she had already put up her hair, and he could not get a single strand. Then they tended the geese until evening.

That evening, after they had returned home, Conrad went to the old king and said, "I won't tend geese with that girl any longer."

"Why not?" asked the old king.

"Oh, because she angers me all day long."

Then the old king ordered him to tell what it was that she did to him. Conrad said, "In the morning when we pass beneath the dark gateway with the flock, there is a horse's head on the wall, and she says to it, 'Alas, Falada, hanging there!' And the head replies:

Alas, young queen, passing by,

If this your mother knew,

Her heart would break in two." Then Conrad went on to tell what happened at the goose pasture, and how he had to chase his hat.

The old king ordered him to drive his flock out again the next day. As soon as morning came, he himself sat down behind the dark gateway, and heard how the girl spoke with Falada's head. Then he followed her out into the country and hid himself in a thicket in the meadow. There he soon saw with his own eyes the goose-girl and the goose-boy bringing their flock, and how after a while she sat down and took down her hair, which glistened brightly. Soon she said:

Blow, wind, blow,

Take Conrad's hat,

And make him chase it,

Until I have braided my hair,

And tied it up again. Then came a blast of wind and carried off Conrad's hat, so that he had to run far away, while the maiden quietly went on combing and braiding her hair, all of which the king observed. Then, quite unseen, he went away, and when the goose-girl came home in the evening, he called her aside, and asked why she did all these things.

"I am not allowed to tell you, nor can I reveal my sorrows to any human being, for I have sworn under the open heaven not to do so, and if I had not so sworn, I would have been killed."

He urged her and left her no peace, but he could get nothing from her. Finally he said, "If you will not tell me anything, then tell your sorrows to the iron stove there," and he went away.

So she crept into the iron stove, and began to cry sorrowfully, pouring out her whole heart. She said, "Here I sit, abandoned by the whole world, although I am the daughter of a king. A false chambermaid forced me to take off my royal clothes, and she has taken my place with my bridegroom. Now I have to do common work as a goose-girl. If my mother this, her heart would break in two."

The old king was standing outside listening by the stovepipe, and he heard what she said. Then he came back inside, and asked her to come out of the stove. Then they dressed her in royal clothes, and it was marvelous how beautiful she was.

The old king summoned his son and revealed to him that he had a false bride who was only a chambermaid, but that the true one was standing there, the one who had been a goose-girl. The young king rejoiced with all his heart when he saw her beauty and virtue. A great feast was made ready to which all the people and all good friends were invited.

At the head of the table sat the bridegroom with the king's daughter on one side of him, and the chambermaid on the other. However, the chambermaid was deceived, for she did not recognize the princess in her dazzling attire. After they had eaten and drunk, and were in a good mood, the old king asked the chambermaid as a riddle, what punishment a person deserved who had deceived her master in such and such a manner, then told the whole story, asking finally, "What sentence does such a person deserve?"

The false bride said, "She deserves no better fate than to be stripped stark naked, and put in a barrel that is studded inside with sharp nails. Two white horses should be hitched to it, and they should drag her along through one street after another, until she is dead."

"You are the one," said the old king, "and you have pronounced your own sentence. Thus shall it be done to you."

After the sentence had been carried out, the young king married his true bride, and both of them ruled over their kingdom in peace and happiness.

THE WINGED HORSE OF THE MUSES
JAMES BALDWIN

I. THE FOUNTAIN OF THE HORSE

PEOPLE SAID THAT THE GODS SENT HIM TO THE EARTH. OF COURSE IT was very desirable to account in some way for the appearance of so wonderful a creature, and there was no easier way to do it. But to this day nobody knows anything about his origin. When first seen he was simply a beautiful horse with wings like a great bird's, and he could travel with equal ease in the air and on the ground.

A good many years ago — so many that we shall not bother about the date — this wonderful animal, after a long and wearisome flight above the clouds, alighted at a pleasant spot near the foot of Mount Helicon, in Boeotia. He was hot and thirsty, and having seen some reeds growing at that spot, he hoped that he would find there a stream of water, or at least a small pool, from which he could drink. But to his disappointment there wasn't a drop of water to be seen — nothing but a little patch of boggy ground where the tall grass grew rank and thick. In his anger he spread his wings and gave the earth a tremendous kick with both of his hind feet together. The ground was soft, and the force of the blow was such that a long, deep trench was opened in the boggy soil. Instantly a stream of water, cool and sweet and clear, poured out and filled the trench and ran as a swift brook across the plain toward the distant river. The horse drank his fill from the pleasant fountain which he himself had thus hollowed out; and then, greatly refreshed, unfolded his wings again and rose high in the air, ready for a flight across the sea to the distant land of Lycia.

Men were not long in finding out that the waters of the new spring at the foot of Mount Helicon had some strange properties, filling their hearts with a wonderful sense of whatever is beautiful and true and good, and putting music into their souls and new songs into their mouths. And so they called the spring Hippocrene, or the Fountain of the Horse, and poets from all parts of the world went there to drink. But in later times the place fell into neglect, for, somehow, people were so busy with other things that they forgot the difference between poetry and doggerel, and nobody cared to drink from Hippocrene. And so the fountain was allowed to become choked with the stones and dirt that rolled down from the mountain; and soon wild grass and tall reeds hid the spot from view, and nobody from that day to this has been able to point out just where it is.

II. THE YOUNG TRAVELER

BUT THE HORSE?

We left him poised high in the air, with his head turned toward the sea and the distant land of Lycia. I do not know how long it took him to fly across, nor does it matter ; but one day, full of vigor and strength, and beautiful as a poet's dream, he alighted on the great road that runs eastward a little way from the capital city of Lycia. So softly had he descended, and so quietly had he folded his great wings and set his feet upon the ground, that a young man who was walking thoughtfully along the way did not know of his presence until he had cantered up quite close to him. The young man stopped and turned to admire the beautiful animal, and when he came quite near reached out his hand to stroke his nose. But the horse wheeled about and was away again as quick as an arrow sent speeding from a bow. The young man walked on again, and the horse soon returned and gamboled playfully around him, sometimes trotting swiftly back and forth along the roadway, sometimes rising in the air and sailing in circles round and round him. At last, after much whistling and the offer of a handful of sweetmeats, the young man coaxed the horse so near to him that by a sudden leap he was able to throw himself astride of his back just in front of his great gray wings.

"Now, my handsome fellow," he cried, "carry me straight forward to the country that lies beyond the great northern mountains. I would not be afraid of all the wild beasts in Asia if I could be sure of your help."

But the horse did not seem to understand him. He flew first to the north, then to the south, then to the north again, and sailed hither and thither gaily among the white clouds. At the end of an hour he alighted at the very spot from which he had risen, and his rider, despairing of making any progress with him, leaped to the ground and renewed his journey on foot. But the horse, who seemed to have taken a great liking to the young man, followed him, frisking hither and thither like a frolicsome dog, not afraid of him in the least, but very timid of all other travelers on the road. Late in the afternoon, when they had left the pleasant farm-lands of Lycia behind them and had come to the border of a wild, deserted region, an old man, with a long white beard and bright glittering eyes, met them and stopped, as many others had already done, to admire the beautiful animal.

"Who are you, young man," he inquired, "and what are you doing with so handsome a steed here in this lonely place?"

"My name is Bellerophon," answered the young man, "and I am going by order of King Iobates to the country beyond the northern mountains, where I expect to slay the Chimaera, which lives there. But as for this horse, all I know is that he has followed me since early morning. Whose he is and from whence he came I cannot tell."

The old man was silent for a few moments as if in deep thought, while Bellerophon, very weary with his long walk, sat down on a stone to rest, and the horse strolled along by the roadside nipping the short grass.

"Do you see the white roof over there among the trees?" finally asked the old man. "Well, under it there is a shrine to the goddess Athena, of which I am the keeper. A few steps beyond it is my own humble cottage, where I spend my days in study and meditation. If you will go in and lodge with me for the night, I may be able to tell you something about the task that you have undertaken."

Bellerophon was very glad to accept the old man's invitation, for the sun had already begun to dip below the western hills. The hut contained only two rooms, but everything about it was very clean and cozy, and the kind host spared no pains to make his guest comfortable and happy. After they had eaten supper and were still reclining on couches at the side of the table, the old man looked Bellerophon sharply in the face and said:

"Now tell me all about yourself and your kindred, and why you are going thus alone and on foot into the country of the Chimaera."

III. BELLEROPHON'S STORY

"My father," answered Bellerophon, "is Glaucus, the king of far-off Corinth, where he has great wealth in horses and in ships; and my grandfather was Sisyphus, of whom you have doubtless heard, for he was famed all over the world for his craftiness and his fine business qualities, that made him the richest of men. I was brought up in my father's house, and it was intended that I should succeed him as king of Corinth; but three years ago a sad misfortune happened to me. My younger brother and I were hunting among the wooded hills of Argos, and we were having fine sport, for we had taken much game. We had started home with our booty, and I, who was the faster walker, was some distance ahead of my brother, when, suddenly, a deer sprang up between me and the sun. Half -blinded by the light, I turned and let fly an arrow quickly. The creature bounded swiftly away, unhurt, but a cry of anguish from the low underbrush told me that I had slain my brother.

"Vainly did I try to stanch the flow of blood; vainly did I call upon the gods to save him and me. He raised his eyes to mine, smiled feebly, pressed my hand as in forgiveness, and was no more.

"I knew that I dared not return home, for the laws of our country are very severe against anyone who, though by accident, causes the death of another. Indeed, until I could be purified from my brother's blood, I dared not, as you know, look any man in the face. For a long time I wandered hither and thither, like a hunted beast, shunning the sight of every human being, and living upon nuts and fruits and such small game as I could bring down with my arrows. At length I bethought me that perhaps old King Proetus of Tiryns, in whose land I then was, might purify me; or if not, he might at least slay me at the altar, which would be better than living longer as a fugitive ; and so, under the cover of night, I went down into Tiryns, and entering the temple with my cloak thrown over my head, knelt down at the shrine where penitent men are wont to seek purification.

"I need not tell you how the king found me and purified me and took me into his own house and treated me for a long time as his own son; it would make my story too long. . . . But a few weeks ago I noticed that a great change had come over him, for he no longer showed me the kind attention which I had learned to expect of him. The queen, too, seemed to have become my enemy, and treated me with the haughtiest disdain. Indeed, I began to suspect that she was urging her husband to put me out of the way, and I should not have been surprised if he had banished me from his court. I was, of course, uncomfortable, and was trying to think of some excuse for leaving Tiryns, when the king, very early one morning, called me into his private chamber. He held in his hand a wooden tablet, sealed with his own signet, and he seemed to be greatly excited about something.

"'Bellerophon,' he said, 'I have written on this tablet a letter of very great importance, which I wish to send to my father-in-law. King Iobates, of Lycia, beyond the sea. You are the only man whom I can trust to carry this letter, and so I beg that you will get ready to go at once. A ship is in the harbor already manned for the voyage, and the wind is fair. Before the sun rises you may be well out at sea.'

"I took the tablet and embarked, as he wished, without so much as bidding good-by to any of his household. A good ship and fresh breezes carried me over the sea to Lycia, where I was welcomed most kindly by your good king Iobates. For he had known both my father and my grandfather, and he said that he owed me honor for their sakes. Nine days he held a great feast in his palace, and all the most famous philosophers, merchants, and warriors were invited to his table, in order that I might meet them and hear them talk. I had not forgotten the tablet that King Proetus had given me, and several times I had made a start to give it to Iobates ; but I knew that it would be bad taste to speak of business at such a time. On the tenth day, however, after all the guests had gone home, he said to me:

"'Now tell me what message you have brought from my son-in-law Proetus and my dear daughter Anteia. For I know that they have sent me some word.'

"Then I gave him the tablet. He untied the ribbon which bound the two blocks of wood together, and when he had broken the seal he lifted them apart and read that which was engraved on the wax between them. I do not know what this message was, but it must have been something of great importance, for the king's face grew very pale, and he staggered as if he would fall. Then he left the room very quickly, and I did not see him again until this morning, when he called me into his council-chamber. I was surprised to notice how haggard and worn he was, and how very old he seemed to have become within the past three days.

"'Young man,' he said, speaking rather sharply, I thought, — 'Young man, they tell me that you are brave and fond of hunting wild beasts, and that you are anxious to win fame by doing some daring deed. I have word, only this morning, that the people who live on the other side of the northern mountains are in great dread of a strange animal that comes out of the caves and destroys their flocks, and sometimes carries their children off to its lair. Some say it is a lion, some a dragon, and some laugh at the whole affair and call it a goat. I think myself that it must be the very same beast that infested the mountain valleys some years ago, and was called by our wise men a Chimaera ; and for the sake of the good people whom it annoys, I should like to have it killed. Every one to whom I have spoken about it, however, is afraid to venture into its haunts.'

"'I am not afraid said I. I will start to the mountains this very hour, and if I don't bring you the head of the Chimaera to hang up in your halls, you may brand me as a coward.'

"'You are a brave young man,' said the king, "and I will take you at your word, but I would advise you to lose no time in starting.'

"I was surprised at the way in which the king dismissed me, and the longer I thought about the matter the stranger it all seemed. But there was only one thing to do. I walked out of the king's palace, found the shortest road to Mount Climax, and — here I am!"

IV. THE DREAM AND THE GIFTS

"Do you have any idea what it was that King Proetus wrote to King Iobates?" asked the old man.

"Why should I?"

"Then I will tell you. He wrote to say that you had been accused of treasonable crimes in Tiryns, and that, not wishing to harm you himself, he had sent you to Lycia to be put to death. King Iobates was loath to have this done, and so he has sent you out against the Chimaera, knowing that no man ever fought with that monster and lived. For she is a more terrible beast than you would believe. All the region beyond the mountains has been laid waste by her, hundreds of people have been slain by her fiery breath alone, and a whole army that was lately sent out against her was routed and put to flight. The king knows very well that she will kill you."

"But what kind of a beast is this Chimaera?" asked Bellerophon.

"She is a strange kind of monster," was the answer. "Her head and shoulders are those of a lion, her body is that of a goat, and her hinder parts are those of a dragon. She fights with her hot breath and her long tail, and she stays on the mountains by night, and goes down into the valleys by day."

"If I had only a shield, and my bow and arrows, and could ride the good winged horse whithersoever I wished him to go, I would not be afraid of all the Chimaeras in the world," said Bellerophon.

"Let me tell you something," said the old man. " Do you go out to the little temple in the grove before us and lie down to sleep at the

foot of the shrine. Everybody knows that to people who are in need
of help Athena often comes in dreams to give good advice. Perhaps
she will favor you with her counsel and aid, if you only show that
you have faith in her."

Bellerophon went at once to the little temple and stretched himself out on the floor close to the shrine of the goddess. The winged
horse, who had been feeding on the grass, followed him to the door,
and then lay down on the ground outside.

It was nearly morning when Bellerophon dreamed that a tall
and stately lady, with large round eyes, and long hair that fell in
ringlets upon her shoulders, came into the temple and stood beside
him.

"Do you know who the winged steed is that waits outside the
door for you ? " she asked.

"Truly, I do not," answered Bellerophon. " But if I had some
means of making him understand me, he might be my best friend
and helper."

"His name is Pegasus," said the lady, " and he was born near the
shore of the great western ocean. He has come to help you in your
fight with the Chimaera, and you can guide him anywhere you wish
if you will only put this ribbon into his mouth, holding on to the
ends yourself."

With these words, she placed a beautiful bridle in Bellerophon's
hands, and, turning about, walked silently away.

When the sun had risen and Bellerophon awoke, the bridle was
lying on the floor beside him, and near it were a long bow with
arrows and a shield. It was the first bridle that he had ever seen —
some people say that it was the first that was ever made — and the
young man examined it with great curiosity. Then he went out and
quickly slipped the ribbon bit into the mouth of Pegasus, and leaped
upon his back. To his great joy, he saw that now the horse understood all his wishes.

"Here are your bow and arrows and your shield," cried the old
man, handing them to him. "Take them, and may Athena be with
you in your fight with the Chimaera!"

V. THE FIGHT WITH THE CHIMAERA

AT A WORD FROM BELLEROPHON, PEGASUS ROSE HIGH IN THE AIR, AND then, turning, made straight northward toward the great mountains. It was evening when they reached Mount Climax, and quite dark when they at last hovered over the spot which the Chimsera was said to visit at night. Bellerophon would have passed on without seeing her, had not a burning mountain sent out a great sheet of flame, that lighted up the valleys and gave him a plain view of the monster crouching in the shadow of a cliff. He fitted an arrow quickly in his bow and, as Pegasus paused above the edge of the cliff, he let fly directly at her fear ful head. The arrow missed the mark, however, and struck the beast in the throat, giving her an ugly wound. Then you should have seen the fury of the Chimaera, how she reared herself on her hind feet; how she leaped into the air; how she beat the rocks with her long dragon's tail; how she puffed and fumed and roared and blew her fiery breath toward Pegasus, hoping to scorch his wings or smother both horse and rider with its poisonous fumes. Bellerophon, when he saw her in her mad rage, could no longer wonder that the whole country had been in terror of her.

"Now, my good Pegasus," he said, stroking the horse's mane, "steady yourself just out of her reach, and let me send her another keepsake!"

This time the arrow struck the beast in the back, and instead of killing her, only made her more furious than ever. She attacked everything that was in her reach, clawed the rocks, knocked trees down with her tail, and filled all the mountain valleys with the noise of her mad roarings. The third arrow, however, was sent with a better aim, and the horrid creature, pierced to the heart, fell backward lifeless, and rolled over and over down the steep mountain side, and far out into the valley below.

Bellerophon slept on the mountain that night, while his steed kept watch by his side. In the morning he went down and found the Chimaera lying stiff and dead in the spot where she had rolled, while a score of gaping countrymen stood around at a safe distance, rejoicing that the monster which had laid waste their fields and desolated their homes had at last been slain. Bellerophon cut off the creature's head, and remounting Pegasus, set out on his return to King Iobates.

Of course old Iobates was astonished to see Bellerophon come back with the monster's head in his arms. All that he did was to thank the young hero for the great service which he had done for his country; and then he began to study up some other means of putting him out of the way.

At length, Bellerophon bethought him that, since this world was beset with so many distressing things, worse even than Chimaeras, he would leave it and ride on the back of Pegasus to heaven. There is no knowing what he might have done, had not Zeus, just in the nick of time, sent a gadfly to sting the horse. Pegasus made a wild plunge to escape the fly, and Bellerophon, taken by surprise, was tumbled to the earth. Strange to say, the hero was not killed, but only blinded by his fall; and he never heard of Pegasus again.

HORSEMAN
RENEE
CARTER
HALL

THE BIRTH WAS NOT GOING WELL. HE WATCHED ON THE BLACK-AND-white closed-circuit monitor as the dapple gray mare, Carolina Moon, strained and panted through what should have been the shortest and final stage of labor. Nothing was happening, and that wasn't good.

He scrubbed his face with his hands, feeling two days' worth of stubble. He'd hoped that having a new life to look after, a knobby-kneed foal to run around the pasture, would somehow begin to heal him. But so far, everything was just a reminder of why Katie should have been there. She would have known exactly what to do, now, when he didn't.

For one brief, bitter moment he wished he could just turn the monitor off and walk away from all of it, out of the house and down the long driveway and then... wherever. Anywhere he could forget, but that place didn't exist.

And he could never leave Carolina, of course. She had been Katie's horse, the only part of her he had left now. He'd joked sometimes that she loved the mare more than him, and she'd grin back at him and say something like "Of course I do. She smells better, for one thing."

He realized his hands were clenched. He'd grown so used to the anger that it was simply there now, essential and unnoticed, like the breath held tight in his chest.

If he waited any longer, he could lose both Carolina and the foal, and he didn't think he could stand that, not now. He was headed for the phone to call the vet when he caught movement on the monitor from the corner of his eye. A dark, wet shape was emerging as Carolina pushed. He grabbed the battery-powered lantern and raced to the stable, his breath steaming in the April night.

Halfway there, he heard the mare scream.

He had never heard a horse make a sound like that, not even ones that were panicked or in pain. It was a long, shrill, desperate cry, and his skin prickled as he pushed the stall door open.

The straw beneath the mare was soaked with blood. Too much blood. His first impulse was to run back for the phone--damn it, he should have brought it out with him--but the mare's breaths were shallow, spaced further and further apart, and as he knelt over her, stroking her neck, he knew there wouldn't be enough time for the vet to get there, much less do anything. "Oh, God, I'm sorry," he said, not sure whether he was apologizing to Carolina or Katie or himself. "I'm sorry." He said it over and over, and then she wasn't breathing, and then she was still.

He sat there for a long moment, the emptiness of it pulling him in, draining him. He might have cried, but he had cried so much before that it seemed there was nothing left in him for tears. At last he turned to the foal, expecting it to be dead, too.

It wasn't. It was struggling its way clear of the birth sac, its dark coat wet and tousled. It was male, a little colt. He reached for one of the old towels he'd left there the day before, then stopped and looked closer at the foal. Its coat was not merely dark but black, and it looked oddly glossy in spots, more than he would have expected for it just being wet. As the foal tried to stand, he moved the lantern a little closer. "What the hell...?"

It had scales, he saw now, ebony patches shining here and there among the horsehair. The hooves were wrong as well, oddly cloven and pointed. The head was the right shape, but its eyes were almost red, and its mouth--

He swore and backed up fast. The damned thing had fangs curving out from its upper lip.

The foal got to its feet, far steadier than a newborn should have been. Its eyes focused on him, and for a moment he knew nothing but that strange gaze and his own blood roaring in his ears.

It was when the forked tongue slipped from the foal's mouth that he turned and ran.

Back in the house, hands shaking, he cupped cold water at the kitchen sink and splashed his face once, twice, three times. When that didn't work, he took a knife from the drawer and pressed his thumb against the point. He drew in a sharp breath as it nicked the skin, but he did not wake up.

"Okay," he said, his voice sounding far away. "Fine."

They kept the rifle over the mantel. It was kind of a joke, really, the kind Katie would make about them living out here in the wilderness, needing a gun to keep varmints off the farm, when the farmhouse had central air and he could see the Lowells' house from the kitchen window. He took the rifle down and tried to remember where they'd put the bullets. He finally found them in the kitchen junk drawer, shoved in the back behind the stray rubber bands, a box of toothpicks, and several sizes of batteries.

Whatever it was, he told himself, it would probably be dead by the time he got back out there. It was probably already dead. Things like that happened sometimes, throwbacks or weird mutations. Maybe there'd been something off with Carolina's feed--hormones or some chemical crap they were pumping into everything these days.

He went to the monitor. Carolina's bright shape was still there, taking up most of the image. The foal was there, too, still alive, standing over her. It was nosing at her body, and beneath his revulsion he felt a certain vague pity; no doubt it was trying to suckle. It bent its head to her belly and--

No. No, he hadn't seen that. He stared at the screen.

The foal drew its head up again, and he saw the sudden dark

gash in the mare's light gray coat. The foal had something in its mouth, and as he watched, it tossed its head back a bit, mouth gaping.

Like a lizard swallowing--

The foal spread its long forelegs and bent its head down again, tearing off another mouthful of flesh.

His stomach clenched, and he tasted sour coffee in the back of his throat. He swallowed hard, gripped the rifle in damp palms, and went back out to the stable.

The foal did not look up when he entered. It kept tearing at the mare's flesh, a wet, thick sound followed by gulps as it swallowed.

He cocked the rifle. The foal turned at the sound and met his gaze again. It looked like it knew what he meant to do, but there was no fear in its eyes when he took aim and tightened his finger on the trigger.

In one swift strike, the foal lunged and sank its fangs into his arm, clamping down through his flannel shirt. Pain lanced through his arm, and he struggled to throw the creature off, trying to get at an angle where he could shoot it. At last the foal let go, scuttling back to the far corner of the stable, behind Carolina.

His arm burned all the way to the shoulder. How had the thing moved that fast? He'd been looking right at it, and he hadn't even seen--

Never mind it. It was off him, and the gun was still loaded. Panting, he leveled the barrel at the foal and pulled the trigger.

Click.

He took a few steps back, keeping an eye on the foal, and checked the rifle. The shell was still there, everything as it should be.

He tried again. Click.

The foal watched him, its gaze steady and deep.

The world spun and tilted around him, and he stumbled backwards out of the stable. It felt like his bones were on fire. *Goddamn thing probably gave me an infection.* He wasn't sure where the rifle was, but he didn't have it and didn't want to go back to look for it. *Bacteria or venom or God knows what...*

His chest felt tight by the time he got back to the house. He fumbled through the kitchen cabinet, knocking over bottles of

Katie's vitamins he still hadn't thrown away, and managed to get the top off the aspirin. He swallowed two dry and was halfway to the phone when he passed out.

WHEN HE WOKE, HE WAS STILL ON THE KITCHEN FLOOR, AND SEVERAL minutes passed before he could remember what had happened. He picked himself up slowly, testing, but besides his back and knees being stiff, he felt fine.

It was dark outside. He squinted at the clock on the stove, not believing the numbers. Nine-thirteen. At night. He'd been out the whole day.

He gingerly pulled back his shirt sleeve. The twin punctures were deep and neat, and around them the skin was raw, as if he'd been burned. But the wounds didn't hurt, not even when he pressed them, though he still had feeling in the skin. He bandaged his arm anyway, tearing the gauze off with his teeth.

The monitor was still on, though the camera's battery should have been dead by now. The mare's white ribs curved out from what remained of her body. He could not see the foal, and he shivered at the thought of the thing getting out of the stable.

He turned on the back porch light and went out to the shed, searching through snow shovels and rakes before he found the axe. The weight of it felt good in his hands, solid and simple and real.

He rounded the house and stopped. Light was flickering from the front pasture.

Fire. He broke into a run. As he got closer, he saw that the grass itself wasn't burning; instead, a bonfire rose from the bales of hay he'd left there months before. He'd meant to take them in to the barn, but... well, it was another thing that hadn't happened since the accident.

A dark shape darted around the orange flames. He clutched the axe handle a little tighter.

It was no longer a foal. There was no question it was the same creature, but it was as large as a yearling now, grown strong on its mother's flesh, and it was... Well, there was nothing else he could call it. It was dancing in tightening circles around the fire, picking up its hooves, kicking its heels, churning the earth as it pounded out rhythms in double time, triple time, cadences he'd never heard before. Sparks rose where each hoof struck the ground, and for a moment, it looked as if the fire was coming not from the hay, but from within the earth itself.

The colt slowed, then stopped. Its coat was lathered with sweat, but it did not seem tired. It turned its head and held his gaze for a long moment.

Something in him could feel that rhythm continuing even though the hoofbeats had ceased. It was something ancient, something passed into legend, and even as he stood shaking, his own sweat chilling his skin, he fought the desire to go to the fireside himself, to dance before it as men might have in elder days when speech was gesture and reason only a dream.

The fire was dying down. The colt shook itself and lowered its head as if to graze on the embers.

He turned and walked slowly back to the house. When he got back into the kitchen, he was still holding the axe, and he looked down at it dully for a moment, trying to remember what it was for.

A distant light burned in the black square of the kitchen window, and he thought of fire again before he remembered the Lowells' porch light, the one they kept on even during the day.

Was Frank asleep? He hoped not. He hoped the bastard hadn't slept since that night. It was what he deserved.

He stared at the house, the same familiar rage rising in him like bile. If it were possible to set a house on fire by sheer will, he would have expected to see flames licking at the shutters.

He hadn't been there when she'd died. He hadn't even known. He would have thought that loving a person more than a decade meant that you would know, somehow, when they needed you, know when something was wrong, just *know*. Wasn't that what people talked about?

But he hadn't felt a thing.

Neither had she; that was what they all tried to tell him. It had been quick, and he was supposed to think that was a blessing, that it was so much better she hadn't suffered, hadn't had the kind of death everyone feared, with hospital monitors and tubes and a slow march of pain. But at least then he might have had some warning, might have had some chance to prepare himself, to know that what he was saying was being said for the last time.

He couldn't remember what he had said to her last. He was afraid it was something about the electric bill. He had lain awake several nights, trying to remember, afraid to remember. He couldn't remember what she had said either. It was the last time he'd ever seen her alive, and he wanted to enclose that memory in crystal, keep it safe, and he couldn't even remember, and he hated that, hated himself for not paying more attention.

He hadn't seen Frank since the sentencing. Apparently drinking so much you could barely walk, getting behind the wheel anyway, and slamming into someone at seventy miles an hour on a rural road could be paid for with sixty days in jail and a smattering of community service hours afterward.

Saying it wasn't fair was obvious. Of course it wasn't. If it had been fair, he would have been resting a hand comfortingly on the arm of Frank's widow as she dabbed at her eyes with a handkerchief, telling her that we don't know why these things happen, but there's a reason we just can't see, that things are meant to be this way.

He realized he was still holding the axe. He forced himself to release it, hands aching as he propped it against the wall and went to bed.

When he woke up, it was dark again—or dark still. He felt his stubble and decided it was the same night. The monitor in the kitchen was finally blank, and he turned it off.

He unwrapped the gauze around his arm. The puncture wounds were almost gone, just two purplish-black marks there, each about the size of a dime. The skin around them was less raw, but a set of odd welts had risen, curving slashes of raised flesh, as if he'd been burned with a brand. He touched them hesitantly, but they didn't hurt.

He went outside. The pasture was gray under a gray sky. In the stable, nothing was left of the mare but bones and twisted hide. Her skull stared back at him.

He felt the horse's presence before he turned and saw it. It was grown now, a stallion, a twisted mockery of fine equine form, hideous and mesmerizing. It stood as if waiting for him, tossing its head eagerly as he came near. It smelled of horse-sweat and moldy hay, of wet leaves and rotten meat, of something burned and something long dead.

It was beautiful.

He reached his hand out to stroke its neck. Steam rose when he touched its flesh, but he felt no pain.

He found the tack where Carolina's had been kept. At first the saddle and bridle looked like black leather, but the texture was strangely pebbled and thin, the hide of nothing he knew on earth. The bit looked like old bone.

The horse stood calmly while he saddled it and slipped the bridle on. The brand on its flank matched the raised flesh on his arm. He traced the marks with his fingers and felt himself smile. He didn't know what the symbols said, but he knew what they meant. This creature was part of him, as he was part of it. The selfsame darkness laid claim to them both.

The horse snorted and pawed at the ground. He knew what it wanted. He wanted it too.

He led the horse out of the stable. The sun would be rising soon, though all he could see of it now was a smudge of lighter gray at the horizon. When he mounted up, the stallion went forward, needing no command, and as dawn broke, they rode out of the pasture together, heading for the house just up the hill, the one where the light still burned.

JACK PUMPKINHEAD AND THE SAWHORSE
L. FRANK BAUM

IN A ROOM OF THE ROYAL PALACE OF THE EMERALD CITY OF OZ hangs a Magic Picture, in which are shown all the important scenes that transpire in those fairy dominions. The scenes shift constantly and by watching them, Ozma, the girl Ruler, is able to discover events taking place in any part of her kingdom.

One day she saw in her Magic Picture that a little girl and a little boy had wandered together into a great, gloomy forest at the far west of Oz and had become hopelessly lost. Their friends were seeking them in the wrong direction and unless Ozma came to their rescue the little ones would never be found in time to save them from starving.

So the Princess sent a message to Jack Pumpkinhead and asked him to come to the palace. This personage, one of the queerest of the queer inhabitants of Oz, was an old friend and companion of Ozma. His form was made of rough sticks fitted together and dressed in ordinary clothes. His head was a pumpkin with a face carved upon it, and was set on top a sharp stake which formed his neck.

Jack was active, good-natured and a general favorite; but his pumpkin head was likely to spoil with age, so in order to secure a good supply of heads he grew a big field of pumpkins and lived in the middle of it, his house being a huge pumpkin hollowed out. Whenever he needed a new head he picked a pumpkin, carved a face on it and stuck it upon the stake of his neck, throwing away the old head as of no further use.

The day Ozma sent for him Jack was in prime condition and was glad to be of service in rescuing the lost children. Ozma made him a map, showing just where the forest was and how to get to it and the paths he must take to reach the little ones. Then she said:

"You'd better ride the Sawhorse, for he is swift and intelligent and will help you accomplish your task."

"All right," answered Jack, and went to the royal stable to tell the Sawhorse to be ready for the trip.

This remarkable animal was not unlike Jack Pumpkinhead in form, although so different in shape. Its body was a log, with four sticks stuck into it for legs. A branch at one end of the log served as a tail, while in the other end was chopped a gash that formed a mouth. Above this were two small knots that did nicely for eyes. The Sawhorse was the favorite steed of Ozma and to prevent its wooden legs from wearing out she had them shod with plates of gold.

Jack said "Good morning" to the Sawhorse and placed upon the creature's back a saddle of purple leather, studded with jewels.

"Where now?" asked the horse, blinking its knot eyes at Jack.

"We're going to rescue two babes in the wood," was the reply. Then he climbed into the saddle and the wooden animal pranced out of the stable, through the streets of the Emerald City and out upon the highway leading to the western forest where the children were lost.

Small though he was, the Sawhorse was swift and untiring. By nightfall they were in the far west and quite close to the forest they sought. They passed the night standing quietly by the roadside. They needed no food, for their wooden bodies never became hungry; nor did they sleep, because they never tired. At daybreak they continued their journey and soon reached the forest.

Jack now examined the map Ozma had given him and found the right path to take, which the Sawhorse obediently followed.

Underneath the trees all was silent and gloomy and Jack beguiled the way by whistling gayly as the Sawhorse trotted along.

The paths branched so many times and in so many different ways that the Pumpkinhead was often obliged to consult Ozma's map, and finally the Sawhorse became suspicious.

"Are you sure you are right?" it asked.

"Of course," answered Jack. "Even a Pumpkinhead whose brains are seeds can follow so clear a map as this. Every path is plainly marked, and here is a cross where the children are."

Finally they reached a place, in the very heart of the forest, where they came upon the lost boy and girl. But they found the two children bound fast to the trunk of a big tree, at the foot of which they were sitting.

When the rescuers arrived, the little girl was sobbing bitterly and the boy was trying to comfort her, though he was probably frightened as much as she.

"Cheer up, my dears," said Jack, getting out of the saddle. "I have come to take you back to your parents. But why are you bound to that tree?"

"Because," cried a small, sharp voice, "they are thieves and robbers. That's why!"

"Dear me!" said Jack, looking around to see who had spoken. The voice seemed to come from above.

A big grey squirrel was sitting upon a low branch of the tree. Upon the squirrel's head was a circle of gold, with a diamond set in the center of it. He was running up and down the limbs and chattering excitedly.

"These children," continued the squirrel, angrily, "robbed our storehouse of all the nuts we had saved up for winter. Therefore, being King of all the Squirrels in this forest, I ordered them arrested and put in prison, as you now see them. They had no right to steal our provisions and we are going to punish them."

"We were hungry," said the boy, pleadingly, "and we found a hollow tree full of nuts, and ate them to keep alive. We didn't want to starve when there was food right in front of us."

"Quite right," remarked Jack, nodding his pumpkin head. "I

don't blame you one bit, under the circumstances. Not a bit."

Then he began to untie the ropes that bound the children to the tree.

"Stop that!" cried the King Squirrel, chattering and whisking about. "You mustn't release our prisoners. You have no right to."

But Jack paid no attention to the protest. His wooden fingers were awkward and it took him some time to untie the ropes. When at last he succeeded, the tree was full of squirrels, called together by their King, and they were furious at losing their prisoners. From the tree they began to hurl nuts at the Pumpkinhead, who laughed at them as he helped the two children to their feet.

Now, at the top of this tree was a big dead limb, and so many squirrels gathered upon it that suddenly it broke away and fell to the ground. Poor Jack was standing directly under it and when the limb struck him it smashed his pumpkin head into a pulpy mass and sent Jack's wooden form tumbling, to stop with a bump against a tree a dozen feet away.

He sat up, a moment afterward, but when he felt for his head it was gone. He could not see; neither could he speak. It was perhaps the greatest misfortune that could have happened to Jack Pumpkinhead, and the squirrels were delighted. They danced around in the tree in great glee as they saw Jack's plight.

The boy and girl were indeed free, but their protector was ruined. The Sawhorse was there, however, and in his way he was wise. He had seen the accident and knew that the smashed pumpkin would never again serve Jack as a head. So he said to the children, who were frightened at this accident to their new found friend:

"Pick up the Pumpkinhead's body and set it on my saddle. Then mount behind it and hold on. We must get out of this forest as soon as we can, or the squirrels may capture you again. I must guess at the right path, for Jack's map is no longer of any use to him since that limb destroyed his head."

The two children lifted Jack's body, which was not at all heavy, and placed it upon the saddle. Then they climbed up behind it and the Sawhorse immediately turned and trotted back along the path he had come, bearing all three with ease. However, when the path began to branch into many paths, all following different directions, the wooden animal became puzzled and soon was wandering aimlessly about, without any hope of finding the right way. Toward evening they came upon a fine fruit tree, which furnished the children a supper, and at night the little ones lay upon a bed of leaves while the Sawhorse stood watch, with the limp, headless form of poor Jack Pumpkinhead lying helpless across the saddle.

Now, Ozma had seen in her Magic Picture all that had happened in the forest, so she sent the little Wizard, mounted upon the Cowardly Lion, to save the unfortunates. The Lion knew the forest well and when he reached it he bounded straight through the tangled paths to where the Sawhorse was wandering, with Jack and the two children on his back.

The Wizard was grieved at the sight of the headless Jack, but believed he could save him. He first led the Sawhorse out of the forest and restored the boy and girl to the arms of their anxious friends, and then he sent the Lion back to Ozma to tell her what had happened.

The Wizard now mounted the Sawhorse and supported Jack's form on the long ride to the pumpkin field. When they arrived at Jack's house the Wizard selected a fine pumpkin--not too ripe--and very neatly carved a face on it. Then he stuck the pumpkin solidly on Jack's neck and asked him:

"Well, old friend, how do you feel?"

"Fine!" replied Jack, and shook the hand of the little Wizard gratefully. "You have really saved my life, for without your assistance I could not have found my way home to get a new head. But I'm all right, now, and I shall be very careful not to get this beautiful head smashed." And he shook the Wizard's hand again.

"Are the brains in the new head any better than the old ones?" inquired the Sawhorse, who had watched Jack's restoration.

"Why, these seeds are quite tender," replied the Wizard, "so they will give our friend tender thoughts. But, to speak truly, my dear Sawhorse, Jack Pumpkinhead, with all his good qualities, will never be noted for his wisdom."

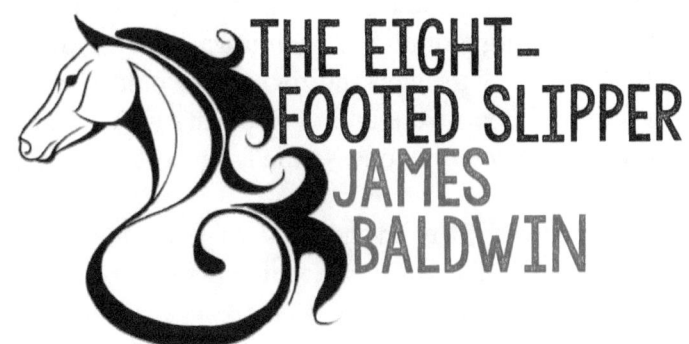

THE EIGHT-FOOTED SLIPPER
JAMES BALDWIN

DID YOU EVER HEAR OF THE CURIOUS RIDDLE WHICH OLD-FASHIONED people in the North used to tell one another on Wednesday mornings? It was something like this:

"Who are the two that ride over the rainbow? Three eyes have they together, ten feet, two arms, and a tail. And thus they journey through the world."

You can't guess it, and it will be of no use for you to try. But all those old-fashioned people knew the answer; and everybody repeated the question to everybody else, not as a puzzle nor to gain information, but simply because it was the custom, and therefore the right thing to do. In that respect it was like the briefer and more matter-of-fact riddle which people propound to one another nowadays:" It's a fine morning, isn't it?" But it didn't mean the same. The answer which everybody gave to everybody was this:

"The two who ride over the rainbow are Odin and his steed Sleipnir. Odin has one eye, the horse two; the horse runs on eight feet, Odin has two; two arms has Odin, and the horse has a tail."

A horse with eight feet would of course have many advantages over the commoner kind that have only four. If a heavy load had to be drawn, only think what a wonderful leverage his long legs would give him ! If a long journey were to be taken, how nicely he could hold up half of his feet and give them a rest while the other four were steadily jogging along! And then in racing and jumping, what an impetus all those legs, working together, would give him! Many tales are told of his prowess and of the feats which he performed, but I will repeat to you only one — the famous story of his journey to the underworld.

There was great grief in the house of Odin, for word had been brought that Balder, his best-loved son, was dead. Balder, the white, the pure, the good, the fair, had been treacherously slain, and all the world was in mourning. Who now would bring good gifts to men? Who would bless them with smiles and sunlight, as Balder had done? Out by the shore of the sea the people had gathered to perform the last sad rites for the dead hero. Balder's own ship, the Ringhorn, had been drawn up on the beach, and in it were placed all the most precious things that had been his. The deck was piled with cedar-wood, and between the layers of sticks were placed gums and rich spices and fragrant leaves, and the whole pile was covered with fine robes, and a couch was made whereon to lay the body of the dead. Then Balder's horse, Gyller the Golden, was led on board, saddled and bridled as if for a long journey. His arms also were brought — his shield and sword and bow and quiver — and laid by the side of the ouch. Finally the hero himself was borne to his last resting-place, and Nanna, his young wife who had died of grief, was laid beside him. The great ship was pushed into the sea and set on fire. Wrapped in flames and hidden by dense clouds of smoke, it drifted far away from the shore.

"Alas! alas!" cried the people, "what will become of us, now that Balder is dead — now that the sunlight is gone out of the world?" And they went to their homes weeping, and sat down in the darkness and cold, and could not believe that aught of joy would ever come to them again.

And other things sorrowed, too. The trees bent their heads, and the leaves upon them fell withered to the ground. The meadows doffed their green summer coats and dressed themselves in sober suits of russet. The birds forgot to sing. The small creatures of the woods hid themselves in the ground or in the hollow trunks of the trees. The cicadas no longer made merry in the groves. The music of the busy world was hushed. Nowhere could be heard the sound of the spindle or the loom, of ax or flail, of the harvesters' song, of the huntsmen's horn, of the warriors' battle-cry; but only the dull thud of the waves beating against the shore, or the wild whistling of the winds among the dead branches of the trees.

In the King's high halls Balder's mother lamented his untimely fate, and his sisters were beside themselves with grief. Odin, with his blue hood pulled down over his face, sat silent in the twilight and listened to the moaning of the sea. He was not only troubled because of the death of his son, but the sadness of the world oppressed him. What if the universal grief should continue and joy never return? Frost and ice and darkness would at length overwhelm the earth, and the race of mankind would perish.

"We must bring lost Balder back to us!" he cried. "He must not stay in the gloomy halls of the underworld. And yet how can we persuade Hela, the pale-faced Queen of that region, to give him up?"

"Hela is deaf to prayers," answered one of his councilors; "and, moreover, she will be glad to keep the bright Balder in order that perchance some joy may be known to the dwellers in her own domains. And yet, mayhap, if someone of your own household shall go down and carry your prayers to her, she will relent and give him up."

"Ah, so she may!" cried the Queen-mother. "But who among his brothers will dare undertake so fearful a journey?"

"I will dare!" cried Hermod, Balder's younger brother. He was only a little fellow, but he was famous all over the world for the quickness of his movements and for his horsemanship. "I will go down to Hela's house with your prayers, if only I may ride Sleipnir, who is both fleet and sure-footed."

Gray Sleipnir was at once led out and saddled with the greatest care; and food and drink were given him, enough for eighteen days. Then Hermod, booted and spurred, sprang upon him and rode fearlessly away along the shadowy highroad that leads toward the land of the stern-faced Hela. Nine days through mists and fogs, nine

nights amid darkness and unseen perils, did the good steed gallop
steadily onward; and his eight iron hoofs, clattering upon the rocky
roadway, roused strange echoes among the barren hills and frowning mountain passes. Nine days and nine nights did bold Hermod sit
in the saddle with his face bared to the chilling winds and his heart
set firm upon his errand. Many were the sad-eyed travelers whom
they overtook, all journeying toward the same goal, but not one did
they meet returning. And pale specters flitted in the air above them,
and ogres grinned in the darkness, and owls hooted from the clefts
of the rock. But none of these things could frighten Sleipnir; for
were not the mystic runes of Odin engraved on his teeth? And no
terror could make Hermod falter; for was not his errand one of love
and mercy?

At length, having passed through a dark and narrow valley
where there were many unknown and fearful things, they came out
upon a broad plain which is the beginning of the great silent land. A
dim yellow light illumined the sky, and the air seemed soft and mild,
and a restful peace abode there. But no sound of any kind was heard;
even the striking of Sleipnir's hoofs upon the pavement was noise-
less; and when Hermod tried to sing, he found that he could not hear
his own voice. On the farther side of the plain they came to a broad
river that flowed silently toward the sea. It was the river Gjol, and
across it was the long Gjallar Bridge, a narrow roadway roofed with
shining gold. Here Sleipnir slacked his pace, and Hermod found that
the great silence had been left behind. At the end of the bridge was
a gate behind which stood a maiden named Modgud, whose duty it
was to take toll of all the travelers who passed that way.

"Who are you," she asked, "who ride so heavily across the frail
Gjallar Bridge, and what kind of beast is that which you bestride?"

"I am Hermod, of the house of mighty Odin," was the answer;
"and this beast is Sleipnir the Glider, the fleetest and the wisest of
all horses."

"Why do you ride so hard, and why are you so wondrous
heavy?" asked the maiden. "Never have I seen this golden bridge
shake and sag as it did under your weight. Only yesterday five thousand passengers were crowded upon it at once, and yet it trembled

not in the least. Surely you are not the kind of man that should travel this road. There is too much color in your face, and too much strength in your arm. Why do you ride into the land of Hela?"

"I am on my way to Hela's halls to find my brother Balder," answered Hermod." He has but lately passed this way, and I doubt not but that among all the multitudes who have given you toll you remember him." "Indeed, I do remember him. Two days ago he came, riding his good steed Gyller the Golden, and his sweet-faced wife Nanna was beside him. Never before did such brightness cross this river; never before did beauty such as his pass over into the land of Hela. If you will promise to bring him back this way, I will lift the gate and allow you to ride on, for I see you have nothing to give me for toll."

"I promise," said Hermod. "But which way shall I ride to find Hela's halls?"

"The way lies downward and northward," answered Modgud. "It is not far, and you cannot miss the road. Farewell!"

Hermod gave the word to Sleipnir, and the horse galloped swiftly onward down the steep way that the maiden had pointed out. In a little while they came to the walls of a huge castle that stood gloomy and dark among the hills. On the outside was a deep moat filled with water. The drawbridge was up and the gate was shut. Hermod tried to call to the watchman, but the sound of his voice died away before it left his mouth. He looked around in the hope that he might attract the notice of some ne in the towers or on the walls. But there was not a soul in sight. At length he dismounted and gave Sleipnir a good breathing spell, while he measured with his eye the distance to the top of the castle wall. Then he stroked the horse's gray mane, read the runes on his teeth, and whispered them in his ear. At last he carefully tightened the saddle-girths and remounted.

"Good Sleipnir," he said, " you have borne me thus far, and have not failed me. Stand me instead this one time, I bid you. Let those eight long limbs of yours be wings as well as legs!"

Then, at a touch of the spur, Sleipnir sped with lightning swiftness down the narrow roadway toward the edge of the moat, and in another moment was flying through the air right over the gate and into the courtyard beyond. It was a wonderful leap; but then it was a wonderful horse that made it. No sportsman's trained hunter ever cleared ditch and hedge with half the ease and grace that great Sleipnir cleared the high wall of Hela's castle. Safe within the courtyard, Hermod alighted and tied the horse to an iron post that stood by the side of a fountain. Then, seeing that all the doors were open, he walked boldly in without asking leave of any one, and made his way to the long banquet-hall where Hela and her guests were feasting. Whom should he see, sitting in the foremost seat at the Queen's right hand, but his brother Balder ! The light which shone in Balder's countenance and glittered in his eyes shed a soft radiance over the entire hall, such as its gloomy walls had never seen before; and the faces of the guests were wreathed in smiles, and the Queen herself seemed to have forgotten all her sternness. Hermod, unbidden though he was, was welcomed very kindly, and a seat was given him at the table. All that evening he mingled with the guests in the hall.

He talked with his brother, or told wondrous stories in the hearing of the Queen, but not once did he speak of the business upon which he had come.

The next morning, when he thought that Hela was in her pleasantest mood, Hermod asked whether Balder might not ride home with him to his sorrowing mother, whose heart would be broken if he did not return.

"Does she weep for him?" asked the Queen. "Yes, and not only she, but my father and his counselors, and our brothers and sisters — all the household of Odin weep."

"There are so many such households that, if weeping availed anything, I should soon be deprived of all my subjects. There is no home that does not weep for its loved ones."

"But all mankind weeps for Balder."

"All mankind? Well, if that be true, there is some reason for your request, but not enough."

"All living creatures mourn for him," added Hermod.

"Indeed ! But I should weep if you were to take him away from me. Do things that are lifeless also grieve for him?"

"Truly they do. The very rocks shed tears, as do also the mountains and the clouds. There is nothing that does not weep."

"Do you know that this is true? Will you swear it?" asked the Queen, earnestly.

Hermod hesitated. "I am quite sure that it is true," he finally answered. "But, not having seen everything, I cannot now make oath to it."

"I will tell you what I will do," said Hela. "Do you return to your home, and let Odin send into all the earth and find out for a truth whether everything really weeps for Balder. If he shall find that this is the case, then come to me again, and I will give your brother up. But if a single thing shall refuse to shed tears, then Balder shall stay with me."

Hermod was not altogether pleased with this answer, but he knew that it was useless to plead any further with the Queen, and so he took leave of her, and made ready to return. Balder took from his finger a precious golden ring, and gave it to him to carry to Odin as a keepsake; and Nanna sent a kerchief of green and some flowers to her mother. Then Hermod mounted good Sleipnir again and rode back, along the fearful way, out of the land of Hela, and came on the tenth day to Odin's palace. There was, of course, still greater grief in the King's household when it was seen that Hermod returned alone. But when he made known the conditions on which Hela would give Balder back to them, all were glad, for they felt sure that, at the worst, it would be but a few months until they should see his bright face again.

And so messengers were sent into all the world, praying that everything should weep for white Balder. And everything did weep — men and beasts and birds, trees and plants, rivers and mountains, sticks and stones, and all metals. At the end of a year the messengers returned, very glad to report the result. But just before reaching Odin's halls they passed the mouth of a cavern wherein sat a toothless old hag named Thok. They asked her kindly to weep for Balder. She shook her head, and mumbled between curses:

"Bah! Why should such as I weep? Little good did he ever do me; little good will I do him. Go and tell him to stay where he is."

The joy of the messengers was turned to sadness, and with

bowed heads they went up the hill whereon Odin's palace stood, and told the whole story.

When kind Hela heard, however, that not anything save the wicked hag had refused to weep for Balder, she was moved to be better than her word. For she consented that Balder, for six months in every twelve, might gladden the earth with his presence. But during the other six she would keep him in her own halls. And this is why the sun shines, and the trees are green, and the birds sing, and men rejoice from April to October, for that is the season of Balder's stay with them; but during the other months the sun seldom shows his face, and all things are silent and sad, because Balder has gone back to the underworld.

But we must not forget the good steed Sleipnir. Although he never made another journey to the under-world, there was scarcely any part of the earth to which his long legs did not sometimes carry him; and especially in the far North he was a familiar figure long after Odin had gone from the earth.

In some parts of Sweden the old horse had, until quite recently, a troublesome habit of running through the harvest fields and making sad tangles of the standing grain. But by and by the cunning farmers learned a trick that saved them from all further trouble. As soon as the oats or barley was tall enough they would cut and tie up a fair sheaf of it, and lay it high up on a fence where the frolicsome old fellow would be sure to see it before getting into the field.

"Ah! How kind the dear farmer is to provide this sheaf of sweet barley for me," Sleipnir would say to himself. "I really cannot have the heart to tangle his grain." And then he would gallop away to the next farm. Wednesday night was — and still is, for all I know — his favorite time for visiting the fields; for Wednesday, as you know, is Odin's day. And that, I suppose, is the reason why people always selected Wednesday as the best time in the week for puzzling one another with the question:

"Who are the two that ride over the rainbow?"

DAPPLEGRIM
NORWEGIAN
FAIRY
TALE

THERE WAS ONCE UPON A TIME A COUPLE OF RICH FOLKS WHO HAD twelve sons, and when the youngest was grown up he would not stay at home any longer, but would go out into the world and seek his fortune. His father and mother said that they thought he was very well off at home, and that he was welcome to stay with them; but ho could not rest, and said that he must and would go, so at last they had to give him leave. When he had walked a long way, he came to a King's palace. There he asked for a place and got it.

Now the daughter of the King of that country had been carried off into the mountains by a Troll, and the King had no other children, and for this cause both he and all his people were full of sorrow and affliction, and the King had promised the Princess and half his kingdom to anyone who could set her free; but there was no one who could do it, though a great number had tried. So when the youth had been there for the space of a year or so, he wanted to go home again to pay his parents a visit; but when he got there his father and mother were dead, and his brothers had divided everything that their parents possessed between themselves, so that there was nothing at all left for him.

'Shall I, then, receive nothing at all of my inheritance?' asked the youth.

'Who could know that you were still alive — you who have been a wanderer so long?' answered the brothers. 'However, there are twelve mares upon the hills which we have not yet divided among us, and if you would like to have them for your share, you may take them.'

So the youth, well pleased with this, thanked them, and at once set off to the hill where the twelve mares were at pasture. When he got up there and found them, each mare had her foal, and by the side of one of them was a big dapple-grey foal as well. which was so sleek that it shone again.

'Well, my little foal, you are a fine fellow!' said the youth.

'Yes, but if you will kill all the other little foals so that I can suck all the mares for a year, you shall see how big and handsome I shall be then!' said the Foal.

So the youth did this — he killed all the twelve foals, and then went back again.

Next year, when he came home again to look after his mares and the foal, it was as fat as it could be, and its coat shone with brightness, and it was so big that the lad had the greatest difficulty in getting on its back, and each of the mares had another foal.

'Well, it's very evident that I have lost nothing by letting you suck all my mares,' said the lad to the yearling; 'but now you are quite big enough, and must come away with me.'

'No,' said the Colt, 'I must stay here another year; kill the twelve little foals, and then I can suck all the mares this year also, and you shall see how big and handsome I shall be by summer.'

So the youth did it again, and when he went up on the hill next year to look after his colt and the mares, each of the mares had her foal again; but the dappled colt was so big that when the lad wanted to feel its neck to see how fat it was, he could not reach up to it, it was so high? and it was so bright that the light glanced off its coat.

'Big and handsome you were last year, my colt, but this year you are ever so much handsomer,' said the youth; 'in all the King's court no such horse is to be found. But now you shall come away with me.'

'No,' said the dappled Colt once more; 'here I must stay for another year. Just kill the twelve little foals again, so that I can suck the mares this year also, and then come and look at me in the summer.'

So the youth did it — he killed all the little foals, and then went home again.

But next year, when he returned to look after the dappled colt and the mares, he was quite appalled. He had never imagined that any horse could become so big and overgrown, for the dappled horse had to lie down on all fours before the youth could get on his back, and it was very hard to do that even when it was lying down, and it was so plump that its coat shone and glistened just as if it had been a looking-glass. This time the dappled horse was not unwilling to go away with the youth, so he mounted it, and when he came riding home to his brothers they all smote their hands together and crossed themselves, for never in their lives had they either seen or heard tell of such a horse as that.

'If you will procure me the best shoes for my horse, and the most magnificent saddle and bridle that can be found,' said the youth, 'you may have all my twelve mares just as they are standing out on the hill, and their twelve foals into the bargain.' For this year also each mare had her foal. The brothers were quite willing to do this; so the lad got such shoes for his horse that the sticks and stones flew high up into the air as he rode away over the hills, and such a gold saddle and such a gold bridle that they could be seen glittering and glancing from afar.

'And now we will go to the King's palace,' said Dapplegrim — that was the horse's name, 'but bear in mind that you must ask the King for a good stable and excellent fodder for me.'

So the lad promised not to forget to do that. He rode to the palace, and it will be easily understood that with such a horse as he had he was not long on the way.

When he arrived there, the King was standing out on the steps, and how he did stare at the man who came riding up!

'Nay,' said he, 'never in my whole life have I seen such a man and such a horse.'

And when the youth inquired if he could have a place in the King's palace, the King was so delighted that he could have danced on the steps where he was standing, and there and then the lad was told that he should have a place.

'Yes; but I must have a good stable and most excellent fodder for my horse,' said he.

So they told him that he should have sweet hay and oats, and as much of them as the dappled horse chose to have, and all the other riders had to take their horses out of the stable that Dapplegrim might stand alone and really have plenty of room.

But this did not last long, for the other people in the King's Court became envious of the lad, and there was no bad thing that they would not have done to him if they had but dared. At last they bethought themselves of telling the King that the youth had said that, if he chose, he was quite able to rescue the Princess who had been carried off into the mountain a long time ago by the Troll.

The King immediately summoned the lad into his presence, and said that he had been informed that he had said that it was in his power to rescue the Princess, so he was now to do it. If he succeeded in this, he no doubt knew that the King had promised his daughter and half the kingdom to anyone who set her free, which promise should be faithfully and honourably kept, but if he failed he should be put to death. The youth denied that he had said this, but all to no purpose, for the King was deaf to all his words; so there was nothing to be done but say that he would make the attempt.

He went down into the stable, and very sad and full of care he was. Then Dapplegrim inquired why he was so troubled, and the youth told him, and said that he did not know what to do, 'for as to setting the Princess free, that was downright impossible.'

'Oh, but it might be done,' said Dapplegrim. 'I will help you; but you must first have me well shod. You must ask for ten pounds of iron and twelve pounds of steel for the shoeing, and one smith to hammer and one to hold.'

So the youth did this, and no one said him nay. He got both the iron and the steel, and the smiths, and thus was Dapplegrim

shod strongly and well, and when the youth went out of the King's
palace a cloud of dust rose up behind him. But when he came to the
mountain into which the Princess had been carried, the difficulty
was to ascend the precipitous wall of rock by which he was to get on
to the mountain beyond, for the rock stood right up on end, as steep
as a house side and as smooth as a sheet of glass. The first time the
youth rode at it he got a little way up the precipice, but then both
Dapplegrim's fore legs slipped, and down came horse and rider with
a sound like thunder among the mountains. The next time that he
rode at it he got a little farther up, but then one of Dapplegrim's
fore legs slipped, and down they went with the sound of a landslip.
But the third time Dapplegrim said: 'Now we must show what we
can do,' and went at it once more till the stones sprang up sky high,
and thus they got up. Then the lad rode into the mountain cleft at
full gallop and caught up the Princess on his saddle-bow, and then
out again before the Troll even had time to stand up, and thus the
Princess was set free.

When the youth returned to the palace the King was both
happy and delighted to get his daughter back again, as may easily be
believed, but somehow or other the people about the Court had so
worked on him that he was angry with the lad too. 'Thou shalt have
my thanks for setting my Princess free,' he said, when the youth
came into the palace with her, and was then about to go away.

She ought to be just as much my Princess as she is yours now,
for you are a man of your word,' said the youth.

'Yes, yes,' said the King. 'Have her thou shalt, as I have said it;
but first of all thou must make the sun shine into my palace here.'

For there was a large and high hill outside the windows which
overshadowed the palace so much that the sun could not shine in.

'That was no part of our bargain,' answered the youth. 'But as
nothing that I can say will move you, I suppose I shall have to try to
do my best, for the Princess I will have.'

So he went down to Dapplegrim again and told him what the
King desired, and Dapplegrim thought that it might easily be done;
but first of all he must have new shoes, and ten pounds of iron and
twelve pounds of steel must go to the making of them, and two

smiths were also necessary, one to hammer and one to hold, and then it would be very easy to make the sun shine into the King's palace.

The lad asked for these things and obtained them instantly, for the King thought that for very shame he could not refuse to give them, and so Dapplegrim got new shoes, and they were good ones. The youth seated himself on him, and once more they went their way, and for each hop that Dapplegrim made, down went the hill fifteen ells into the earth, and so they went on until there was no hill left for the King to see.

When the youth came down again to the King's palace he asked the King if the Princess should not at last be his, for now no one could say that the sun was not shining into the palace. But the other people in the palace had again stirred up the King, and he answered that the youth should have her, and that he had never intended that he should not; but first of all he must get her quite as good a horse to ride to the wedding on as that which he had himself. The youth said that the King had never told him he was to do that, and it seemed to him that he had now really earned the Princess; but the King stuck to what he had said, and if the youth were unable to do it he was to lose his life, the King said. The youth went down to the stable again, and very sad and sorrowful he was, as anyone may well imagine. Then he told Dapplegrim that the King had now required that he should get the Princess as good a bridal horse as that which the bridegroom had, or he should lose his life. 'But that will be no easy thing to do,' said he, 'for your equal is not to be found in all the world,'

'Oh yes, there is one to match me,' said Dapplegrim. 'But it will not be easy to get him, for he is underground. However, we will try. Now you must go up to the King and ask for new shoes for me, and for them we must again have ten pounds of iron, twelve pounds of steel, and two smiths, one to hammer and one to hold, but be very particular to see that the hooks are very sharp. And you must also ask for twelve barrels of rye, and twelve slaughtered oxen must we have with us, and all the twelve ox-hides with twelve hundred spikes set in each of them; all these things must we have, likewise a barrel of tar with twelve tons of tar in it. The youth went to the King and asked for all the things that Dapplegrim had named, and once more, as the King thought that it would be disgraceful to refuse them to him, he obtained them all.

So he mounted Dapplegrim and rode away from the Court, and when he had ridden for a long, long time over hills and moors, Dapplegrim asked: 'Do you hear anything?'

'Yes; there is such a dreadful whistling up above in the air that I think I am growing alarmed,' said the youth.

'That is all the wild birds in the forest flying about; they are sent to stop us,' said Dapplegrim. 'But just cut a hole in the corn sacks, and then they will be so busy with the corn that they will forget us.'

The youth did it. He cut holes in the corn sacks so that barley and rye ran out on every side, and all the wild birds that were in the forest came in such numbers that they darkened the sun. But when they caught sight of the corn they could not refrain from it, but flew down and began to scratch and pick at the corn and rye, and at last they began to fight among themselves, and forgot all about the youth and Dapplegrim, and did them no harm.

And now the youth rode onwards for a long, long time, over hill and dale, over rocky places and morasses, and then Dapplegrim began to listen again, and asked the youth if he heard anything now.

'Yes; now I hear such a dreadful crackling and crashing in the forest on every side that I think I shall be really afraid,' said the youth.

'That is all the wild beasts in the forest,' said Dapplegrim; 'they are sent out to stop us. But just throw out the twelve carcasses of the oxen, and they will be so much occupied with them that they will quite forget us.' So the youth threw out the carcasses of the oxen, and then all the wild beasts in the forest, both bears and wolves, and lions, and grim beasts of all kinds, came. But when they caught sight of the carcasses of the oxen they began to fight for them till the blood flowed, and they entirely forgot Dapplegrim and the youth.

So the youth rode onwards again, and many and many were the new scenes they saw, for travelling on Dapplegrim's back was not travelling slowly, as may be imagined, and then Dapplegrim neighed.

'Do you hear anything? he said.

'Yes; I heard something like a foal neighing quite plainly a long, long way off,' answered the youth.

'That's a full-grown colt,' said Dapplegrim, 'if you hear it so plainly when it is so far away from us.'

So they travelled onwards a long time, and saw one new scene after another once more. Then Dapplegrim neighed again.

'Do you hear anything now?' said he.

'Yes; now I heard it quite distinctly, and it neighed like a full-grown horse,' answered the youth.

'Yes, and you will hear it again very soon,' said Dapplegrim; 'and then you will hear what a voice it has.' So they travelled on through many more different kinds of country, and then Dapplegrim neighed for the third time; but before he could ask the youth if he heard anything, there was such a neighing on the other side of the heath that the youth thought that hills and rocks would be rent in pieces.

'Now he is here!' said Dapplegrim. 'Be quick, and fling over me the ox-hides that have the spikes in them, throw the twelve tons of tar over the field, and climb up into that great spruce fir tree. When he comes, fire will spurt out of both his nostrils, and then the tar will catch fire. Now mark what I say — if the flame ascends I conquer, and if it sinks I fail; but if you see that I am winning, fling the bridle, which you must take off me, over his head, and then he will become quite gentle.'

Just as the youth had flung all the hides with the spikes over Dapplegrim, and the tar over the field, and had got safely up into the spruce fir, a horse came with flame spouting from his nostrils, and the tar caught fire in a moment; and Dapplegrim and the horse began to fight until the stones leapt up to the sky. They bit, and they fought with their fore legs and their hind legs, and sometimes the youth looked at them. and sometimes he looked at the tar, but at last the flames began to rise, for wheresoever the strange horse bit or wheresoever he kicked he hit upon the spikes in the hides, and at length he had to yield. When the youth saw that, he was not long in getting down from the tree and flinging the bridle over the horse's head, and then he became so tame that he might have been led by a thin string.

This horse was dappled too, and so like Dapplegrim that no one could distinguish the one from the other. The youth seated himself on the dappled horse which he had captured, and rode home again to the King's palace, and Dapplegrim ran loose by his side. When he got there, the King was standing outside in the courtyard.

'Can you tell me which is the horse I have caught, and which is the one I had before?' said the youth. 'If you can't, I think your daughter is mine.'

The King went and looked at both the dappled horses; he looked high and he looked low, he looked before and he looked behind, but there was not a hair's difference between the two.

'No,' said the King; 'that I cannot tell thee, and as thou hast procured such a splendid bridal horse for my daughter thou shalt have her; but first we must have one more trial, just to see if thou art fated to have her. She shall hide herself twice, and then thou shalt hide thyself twice. If thou canst find her each time that she hides herself, and if she cannot find thee in thy hiding-places, then it is fated, and thou shalt have the Princess.'

'That, too, was not in our bargain,' said the youth. 'But we will make this trial since it must be so.'

So the King's daughter was to hide herself first.

Then she changed herself into a duck, and lay swimming in a lake that was just outside the palace. But the youth went down into the stable and asked Dapplegrim what she had done with herself.

'Oh, all that you have to do is to take your gun, and go down to the water and aim at the duck which is swimming about there, and she will soon discover herself,' said Dapplegrim.

The youth snatched up his gun and ran to the lake. 'I will just have a shot at that duck,' said he, and began to aim at it.

'Oh, no, dear friend, don't shoot! It is I,' said the Princess. So he had found her once.

The second time the Princess changed herself into a loaf, and laid herself on the table among four other loaves; and she was so like the other loaves that no one could see any difference between them.

But the youth again went down to the stable to Dapplegrim, and told him that the Princess had hidden herself again, and that he had not the least idea what had become of her.

'Oh, just take a very large bread-knife, sharpen it, and pretend that you are going to cut straight through the third of the four loaves which are lying on the kitchen table in the King's palace — count them from right to left — and you will soon find her,' said Dapplegrim.

So the youth went up to the kitchen, and began to sharpen the largest bread-knife that he could find; then he caught hold of the third loaf on the left-hand side, and put the knife to it as if he meant to cut it straight in two. 'I will have a bit of this bread for myself,' said he.

'No, dear friend, don't cut, it is I!' said the Princess again; so he had found her the second time.

And now it was his turn to go and hide himself; but Dapplegrim had given him such good instructions that it was not easy to find him. First he turned himself into a horse-fly, and hid himself in Dapplegrim's left nostril. The Princess went poking about and searching everywhere, high and low, and wanted to go into Dapplegrim's stall too, but he began to bite and kick about so that she was afraid to go there, and could not find the youth. 'Well,' said she, 'as I am unable to find you, you must show yourself,' whereupon the youth immediately appeared standing there on the stable floor.

Dapplegrim told him what he was to do the second time, and he turned himself into a lump of earth, and stuck himself between the hoof and the shoe on Dapplegrim's left fore foot. Once more the King's daughter went and sought everywhere, inside and outside, until at last she came into the stable, and wanted to go into the stall beside Dapplegrim. So this time he allowed her to go into it, and she peered about high and low, but she could not look under his hoofs, for he stood much too firmly on his legs for that, and she could not find the youth.

'Well, you will just have to show where you are yourself, for

I can't find you,' said the Princess, and in an instant the youth was standing by her side on the floor of the stable.

'Now you are mine!' said he to the Princess.

'Now you can see that it is fated that she should be mine,' he said to the King.

'Yes, fated it is,' said the King. 'So what must be, must.'

Then everything was made ready for the wedding with great splendour and promptitude, and the youth rode to church on Dapplegrim, and the King's daughter on the other horse. So everyone must see that they could not be long on their way thither.

A HORSEMAN IN THE SKY
AMBROSE BIERCE

I

ONE SUNNY AFTERNOON IN THE AUTUMN OF THE YEAR 1861 A SOLDIER lay in a clump of laurel by the side of a road in western Virginia. He lay at full length upon his stomach, his feet resting upon the toes, his head upon the left forearm. His extended right hand loosely grasped his rifle. But for the somewhat methodical disposition of his limbs and a slight rhythmic movement of the cartridge-box at the back of his belt he might have been thought to be dead. He was asleep at his post of duty. But if detected he would be dead shortly afterward, death being the just and legal penalty of his crime.

The clump of laurel in which the criminal lay was in the angle of a road which after ascending southward a steep acclivity to that point turned sharply to the west, running along the summit for perhaps one hundred yards. There it turned southward again and went zigzagging downward through the forest. At the salient of that second angle was a large flat rock, jutting out northward, overlooking the deep valley from which the road ascended. The rock capped a high cliff; a stone dropped from its outer edge would have fallen sheer downward one thousand feet to the tops of the pines.

The angle where the soldier lay was on another spur of the same cliff. Had he been awake he would have commanded a view, not only of the short arm of the road and the jutting rock, but of the entire profile of the cliff below it. It might well have made him giddy to look.

The country was wooded everywhere except at the bottom of the valley to the northward, where there was a small natural meadow, through which flowed a stream scarcely visible from the valley's rim. This open ground looked hardly larger than an ordinary door-yard, but was really several acres in extent. Its green was more vivid than that of the inclosing forest. Away beyond it rose a line of giant cliffs similar to those upon which we are supposed to stand in our survey of the savage scene, and through which the road had somehow made its climb to the summit. The configuration of the valley, indeed, was such that from this point of observation it seemed entirely shut in, and one could but have wondered how the road which found a way out of it had found a way into it, and whence came and whither went the waters of the stream that parted the meadow more than a thousand feet below.

No country is so wild and difficult but men will make it a theatre of war; concealed in the forest at the bottom of that military rat-trap, in which half a hundred men in possession of the exits might have starved an army to submission, lay five regiments of Federal infantry. They had marched all the previous day and night and were resting. At nightfall they would take to the road again, climb to the place where their unfaithful sentinel now slept, and descending the other slope of the ridge fall upon a camp of the enemy at about midnight. Their hope was to surprise it, for the road led to the rear of it. In case of failure, their position would be perilous in the extreme; and fail they surely would should accident or vigilance apprise the enemy of the movement.

II

THE SLEEPING SENTINEL IN THE CLUMP OF LAUREL WAS A YOUNG Virginian named Carter Druse. He was the son of wealthy parents, an only child, and had known such ease and cultivation and high living as wealth and taste were able to command in the mountain country of western Virginia. His home was but a few miles from where he now lay. One morning he had risen from the breakfast-table and said, quietly but gravely: "Father, a Union regiment has arrived at Grafton. I am going to join it."

The father lifted his leonine head, looked at the son a moment in silence, and replied: "Well, go, sir, and whatever may occur do what you conceive to be your duty. Virginia, to which you are a traitor, must get on without you. Should we both live to the end of the war, we will speak further of the matter. Your mother, as the physician has informed you, is in a most critical condition; at the best she cannot be with us longer than a few weeks, but that time is precious. It would be better not to disturb her."

So Carter Druse, bowing reverently to his father, who returned the salute with a stately courtesy that masked a breaking heart, left the home of his childhood to go soldiering. By conscience and courage, by deeds of devotion and daring, he soon commended himself to his fellows and his officers; and it was to these qualities and to some knowledge of the country that he owed his selection for his present perilous duty at the extreme outpost. Nevertheless, fatigue had been stronger than resolution and he had fallen asleep. What good or bad angel came in a dream to rouse him from his state of crime, who shall say? Without a movement, without a sound, in the profound silence and the languor of the late afternoon, some invisible messenger of fate touched with unsealing finger the eyes of his consciousness--whispered into the ear of his spirit the mysterious awakening word which no human lips ever have spoken, no human memory ever has recalled. He quietly raised his forehead from his arm and looked between the masking stems of the laurels, instinctively closing his right hand about the stock of his rifle.

His first feeling was a keen artistic delight. On a colossal pedestal, the cliff,--motionless at the extreme edge of the capping rock and sharply outlined against the sky,--was an equestrian statue of impressive dignity. The figure of the man sat the figure of the horse, straight and soldierly, but with the repose of a Grecian god carved in the marble which limits the suggestion of activity. The gray costume harmonized with its arial background; the metal of accoutrement and caparison was softened and subdued by the shadow; the animal's skin had no points of high light. A carbine strikingly foreshortened lay across the pommel of the saddle, kept in place by the right hand grasping it at the "grip"; the left hand, holding the bridle rein, was invisible. In silhouette against the sky the profile of the horse was cut with the sharpness of a cameo; it looked across the heights of air to the confronting cliffs beyond. The face of the rider, turned slightly away, showed only an outline of temple and beard; he was looking downward to the bottom of the valley. Magnified by its lift against the sky and by the soldier's testifying sense of the formidableness of a near enemy the group appeared of heroic, almost colossal, size.

For an instant Druse had a strange, half-defined feeling that he had slept to the end of the war and was looking upon a noble work of art reared upon that eminence to commemorate the deeds of an heroic past of which he had been an inglorious part. The feeling was dispelled by a slight movement of the group: the horse, without moving its feet, had drawn its body slightly backward from the verge; the man remained immobile as before. Broad awake and keenly alive to the significance of the situation, Druse now brought the butt of his rifle against his cheek by cautiously pushing the barrel forward through the bushes, cocked the piece, and glancing through the sights covered a vital spot of the horseman's breast. A touch upon the trigger and all would have been well with Carter Druse. At that instant the horseman turned his head and looked in the direction of his concealed foeman--seemed to look into his very face, into his eyes, into his brave, compassionate heart.

Is it then so terrible to kill an enemy in war--an enemy who has surprised a secret vital to the safety of one's self and comrades--an enemy more formidable for his knowledge than all his army for its numbers? Carter Druse grew pale; he shook in every limb, turned faint, and saw the statuesque group before him as black figures, rising, falling, moving unsteadily in arcs of circles in a fiery sky. His hand fell away from his weapon, his head slowly dropped until his face rested on the leaves in which he lay. This courageous gentleman and hardy soldier was near swooning from intensity of emotion.

It was not for long; in another moment his face was raised from earth, his hands resumed their places on the rifle, his forefinger sought the trigger; mind, heart, and eyes were clear, conscience and reason sound. He could not hope to capture that enemy; to alarm him would but send him dashing to his camp with his fatal news. The duty of the soldier was plain: the man must be shot dead from ambush--without warning, without a moment's spiritual preparation, with never so much as an unspoken prayer, he must be sent to his account. But no--there is a hope; he may have discovered nothing--perhaps he is but admiring the sublimity of the landscape. If permitted, he may turn and ride carelessly away in the direction whence he came. Surely it will be possible to judge at the instant of his withdrawing whether he knows. It may well be that his fixity of attention--Druse turned his head and looked through the deeps of air downward, as from the surface to the bottom of a translucent sea. He saw creeping across the green meadow a sinuous line of figures of men and horses--some foolish commander was permitting the soldiers of his escort to water their beasts in the open, in plain view from a dozen summits!

Druse withdrew his eyes from the valley and fixed them again upon the group of man and horse in the sky, and again it was through the sights of his rifle. But this time his aim was at the horse. In his memory, as if they were a divine mandate, rang the words of his father at their parting: "Whatever may occur, do what you conceive to be your duty." He was calm now. His teeth were firmly but not rigidly closed; his nerves were as tranquil as a sleeping babe's-- not a tremor affected any muscle of his body; his breathing, until suspended in the act of taking aim, was regular and slow. Duty had conquered; the spirit had said to the body: "Peace, be still." He fired.

III

AN OFFICER OF THE FEDERAL FORCE, WHO IN A SPIRIT OF ADVENTURE OR in quest of knowledge had left the hidden bivouac in the valley, and with aimless feet had made his way to the lower edge of a small open space near the foot of the cliff, was considering what he had to gain by pushing his exploration further. At a distance of a quarter-mile before him, but apparently at a stone's throw, rose from its fringe of pines the gigantic face of rock, towering to so great a height above him that it made him giddy to look up to where its edge cut a sharp, rugged line against the sky. It presented a clean, vertical profile against a background of blue sky to a point half the way down, and of distant hills, hardly less blue, thence to the tops of the trees at its base. Lifting his eyes to the dizzy altitude of its summit the officer saw an astonishing sight—a man on horseback riding down into the valley through the air!

Straight upright sat the rider, in military fashion, with a firm seat in the saddle, a strong clutch upon the rein to hold his charger from too impetuous a plunge. From his bare head his long hair streamed upward, waving like a plume. His hands were concealed in the cloud of the horse's lifted mane. The animal's body was as level as if every hoof-stroke encountered the resistant earth. Its motions were those of a wild gallop, but even as the officer looked they ceased, with all the legs thrown sharply forward as in the act of alighting from a leap. But this was a flight!

Filled with amazement and terror by this apparition of a horseman in the sky—half believing himself the chosen scribe of some new Apocalypse, the officer was overcome by the intensity of his emotions; his legs failed him and he fell. Almost at the same instant he heard a crashing sound in the trees—a sound that died without an echo—and all was still.

The officer rose to his feet, trembling. The familiar sensation of an abraded shin recalled his dazed faculties. Pulling himself together he ran rapidly obliquely away from the cliff to a point distant from its foot; thereabout he expected to find his man; and thereabout he naturally failed. In the fleeting instant of his vision his imagination had been so wrought upon by the apparent grace and ease and intention of the marvelous performance that it did not occur to him that the line of march of arial cavalry is directly downward, and that he could find the objects of his search at the very foot of the cliff. A half-hour later he returned to camp.

This officer was a wise man; he knew better than to tell an incredible truth. He said nothing of what he had seen. But when the commander asked him if in his scout he had learned anything of advantage to the expedition he answered:

"Yes, sir; there is no road leading down into this valley from the southward."

The commander, knowing better, smiled.

IV

AFTER FIRING HIS SHOT, PRIVATE CARTER DRUSE RELOADED HIS RIFLE and resumed his watch. Ten minutes had hardly passed when a Federal sergeant crept cautiously to him on hands and knees. Druse neither turned his head nor looked at him, but lay without motion or sign of recognition.

"Did you fire?" the sergeant whispered.

"Yes."

"At what?"

"A horse. It was standing on yonder rock--pretty far out. You see it is no longer there. It went over the cliff."

The man's face was white, but he showed no other sign of emotion. Having answered, he turned away his eyes and said no more. The sergeant did not understand.

"See here, Druse," he said, after a moment's silence, "it's no use making a mystery. I order you to report. Was there anybody on the horse?"

"Yes."

"Well?"

"My father."

The sergeant rose to his feet and walked away. "Good God!" he said.

RAFAEL
EVEY
BRETT

I'D ALWAYS BEEN MORE SENSITIVE TO THE PRESENCE OF OTHERS THAN THE average man, which meant large cities with their stifling crowds, often at all hours, left me anxious. Rome I discovered to be one of the most difficult: by the time my taxi pulled up in front of the hotel, I was nearly blind with a migraine. When I stepped out into the air, tainted with vehicle fumes, I had to lean against the taxi until the dizziness subsided.

"*Si sente bene,* Padre?"

It wasn't the driver who'd spoken, but a policeman mounted on a handsome bay mare. Concern radiated from him, which didn't help my poor head, but after so many years in the priesthood, I'd learned how to wear a serene expression no matter the circumstances. "*Sto bene, grazie.*" That was the extent of pure Italian I could speak, though since my native tongue was Catalan and I had studied Latin since I could read, I understood a good deal of the city's babble.

The horse nudged my shoulder with her nose and let out a soft snort, as if she knew I was lying. I stroked her soft muzzle, calmed by her gentle presence. The throbbing in my head eased just enough to be bearable.

"*Buon giorno*," the policeman said and directed his horse through the crowd. By then the driver had fetched my bag, which he handed off to a waiting porter. After a few deep breaths, I was able to steady myself and take stock of my new surroundings. The hotel's façade seemed to glorify the city's history, with stone lions flanking the columns and a gigantic fountain showing a mural of Bacchus in the midst of a wine-fueled orgy. I thought it a work of art, but Generalissimo Franco would have deemed the scene morally reprehensible and had it destroyed.

But this wasn't Spain, and for a little while, at least, I didn't have to worry about internment or being killed if I did or said the wrong thing. My greatest worry now was being able to cope with the crowds while not revealing my affliction.

I followed the porter into a lobby buzzing with guests, mustachioed men and women in lurid dresses and tall *bouffant* hairstyles. It took all of my effort to keep from being overwhelmed by the intensity of their thoughts and emotions, which transformed my headache into a sensation akin to ice picks driving through my skull.

Breathing deeply, I closed my eyes, wishing I'd been able to find an excuse to keep from attending a conference on alternative healing, but my superior had insisted. "*You spend so much time alone, Rafael. Besides, with your dedication to your patients, there's no one better to represent us.*"

The irony was that I was interested in all aspects of healing, though much of it was because I was desperate to ease the pain of others and thus spare myself. So when the Salesian Pontifical University had offered to sponsor a Spanish candidate, I'd been sent. And while it was a relief to be free of Spain's dictatorship, however briefly, I couldn't risk letting my guard down.

The porter led me to the registration desk. A few minutes later I had a key and a room which, the attendant assured me, had an excellent view of Olympic stadium built three years before in 1960. She gestured down the hall. "The conference is to your left and through the double doors. You can't miss it."

The porter held up my bag. "I'll put this in your room and see that everything's perfect."

"Thank you." I handed him a tip and caught a flash of pleasure as he grinned and departed.

The foyer was crowded with doctors, nurses, psychiatrists, and practitioners of every sort of healing including energetic, herbal and spiritual. I checked in at the welcome desk, picked up my name tag which dangled from a lanyard, then wandered around to get my bearings, exchanging nods with a few Vatican priests. Cigarette smoke drifted through the air, increasing my malaise.

I was about to head toward the elevators when my skin tingled. Something uncomfortable, something akin to electricity. The sensation traveled through my body, lodging there and filling me with sickening unease. I lost what little control I had. Emotions tumbled into my mind, nauseating with their intensity. I struggled against my rising terror. There was evil in this place. Someone—something—was filled with an insatiable hunger all too similar to that which I'd gleaned from many of the soldiers and politicians in Spain.

Frightened, I looked around. No one else seemed to have noticed anything amiss. Priests, doctors, laymen—there were so many people present that I couldn't tell from where the vileness emanated. My first impulsive thought was that someone had followed me from Barcelona, intent on exposing me. Then I caught hold of myself. There was no reason for them to tail me. I'd been careful to keep my secret.

Even so, I wasn't going to take any chances. I pushed through the crowd, desperate to be out of the crowd and away from the foul presence. A few of the attendees grumbled at my rudeness, but I pressed on, looking for the exit.

A few more steps and the world spun in sickening circles. I groped blindly in the air, seeking a wall or chair for support when a strong hand caught my arm. "This way, Father," someone said in English.

The background noise in my head went quiet as suddenly as if someone had shut off an irritating radio broadcast. Within moments I was out of the suffocating foyer and in a little garden replete with sunlight and fresh air. My rescuer sat me down on a stone bench and I leaned forward, head down until the ground stopped swaying.

"Are you all right, Father?"

I gazed at my rescuer, surprised at being unable to sense him. He was in his early twenties, about ten years younger than I, and with his jeans and black leather jacket he seemed out of place amidst the well-dressed professionals. I was not entirely adept at English, but I did my best. "I am. Thank you, Mr...?"

"Just call me Lukas. Can I get you something? A glass of water?"

The young man's accent, American English tinged with German, intrigued me. "You are kind, but I wish only my room."

"I'll be happy to—" A fit of coughing cut him off. "Sorry. All that smoke gets to me. I'll take you upstairs. What's the number?"

"I will find it." I wasn't keen on letting a stranger follow me, however well-intentioned he might be.

"I don't think I should leave you on your own."

I searched his blue eyes for a reason but found none. Much as I despised my ability, I didn't trust anyone I couldn't sense. For all I knew, he could have caused the horrible sensations I'd been feeling and this was a ruse to lure me into harm.

"Please don't think—I didn't mean..." Lukas was instantly contrite, and a hint of worry and anxiety leaked through at last, making me feel guilty for presuming the worst. Whoever he was, he had no intention of hurting me and was sincerely interested in my well-being. "Forgive me, Father. I've offended you. Let me apologize by taking you to dinner in the hotel's restaurant. Will you come?"

Lukas wanted something from me. I suppose I shouldn't have been surprised. After working so many years with the underprivileged, ill and abused, I was well aware of how my cassock sometimes acted as a magnet to those in need. "What time?"

"Seven o'clock?"

"As you wish. The hotel restaurant. Seven o'clock."

Lukas beamed, and for an instant I was taken by the roguish smile. "Thank you, Father. I'll take care of the arrangements. Let me walk you to the elevator, at least."

Given his concern, I allowed him that much. As the doors closed between us, I found myself looking forward to the night's engagement.

ONCE I REACHED MY ROOM, THE NAUSEA AND HEADACHE RETURNED WITH such force that I didn't dare return to the foyer. I decided it must be the remnants of whatever I'd sensed, because the rooms nearby were empty and I was on a high enough floor that the crowds outside were little more than static.

A hot shower and a change of clothes did little to improve my symptoms. Neither did an hour of meditation. By six-thirty, I was considering excuses to avoid an evening in a busy restaurant, but at six fifty-five I took the elevator down, propelled only by my sense of duty. To his surprise, the maître d' escorted me to an isolated, candlelit table for two on the patio where we could enjoy the stars and fresh air. My host, already seated, rose when I arrived. "Thank you for coming, Father."

"Please. You may call me Rafael, or Padre Rafael, if that is more comfortable."

"Rafael."

We sat and, as had happened before in Lukas's presence, my awareness of those around me dulled. Grateful to be clear-headed at last, I studied the menu as Lukas requested a bottle of wine. The waiter bowed and departed, returning shortly to pour a little merlot for me to sample. "Delicious," I said, and the waiter filled two glasses.

Once I'd decided on a dish with shrimp and pasta and the waiter had taken our order, I studied Lukas's newly-shaven chin and the blue eyes which regarded me with equal curiosity. "You are... German?" I asked.

"Austrian. From Vienna. I was adopted by an American after the war and left the country when I was sixteen." Lukas turned his attention to pouring more wine, a sign that he found the topic uncomfortable. I waited patiently for him to either change the subject or say more. After setting the bottle down, he glanced at me then gave me a sad smile. "My adopted father found me in a hospital after the war. He convinced the doctors to let him take me north to

Wimsbach, where the Lipizzans had been taken for safekeeping. If it weren't for the horses, I wouldn't be sane."

"Really? How so?"

Lukas smiled. "I was…overly sensitive, you might say. They taught me control."

Anxiety prickled my neck. There was something in Lukas's carefully worded statement that gave me the feeling he knew my secret, but I wasn't going to push too far, both for Lukas's comfort as well as my own. "We have much in common. My parents were killed in in the Spanish civil war. The Salesian brotherhood raised my brother and I."

"Which is why you became a priest?" Lukas asked. I nodded. "What exactly do you do?"

"I work in a hospital in Barcelona, both as a chaplain and as a medic. When I am not there, I offer solace to the homeless and those who are afraid or too ashamed to approach a church."

Lukas swirled his glass, the coy tilt of his mouth hinting at something I daren't consider. "You are a remarkable man, Rafael."

The waiter brought our food, tantalizing piles of pasta and fresh garlic bread. After a brief prayer, I devoured my dinner with pleasure.

As we ate, Lukas rambled on about the conference and Rome, quick to answer my numerous questions as long as they weren't personal. At length I caught a brief, overpowering concern directed straight at me and decided it was time to be blunt. "Will you tell me the reason you wished to speak with me?"

Lukas poured the last of the wine. "I will, but not here. It's better if—"

The scent of a freshly lit cigar drifted over to our table. Lukas coughed, politely covering his mouth with his napkin. The coughing worsened into a long, drawn-out spasm.

Out of instinct, I grasped his arm, meaning to comfort. Instead, an electric shock raced through my body. I had the strangest feeling I could see Lukas inside and out, and he was being swallowed up by a darkness which threatened to—

I snatched my hand back, reeling from the sensation unnervingly similar to what I'd felt that morning. I stood, pushing the chair back with a *screech* against the stone floor. Several patrons had turned to stare, and their interest jabbed like nails into my brain.

Terror drove me to flee from whatever I'd sensed inside Lukas, but a priest abandoning someone in need would be unforgivable. I rounded the table and crouched to be eye level. "Who—what are you?"

Lukas struggled for a few more breaths. He'd gone pale beneath the lanterns on the patio "Take me to my room. Please."

I didn't want to touch him, but he couldn't stand without assistance. Tentatively I offered an arm, relieved when I felt nothing more than pressure as I helped him rise and walk. In the elevator, silence increased the tension. Lukas had gone quiet, impossible to read as he inhaled careful, shallow breaths.

Lukas collapsed into a chair as soon as he entered his suite. His color hadn't returned. Blue tinged her lips as he gazed at me from under half-closed lids. I wanted to leave, to gain as much distance from this strange man as possible, but I could not bring myself to do so. "Is there someone you would like me to call?"

"I'll be fine," Lukas said hoarsely. He waved a hand at me. "I know what you felt in the foyer. I felt it, too."

His words confirmed my suspicion about his extrasensory abilities. Once, I'd been desperate to find someone else like me, but now, I didn't find his admission comforting. Not when it confirmed what I'd been dreading. "They are after me."

I hadn't meant to speak aloud, by after the day's stress my nerves got the better of me. Lukas looked at me, incredulous. "After *you?* Why?"

He was young and American, with no real idea of what Generalissimo Franco would do to those he deemed a threat. I'd been stupid, going out to dinner with Lukas. He was probably bait for a trap. Whether or not he knew it didn't matter. I headed toward the door. "Forgive me. I must return to my room. Are you sure I cannot call—"

Eyes narrowed, he said, "You don't have to be afraid of me."

I wanted to believe him, yet I was not one who easily trusted a man I couldn't sense. "What do you want from me?"

"Your friendship. That's all."

I sat in the chair across from him, still uneasy. "I should not be here. It is not safe for either of us."

He gave me a wry smile. "Whoever you think was following you, isn't. There's an incubus loose in the hotel."

It took me a moment to translate what he said. Incubus. *El íncubo.* After serving in the priesthood during a civil war and a dictatorship, I had a healthy belief in evil and its accompanying spirits. Mythical creatures were another thing entirely. "A…what?"

"An incubus. It's a creature that feeds off the sexual energies of others. It's mostly energy itself and tends to transform into its victim's greatest desire. Most people can't sense them, but a Sensitive can."

I'd never heard the word sensitive used in the way Lukas had, but I knew exactly what he meant. I'd known I was more perceptive of emotions and feelings than others seemed to be but had never given that awareness a name. The Generalissimo had a penchant for hunting those that were *different,* and I was terrified of discovery. Knowing Lukas had the same ability wasn't the relief I'd hoped.

He gave me an odd look then his expression changed to one of pity. "You don't know what you are, but you're afraid of it, aren't you? No wonder…"

I sat, frozen, not knowing whether to be offended by Lukas's presumption or shocked by the way he spoke so casually about something I endeavored to keep hidden. "What I am or am not is none of your business. Please excuse me."

I rose and tried again to leave, but he said, "You *know* things about people. You can sense their emotions and sometimes experience their memories. That's the reason you were ill this afternoon. You were overloaded by all that energy so I blocked it for you. You don't know how deal with such a large crowd or an incubus, do you?"

I turned back to face him. Even though he was ill, there was something in his manner and appearance I found alluring. "Are you an incubus?"

Lukas laughed, a mistake, because it erupted into another fit of coughing. "No," he said after he recovered. "I hunt them. My friends and I do. Part of the reason we came to this conference is because we tracked it here."

This went beyond the bounds of what I could believe, although I had spent a great deal of time with the mentally ill and Lukas did not strike me as such. "You are unwell. I shall leave you to rest."

"Look. I'm sorry about what happened in the restaurant. You caught me off guard. I reacted badly." He held out a trembling hand. "I'll show you something."

I'd had all the strangeness I could take for one night and had no wish to open myself up for more. Besides, he was growing worse by the minute. His labored breathing echoed uncomfortably. "Shall I call a doctor? Surely there is someone here who—"

He shook his head. "No doctors. They can't help."

"One of your friends, then?"

"No. Olivia fusses too much." But after another round of coughing, I asked again and he relented. "She's in room 314."

I called. Within five minutes came a knock at the door. I opened it for a pretty, forty-ish Hispanic woman who hurried into the room and straight to Lukas. They bantered in English too low and fast for me to catch. I slipped out, wishing I could forget everything I'd just heard.

I DREAMED OF LUKAS AND HIS HORSES, GREAT WHITE MARES AND stallions that moved in and out of sight like waves on the sea and filling me with a similar peace. There were long, vivid scenes in which Lukas took my hand, but his touch was more than skin deep. I felt *him*, emotional, physical, and everything else. Smell, touch, and taste roused a passion I'd never believed I'd feel. I didn't want to let him go.

When I woke, the sheets were damp and sticky. Cheeks burning, I hurried into the shower. I'd resigned myself to the idea of never having a lover, but obviously I was not immune to certain…feelings.

Whatever Lukas had done to me, I was determined not to let it happen again. I did my best to avoid him. While attending a panel on the link between emotional and physical illness, I made certain to sit on the opposite side of the room from Lukas, who appeared little better than the night before. Olivia fretted over him whenever he coughed and I couldn't help wondering if he'd slept well or had endured an experience similar to mine.

At noon I fled the hotel and took my lunch on the patio at a nearby café, choosing a somewhat isolated table. I'd ordered simple fare and was reading through the conference program when Olivia pulled out a chair and sat beside me.

"Good afternoon, Padre," she said, her Spanish tinged with a Mexican accent. "I hope you don't mind if I join you,"

Her mind was as impenetrable as Lukas's. Somehow, I wasn't surprised. Inclining my head, I said, "Not at all. Is there something I can do for you, *señorita?*"

She ordered a glass of lemonade from the waiter then said, "I wanted to thank you for calling me last night. I apologize if Lukas got out of hand. He's young and tends to be rather passionate."

I'd noticed. "I fear I'm the one who offended. Please offer him my regrets. Is he feeling better this morning?"

"Somewhat." The waiter delivered the lemonade. She took a sip. "There isn't much a traditional doctor can do. His sickness is of the soul as much as the body."

This was a concept I was all too familiar with. While some struggled to survive after being shot or tortured, others simply gave up and willed themselves to die so they could join their loved ones. Others survived trauma only to have it manifest later as some form of illness, which, I presumed, was what happened with Lukas. "Because of what happened to him in the war?"

She nodded. "I do what I can since I'm a Sensitive too, but I'm not gifted enough to do much." She rested her hand on mine. Her touch tingled though it lacked the danger Lukas's had.

Discomfited, I eased my hand back. A chill passed through me and I glanced around the café, feeling suddenly vulnerable.

A moment later she went blank, as if she wasn't there anymore. "They're not here, Padre. If someone were following you, Lukas and I would know. You're safe with us. I promise you that."

Against my better judgment, I was beginning to believe her,

and more than a small part of me longed to share my worst secret with someone able to understand. "Thank you, *señorita*."

"Forgive me for being so forward. I wasn't thinking. Lukas said this was all new to you. Haven't you ever learned to shield yourself?"

It was no use to dissemble. Like Lukas, she knew too much. "I…no. I didn't know such a thing was possible."

Her mouth dropped open. "Oh, Padre. You must have a strong heart to go through life with it so open. We can teach you, you know. Come with us after the conference. We'll get you asylum."

Tempting as the offer was, I couldn't take it. "Thank you, *señorita*, but I have my duties." Not to mention the certainty that the Generalissimo would hunt me down if I failed to return home.

"Of course you do," she said, although the words were strained. "But if there's any way we can aid you while you're here…"

Fearful that I might do something else to hasten Lukas's illness, I didn't dare ask for their help, although I longed for it. "I do have one question." I hesitated, feeling foolish for even thinking it. "The incubus. Lukas was telling the truth?"

"Yes, he was. Most people only see and feel them as a lover. Sensitives like us can sense their true nature which makes them easier to track, but encounters can be rather unpleasant."

I nodded, still not quite believing such creatures could exist.

She took my program and flipped it open. "This is my lecture on energetic healing. Two o'clock this afternoon. It'll be in Spanish. I think it would be of benefit to you."

"I'll be there." I'd planned on attending anyway.

"Good." She left a few coins on the table before she disappeared as abruptly as she'd come.

HALFWAY BACK TO THE HOTEL, I FELT THE INCUBUS AGAIN.

The tingling began on the back of my neck and creeped along my spine, spreading out until my whole body clenched with pain. The incubus was hungry. Starving. Now that Lukas and Olivia had both assured me I wasn't being followed, I could sense the inhumanness of the creature projecting it, although the greed and single-mindedness were emotions I knew all too well. A brief scan of the people nearby showed me nothing, no one out of the ordinary.

Yet it was *there*. Somewhere. The tingling increased to the point that my skin burned and my head felt ready to burst from pressure. I hurried away, desperate to rid myself of the awful sensation.

Lukas hunted the things, but he'd neglected to mention how he disposed of them. A stake to the heart? A silver bullet? Strangulation? Whichever it was, I was a priest and didn't care to have blood on my hands, evil creature or not.

I meant to track down either Olivia or Lukas and tell them, but by the time I reached the hotel pain had made me so lightheaded that I had to stop several times to balance against a table or chair. The concierge offered to fetch a doctor. I refused. Painkillers wouldn't help this kind of headache. Besides, I was at a conference filled with physicians and healers of all sorts. One call and I could be surrounded by herbs, acupuncture needles and a half dozen people wanting to lay hands on me.

Somehow I reached my room and spent a miserable afternoon in my room meditating and doing breathing exercises in an attempt to control the discomfort. When the aching eased I ordered a light repast and ate alone, wondering how Olivia's panel had gone and if Lukas had been there.

Someone knocked. I answered, expecting room service to clear away the dishes, but it was Lukas, wearing a tight white T-shirt and jeans. He made a point of studying me. "You don't look good."

His bluntness caught me off-guard. My words emerged more sharply than I'd intended. "That *thing* was back. It gave me a headache."

"The incubus? Damn it. Where?"

I gestured vaguely in the direction of the coffee shop. "Out on the street. Hours ago. I meant to tell you, but…"

"It's all right. It's probably gone by now anyway. Anything I can do to help?"

"No. Thank you for your concern." I tried to shut the door but Lukas put his foot in the way.

"Rafael. Wait."

Before I had a chance to respond, Lukas clasped my wrist.

Energy flickered, and for a moment I was caught in a loop of ardor that heated my entire body. It took a great deal of effort to pry Lukas's hand away. "Go to your friend. She will be missing you."

"You and I are more alike than you care to admit. I *know*. Why are you hiding yourself?"

"That is none of your concern."

Lukas pursed his lips, not quite pouting. "Will it make a difference if I say I'm worried about you? I've known other Sensitives who went crazy when they refused to accept it or never learned how to handle it."

He meant himself. Unwillingly, I caught a glimpse of Lukas as a child, lost in the turmoil of his own mind. Several white shapes surrounded him, cooling his torment. I shook my head to clear away the vision, reminded uncomfortably of last night's dream. "I appreciate your concern, but you need not worry."

"Let me help, damn it."

"There is no need." I didn't have the heart to tell him his insistence was making my head worse.

His face crumpled, and he looked like a puppy someone had left in the rain, bedraggled and uncomprehending of why he'd been punished. "But if you only knew…" That was all he could get out before being seized by another terrible round of coughing.

"All right," I said, as much to calm him as to ease my own conscience. "You can help as long as you do not harm yourself in the process."

His face lit up. "Good. Come on. I want to show you something."

"I do not think we ought to—"

But it was too late. He was already in the elevator and holding the door open for me. I joined him, not liking this at all but unsure how to stop him without riling him more. Once in the lobby, he crossed it and headed outside, seemingly oblivious to the cold and wet. Helplessly I followed, cassock clutched tightly at the neck to protect against the rain. We walked for perhaps five blocks before turning toward the police stable. An officer sat sheltered under a dripping eave.

"Good evening Signore Lukas," the officer said in heavily

accented English. "The horses will be happy to see you." He turned his attention to me. "Brought a friend tonight, I see. Welcome, Padre."

I nodded at him and trailed Lukas inside, happy to be out of the wet. The stable was warm and filled with the pleasant scent of horse. There were over two dozen stalls lined up on either side. Several animals arched their heads over the gates to watch us. A sleek bay mare, the same I'd seen when I'd first arrived at the hotel, greeted Lukas with affection, and he slipped inside the stall and scratched her neck.

"Lukas? Will your friend worry if we do not return?"

He sighed. "She's a friend of my father, not mine. Not really. She's so...overprotective . I admit I have issues, but I'm not going to break." A round of coughing belied that statement, thought I agreed he wasn't a child, not in mind and definitely not in body. Rain had soaked his shirt through, leaving nothing to the imagination. His wet jeans clung to his legs.

I looked away, suddenly ashamed by the thoughts going through my mind.

"This is what I wanted to show you." Lukas rubbed the mare's nose. She licked and chewed, a sign of pleasure. "The horses can feel energy too." He patted the mare's shiny neck. "Come in. See for yourself."

Wary of the mare's back legs and the fragrant manure by the door, I slipped inside. Already he was calmer and more grounded than I'd seen him and his breathing was easier. Gingerly, I set a hand next to his, aware of only warm muscle and silky coat. Then, just below the surface, I picked up tingle of energy, strong and pure in contrast to Lukas's tainted stream.

"Let go," Lukas said. "Let it take you deeper."

I was sorely tempted to see where that purity led, but instead of doing what he asked, I snatched my hand away. I didn't dare follow the energy. It was too tempting, and too risky. If I opened that Pandora's Box, there was no telling what demons I might loose and be unable to put back.

"The horses taught me how to control my Sensitivity. Without them, I would have gone crazy. I don't want that to happen to you." He coughed again. "They can help, if you'll let them."

A sympathetic pain sliced at my chest, and I inhaled sharply. This was too like the dream, intense and unforgiving. I had to get a grip on my control before I lost it completely. "We should go back to the hotel. I shall call for soup and hot tea."

Lukas twisted around so he faced me. He curled an around the horse's neck. "Only if you admit what you are."

Words strangled in my throat. At this point, I didn't know who, or what I was. Lukas had turned everything upside down and torn at the fabric of everything I believed in. I caught Lukas's gaze and lost myself in those bold, blue eyes.

"Say it," Lukas urged. The mare tossed her head as if in agreement. Her tail stung my arm.

I wanted to, desperately, but the energetic contact with the horse had kindled a spark I dared not fan lest it grow into a blaze I couldn't control. "I can't."

Lukas tensed, his anger palpable. "You can. You have to." He grabbed my hand and tried to place it once more upon the horse. I resisted. "Please, Rafael. Please."

Energy flared between us. Once again I saw darkness within him, this time focused around his chest, clenching like a claw to cut off his air. It grew, spreading like an oil slick, seeping into every pore, a visible, palpable expression of his suffering.

I jerked away, crashing back into my own body with a jolt of pain. I shivered, reluctant to accept what I'd seen. Lukas was very ill, possibly dying.

Lukas leaned into the mare's shoulder and coughed, long and hard, until he could scarcely breathe. When he looked up, a soft, sad smile spread across his face. "Now you understand."

"No. I don't." I backed away from him, terrified by both the severity of his illness and the doors he'd opened but I could not close. I didn't want to be special or different. Either of those could get me killed.

"Rafael—"

But I raced out of the stall and into the steady, chilling rain. I hadn't gone more than a block before I paused to lean against a lamp post, overcome by a rush of emotions I didn't know how to name. I longed for my quiet life among my brothers, free from temptation. It was cruel of Lukas to taunt me, to offer me the freedom of being myself when such a thing was impossible at home. I'd touched the energy. I wanted more, much in the same way a man who'd been touched by spirits longed for further contact.

I might have wept at the unfairness. It was hard to tell with the raindrops trailing down my cheeks.

"Rafael?"

I trembled, not wanting to see Lukas, but I straightened my shoulders and turned around. He was little more than a silhouette hiding in the shadows of a nearby building. "Lukas?"

But the moment I said the name, I knew I was wrong. The creature stepped out of the shadows. In every physical detail, it looked exactly like Lukas—but he didn't feel the same. The Lukas I knew was tainted, but this one emanated a dark, seductive energy that kept me from doing the smart thing and fleeing. I recalled what Lukas had said about incubi transforming into the lover their victim desired the most and was overcome by a shudder of revulsion. "Get away from me."

Hypnotized, I could only watch as it came toward me. "I know what you want, priest," it said, speaking not only Catalan but possessing the dialect of my very town.

I wondered how but couldn't ask. Then the creature's hands were upon me, stroking in all the right places. I moaned as much from pleasure as from discomfort, for beneath it all was the sickening sense of evil I'd picked up in the foyer. This was a creature of pure evil, and yet...

"Rafael!"

It was Lukas's voice, but to my mind, it didn't make sense. Lukas was here, in front of me, making promises he couldn't possibly keep.

The long, brutal fit of coughing grounded me. The Lukas in my arms was warm, healthy and breathing normally. The Lukas standing a few feet away swayed on his feet and clutched his chest as the spasms continued.

I tried to get to him, but the incubus gripped my arm and filled me with the same painful, sickening sensation I'd felt in the hotel foyer. The world tilted. I struggled and shoved at it until I finally broke free. I stumbled, no steadier than if I was on a ship in a stormy sea.

Someone screamed.

Lukas.

I looked back. The incubus had taken hold of him. Lukas thrashed, but his shriek of pain faded into a hoarse wheezing. His eyes rolled back in his head and he twitched in a seizure. Weak as he was, he wouldn't last long.

"Let him go!"

Not-Lukas gazed at me with eyes that seemed to glow red in the night. A demon's eyes.

"*Enough.*"

I grabbed the thing and wrenched it free from Lukas, who crumpled onto the pavement. That dark, awful force changed its focus back to me.

It was frightening, unreal, but I'd endured worse. Like Lukas, I'd lived through the horrors of war. I bore scars left by bullets. I'd seen bodies lying in the streets and witnessed murders for no reason beyond a difference of philosophy. This creature was no different from the dictators and soldiers I'd known; a predator seeking satiation with no care for its victims. Years of repressed fear and anger burst forth, and I directed it all at the incubus. I'd never participated in an exorcism, but I'd seen one and recalled the extreme calm shown by the priest. I felt much the same, light-headed yet utterly sure of what I must do. "Leave this place."

Our gazes met and locked. Not-Lukas's gaze burned. "I'm not done with you"

"We're finished here. Go, and do not return."

It bent its head and pressed its lips against my cheek. Then it was gone, vanished as if it had never been.

The chill and rain, which I'd forgotten about, suddenly intensified. I shook, both from the chill and the lingering effects of what I had just done. If it hadn't been for Lukas…

I swiveled around in a panic, finally sighting him. I dashed over and knelt on the wet pavement. He was limp as I gathered him gently into my arms. "Lukas. Speak to me."

His rasping voice was difficult to hear. "You're a remarkable man, Rafael." He coughed and I rubbed his chest, wishing I had a better way to aid him. He sagged against me, his ragged breathing a pointed contrast to the gentle, pattering rain.

"Lukas?" I shook him and slapped his face. Neither action roused him. He wasn't dead, but that thing in his chest was as palpable as the incubus had been. Olivia had said it was more spiritual than physical, which was in my line of work, only I hadn't dealt with anything quite this severe. I didn't know what to do.

But I knew who did.

Heart thudding with hope, I draped Lukas over my shoulder and headed back toward the police stable. The guard jumped to his feet. "Padre? What happened?"

I didn't think he'd believe the whole of it, so I gave him the abridged version. "Lukas fell ill on the way back to the hotel. This was the closest shelter I knew."

"Of course, of course, Padre. I will call for a doctor."

"No. Call the hotel. Ask for Signora Olivia Santiago. She's his physician. Tell her to come at once."

The officer disappeared, presumably to find a phone. I hoped I had enough time to do what I needed.

I carried Lukas inside the barn. The mare whickered. "Will you help me?" I asked her. I don't know how much, if anything, she understood, but she licked and chewed and I took that as a sign of her consent.

I propped Lukas in one corner of the stall and buried the thought that this was a stupid idea. The horse could panic and trample or kick us or worse.

But she didn't. Instead, she bent her head to sniff Lukas then looked pointedly at me. I braced myself for the usual anxiety that came when I had to touch someone, but it didn't come. Feeling the same, deep calm as I had when dealing with the incubus, I put a hand against her neck and opened myself to her.

And suddenly I knew what Lukas had been trying to show me. Energy—a force I'd always been aware of but never sure how to manage—surged through me. I became one with the mare, blood and breath and bone. I could see inside her but didn't have the knowledge to understand what I was looking at. At first it was shocking how alien the horse felt until I found organs I could recognize, heart, lungs, guts, all of which seemed to be surrounded by a pale golden light.

Then, still keeping a hand on the horse, I touched Lukas's chest and found the flesh hot, damp, his breathing erratic. A darkness lurked beneath the surface.

I whispered one last prayer for strength and hoped like hell I was doing the right thing. I'd witnessed people die of heartbreak often enough to know the toll of suffering on the body, and it was obvious that the years of trauma and suffering with no real outlet had taken their toll. No wonder he'd latched onto me so desperately. He'd seen in me a kindred spirit, one as wounded as he.

"I'm here," I told him. "I understand."

I'd been a fool to be so afraid. Energy meant life and beauty and wholeness, something Spain had nearly forgotten about in the past few decades. The horses knew it instinctually, so it was no surprise why Lukas had clung to them as a child and still did now. They were steady and calm and strong in the midst of chaos.

And chaos was what I sensed now within Lukas. I *knew* the trauma which lay tucked inside his body. Loss. Terror. Gunfire. The scent of burnt buildings and charred flesh, the horror of bloody, mutilated bodies. Sensitive as he was, he'd felt it all. His adopted father had taken him to the horses, and while they'd saved his life and his sanity, they could not fully understand what he was and had lived through.

I did. I'd been there. And as I saw and absorbed Lukas's memories and shared my own, the darkness inside his chest gave way. The sensation startled me at first, the slight easing of tension which was almost ticklish. It was like a tug-of-war, a give and take of memory and sentiment that lessened the pain rather than adding to it. Yet try as I might, I couldn't pry the darkness completely loose.

I dropped back into myself just enough to be aware of the outside world. The barn was eerily silent, without a snort or shifting of hooves. "Help me," I whispered. "It's not enough."

Then, one after another, I felt them. The mare was the strongest, since she was the closest, but there were other mares and geldings in the mix. Each added their own particular strength and gave it without question.

I became nothing more than a channel, directing energy into Lukas to tear away at the suffocating darkness with support and love.

Little by little, the sick, sluggish energy cleared and transformed into the golden light I'd seen in the mare. I kept at it, determined to cleanse every last bit from Lukas's body.

The horses dropped out of the mix one by one as unobtrusively as they'd joined.

Exhaustion hit hard. I let go of the mare and slumped down beside Lukas. I'd done all I could. I hoped it was enough.

"PADRE?"

I opened my eyes to find I had an audience. Olivia crouched beside me, one hand on my arm. The stall door was open and several policemen, including the guard from outside, stared at us. Only the mare seemed unperturbed as she flicked her tail and nibbled at a fresh pile of hay.

I looked at Lukas, whose head lay pillowed against my shoulder. Someone had draped a horse blanket over us for warmth. "Is he all right?"

"Thanks to you." She ruffled Lukas's hair which, if he were awake, would probably annoy him.

Already, I could tell his breathing was easier from the steady rise and fall of his chest. It was difficult to tell in the dim light, but I thought his color had improved as well.

The man who'd been guarding the barn handed me a mug of steaming coffee. I took it, grateful for the warmth, and noticed the slight tremor in his hand. "It was a miracle, Padre. I saw him when he came in. I didn't think…"

I hid my surprise by sipping my coffee. Let them think I'd performed a miracle, if that's what they needed to believe. It was, in a way, yet it was also the most natural thing I could have done.

I'd almost finished the mug when Lukas twitched and snuggled against me as if he were a cat. "Thank you," he said.

"You're welcome."

He gazed up at me. For a long time, neither of us spoke. We didn't need to. The bond was still there, sharing everything we needed. At length, he said, "Come home with us. My father will give you asylum."

The offer was tempting, and not just because it meant I could stay with Lukas. "I can't." Duty transcended desire.

Beneath the blanket, he grasped my hand. "Are you still afraid?"

I set the mug aside and ran my fingers through his damp blond hair. "Of what I am? No. Of the Generalissimo? Only a fool would not be." Though I saw now how learning about my gift and using it could save me rather than the opposite.

He looked frightened for a moment, but I was calm and soon he was too. "The conference isn't over for three more days. You still have a lot to learn."

La paciència és la mare de la ciència. "Teach me."

His smile was all the answer I needed.

THE FOX AND THE HORSE
JACOB AND WILHELM GRIMM

A PEASANT HAD A FAITHFUL HORSE WHICH HAD GROWN OLD AND COULD do no more work, so his master would no longer give him anything to eat and said, "I can certainly make no more use of thee, but still I mean well by thee; if thou provest thyself still strong enough to bring me a lion here, I will maintain thee, but now take thyself away out of my stable," and with that he chased him into the open country. The horse was sad, and went to the forest to seek a little protection there from the weather. Then the fox met him and said, "Why dost thou hang thy head so, and go about all alone?" "Alas," replied the horse, "avarice and fidelity do not dwell together in one house. My master has forgotten what services I have performed for him for so many years, and because I can no longer plough well, he will give me no more food, and has driven me out." "Without giving thee a chance?" asked the fox. "The chance was a bad one. He said, if I were still strong enough to bring him a lion, he would keep me, but he well knows that I cannot do that." The fox said, "I will help thee, just lay thyself down, stretch thyself out, as if thou wert dead, and do not stir." The horse did as the fox desired, and the fox went to the lion, who had his den not far off, and said, "A dead horse is lying outside there, just come with me, thou canst have a rich meal." The lion went with him, and when they were both standing by the horse the fox said, "After all, it is not very comfortable for thee here I tell thee what I will fasten it to thee by the tail, and then thou canst drag it into thy cave, and devour it in peace."

This advice pleased the lion: he lay down, and in order that the fox might tie the horse fast to him, he kept quite quiet. But the fox tied the lion's legs together with the horse's tail, and twisted and fastened all so well and so strongly that no strength could break it. When he had finished his work, he tapped the horse on the shoulder and said, "Pull, white horse, pull." Then up sprang the horse at once, and drew the lion away with him. The lion began to roar so that all the birds in the forest flew out in terror, but the horse let him roar, and drew him and dragged him over the country to his master's door. When the master saw the lion, he was of a better mind, and said to the horse, "Thou shalt stay with me and fare well," and he gave him plenty to eat until he died.

AL BORAK — THE NAME IS ARABIC, AND MEANS THE LIGHTNING. AND this is the story which faithful Moslems tell of the wondrous steed.

It was midnight, thirteen hundred years ago, and Mohammed, the prophet, lay asleep in his house in the ancient city of Mecca. Suddenly he was roused by hearing a loud voice crying: "Up, up, thou sleeper ! Arise and make ready for thy journey!"

Mohammed leaped to his feet and looked about him. Before him stood a creature of dazzling radiance whom he took to be an angel. His face was white as the purest marble, his hair was of gold and fell in silk-like waves about his shoulders, his wings reflected all the colors of the rainbow, and his robes of spotless white were embroidered with gold and thickly set with precious gems.

Mohammed was about to speak when he saw that the angel was holding the reins of a steed the most marvelous that any man ever beheld.

It appeared to be a horse, and yet it was not like a horse. Its limbs were slender and long, its body was strong-built and finely formed, its coat sleek and glossy, and its mane so long that it almost swept the ground. Its color was white, intermingled with golden-yellow, and there was a golden star in its forehead. Folded over its back were wings like those of an eagle, amid the plumes of which the lightning gleamed and flashed. Its eyes were brighter than coals of fire, its ears were sharp-pointed and restless, its nostrils were wide, blood-red, and steaming. It had the face of a man, although the cheeks of a horse, and it spoke with a human voice in the purest Arabic.

Mohammed had no sooner seen this wonderful steed than he was filled with a desire to mount it. But when he reached forth his hand and made ready to spring upon its back, it reared high in the air, and would have struck at the prophet with its golden hoofs had not the angel restrained it.

"Be still, Borak!" cried the latter. "Do you not know who this is whom you oppose? It is Mohammed, the son of Abdallah, of one of the tribes of Arabia the Happy. He is the prophet of Allah, and it is through his intercession only that any creature can enter paradise."

Al Borak at once became as gentle as a lamb, and her eyes were filled with beseeching tears as she turned to the prophet and said:

"O thou, the most honored of mortals, I pray thee that thou wilt intercede for me!"

"Be assured that I will," answered Mohammed; "for never was steed more worthy of paradise than thou art!"

Then Al Borak allowed the prophet to mount upon her back, and, rising gently from the ground, she soared aloft above the desert sands and mountains of Arabia. The night was dark — the darkest that any man ever knew; and it was so still that all nature seemed sleeping and dead. There was no sound anywhere of stirring wind or of rippling water. No chirp of wakeful insect, no rustle of creeping reptile, no baying of dogs, no howling of wild beasts among the mountains, disturbed the solemn hour. All Arabia was silent as the grave. And Al Borak, with face directed northward, and at a speed which outdistanced thought, sailed noiselessly through the gloom.

Only thrice did the steed alight upon the earth — first upon Mount Sinai, then in the village of Bethlehem, and finally at the gate of the temple in Jerusalem. There Mohammed dismounted, and, fastening the steed to a ring which was attached to one of the stones of the temple, he left her and went in. But I need not speak of what happened to him there, nor of his further journey, nor of whom or what he saw ; for those things have naught to do with Al Borak. When, at length, he returned to the gate of the temple, he found the steed in the place where he had tethered her, and, having remounted her, he was carried in an instant back to Mecca and set down at his own door. Then Al Borak, having bowed low in honor of the prophet, unfolded her wings again and soared aloft into the upper air, never again to be seen by mortal man.

The distance from Mecca to Jerusalem is about eight hundred miles as the crow flies, or as Al Borak flew. And yet, although Mohammed had not stopped at Jerusalem, but had gone some millions of miles beyond, the whole affair was accomplished in less time than you can think of it. It is easy to prove that this was so. In the first hurry of setting out, a vase of water had been overturned by the angel's wing; but Mohammed returned in time to catch the falling vessel before its contents could be spilled. Could anything have been quicker? Not even thought or a flash of light could have outsped Al Borak.

A HORSE STORY
KATE CHOPIN

HERMINIA, MOUNTED UPON A DEJECTED LOOKING SORREL PONY, WAS climbing the gradual slope of a pine hill one morning in summer. She was a 'Cadian girl of the old Bayou Derbanne settlement. The pony was of the variety known indifferently as Indian, Mustang or Texan. Nothing remained of the spirited qualities of his youth. His coat in places was worn away to the hide. In other spots it grew in long tufts and clumps. To the pommel of the saddle was attached an Indian basket containing eggs packed in cotton seed; and beside, the girl carried some garden truck in a coarse bag.

From the moment of leaving her home on the bayou, Herminia had noticed a slight lump in Ti Démon's left fore foot. But to pay special attention to his peculiarities would have been to encourage him in what she considered an objectionable line of conduct. "Allons donc! You! Ti Démon! W'at's the matter with you?" she exclaimed from time to time. They had long left the bayou road and had penetrated far into the pine forest. The ascent at times was steep and the pony's feet slipped over the pine needles.

"I b'lieve you doin' on purpose!" she exclaimed vexatiously. "If I done right I would walked myse'f f'om the firs' an' lef' you behine." Ti Démon held his leg doubled at a sharp angle and seemed unable to touch it to the ground. At this, Herminia sprang from the saddle, and going forward, lifted the animal's foot to examine it.

The leg was shaggy and might have been swollen; she could not tell. But there was no sign of his having picked up a nail, a stone, or any foreign substance.

"Come 'long, Ti Démon. Courage!" and she tried to lead him by the bridle. But he could not be persuaded to move.

The girl stayed wondering what she should do. The horse could go no further; that was a self evident fact. Her own two legs were as sturdy as steel and could carry her many miles. But the question which confronted her was whether she should turn and go back home or whether she should continue on her way to Monsieur Labatier's. The planter had his summer home in the hills where there were neither flies, mosquitoes, fevers, fleas nor any of the trials which often afflict the bayou dwellers in summer.

It was nearer to go to the planter's – not more than three miles. And Herminia cherished the certainty of being well received up there. Madame Labatier would pay her handsomely for the eggs and vegetables. They would invite her to dine and give her a sip of wine. She would have an opportunityof observing the toilets and manners of the young ladies – two nieces who were spending a month in the hills. But above all there would be young Mr. Prospere Labatier who perhaps would say:

"Ah! Herminia, it is too bad! Allow me to len' you my ho'se to return home," or else:

"Will you permit me the pleasure of escorting you home in my buggy?" These last considerations determined Herminia beyond further hesitancy.

With the piece of rope which she carried on such occasions she tied Ti Démon to a pine tree near the sandy road in a pleasant, shady spot.

"Now, stay there, till I come back. It's yo' own fault if you got to go hungry. You can't expec' me to tote you on my back, grosse bête!" She patted him kindly and turning her back upon him, proceeded to ascend the hill with a little springy step. She wore a calico dress of vivid red and a white sun bonnet from whose depth twinkled two black eyes, quick as a squirrel's.

Ti Démon observed her with his dull eyes and continued to hold his foot from the ground like a veritable martyr. It was still and restful in the forest and if Ti Démon had not been suffering acutely, he would have enjoyed the peaceful moment. Patches of sunlight played upon his back; a couple of red ants crawled up his hind leg; he slowly swished his long, scant tail. The mocking birds began to sing a duet in the top of a pine tree. They were young; they could sing and rejoice; they knew nothing of the tribulations attending upon old age, Ti Démon thought to himself:

"If this thing keeps up, there's no telling where it will land me."

While he understood Herminia's broken English and her mother's 'Cadian French, Ti Démon always thought in his native language, that he had imbibed in his youth in the Indian Nation.

He stood for some hours very still listening to the drowsy noises of the forest. Then a blessed relaxation began to invade the afflicted foreleg. The pain perceptibly died away, and he straightened the limb without difficulty. Ti Démon uttered a deep sigh of relief. But with the consciousness of returning comfort came the realization of his unpleasant situation. He could fancy nothing more uninteresting than to be fastened thus to a tree in the heart of the pine forest. He already began to grow hungry in anticipation of the hunger which would assail him later. He had no means of knowing what hour Herminia would return and release him from his sad predicament. It was then that Ti Démon put into practice one of his chief accomplishments. He began deliberately to unknot the rope with his old, yellow teeth. He had observed Herminia give it an extra knot and had even heard her say:

"There! if you undo that, Ti Démon, they'll have to allow you got mo' sense than Raymond's mule." The remark had offended him. He hated the constant association with Raymond's mule to which he was subjected.

He managed after persistent effort to untie the knot, and Ti Démon soon found himself free to roam whithersoever he chose. If he had been a dog he would have turned his nose uphill and followed in the footsteps of his mistress. But he was only a pony of rather low breeding and almost wholly devoid of sentiment.

Ti Démon walked leisurely down the slope, following the path by which he had come. It was a pleasing diversion to be thus permitted to roam at will. He did not linger, however, to nibble here and there after the manner of stray horses, for he knew well that the pine hill afforded little sustenance to man or beast; and he preferred to wait and whet his appetite with the luscious bits that grew below along the bayou. He appeared like a wise old philosopher plunged in thought.

By frequent stepping upon the rope dangling from his neck, it at length gave way, much to Ti Démon's satisfaction.

"Now! if I could get rid of the saddle as easily!" thought he.

It was impossible to reach the girth with his teeth; he tried that. Then Ti Démon shook himself till his coat bristled; he rubbed himself against the tree; he rolled over on his side, on his back, but the only result which he reached was to turn the saddle so that it dangled beneath him as he walked. At this he swore lustily to himself, as his master, Blanco Bill, used to swear so many years back in the Nation. He did not feel now like nibbling grass or amusing himself in any way. His one thought was to get home to his dinner of soft food and be rid of the hateful encumbrance beating against his legs.

When Ti Démon found himself standing before his home, he viewed the situation with sullen disapproval. The little house was closed and silent. The only living thing to be seen was the cat sleeping in the shade of the gallery. A line of yellow pumpkins gleamed along the boards in the sun. There was a hoe leaning up against the fence where Herminia's mother who had been hoeing the tobacco plants had left it.

"Just as I thought," grumbled Ti Démon. "I could 'a sworn to it. That woman's off gallivanting down the river again; dropped her hoe the minute Herminia's back was turned. An' them kids ought to be back from school; drat 'em! A thousand dollars to a doughnut they gone crawfishing. If I don't shake this whole shootin' match first chance I get, my name ain't Spitfire." It was the name Blanco Bill had given him at birth and the only one he acknowledged officially.

"There's no opening gates or lifting latches or anything since they got them newfangled padlocks on," he further reflected, "if there was, I'd get inside there an' them cabbages an' cowpeas 'ld be nuts for me. Reckon I'll stroll down an' see if I c'n ketch Solistan at home." Ti Démon turned again to the road and with a deliberate stride which sent the saddle bumping and thumping, he headed for the neighboring farm up the bayou.

There was nothing startling to Solistan in seeing Ti Démon staring over his fence. He simply thought Herminia had returned from the pine hill, that the animal had got loose from the "lot" and he went forward to drive him into his own enclosure, intending to take him home later, when he should be at leisure.

But Solistan's astonishment was acute when he discovered Ti Démon's condition; covered with clay and bits of sticks and bark, Herminia's saddle hanging beneath him, and the blanket gone. It was but the work of a moment to drive the pony back in the lot; to throw a measure of corn into the trough; to saddle his own horse and start off at a mad gallop.

"Wonder what all the commotion's about," thought Ti Démon as he attempted to munch the corn from the cob. "He didn't take much trouble to pick an' choose when he gave me this mess. This here corn mus' be a hundred years old; or my teeth ain't what they used to be."

Solistan knew Ti Démon too well to believe that he had cut any capers which could have resulted in harm to Herminia. But the saddle must have turned with her; he might have stumbled and thrown her. A hundred misgivings assailed him, especially after he had been to her house and discovered the place deserted by all save the cat asleep in the shade of the gallery.

Solistan had started away just as he was, in his blue checked shirt and his boots heavy with the damp earth of the fields. He never dreamt of stopping to make a bit of toilet. He could not remember when he had in his life been a prey to such uneasiness. He had known and liked Herminia all her life; but she was always there at hand, seeming to be a natural part of the surroundings to which he was accustomed. It was only at that moment, when the menace of some dreadful and unknown fate hung over her, that he fully realized the depth and nature of his attachment for the girl.

Solistan rode far into the forest, his anxiety growing at every moment, and sick with dread of what any turn or bend in the road might reveal to him. He could not contain himself. He shouted for joy when he saw Herminia standing unharmed and motionless beneath a tall pine tree, as though she were holding a conversation and even some argument with his rugged majesty.

Her sunbonnet hung on her arm and her whole attitude was one of deep dejection. Herminia was in truth helplessly surveying the spot where she had so insecurely fastened Ti Démon, who had disappeared, leaving so much as a hair of his hide or tail to say that he had ever been there. This seeming treachery on the part of Ti Démon marked the culmination of Herminia's mortification, and the tears were suffocating her.

Oh! it had been very fine up at the planter's! Too fine indeed. There was a large house-party congregated for the day, and little Herminia standing on the back gallery with her eggs and garden truck had been scarcely noticed.

She had been permitted to dine with them, wedged in between two stout old people; but she felt like an intruder and even perceived that the servants gave themselves the air of forgetting her. The young ladies' volubility and ease of manners made her feel small and insignificant; and their fluffy summer toilets conveyed to her only the bitter conviction of never being able to reproduce in calico such intricacy of ruffles and puffs. As for Mr. Prospere, he had only exclaimed: "Hello! Herminia!" in passing hastily along the gallery when she sat with her garden truck and eggs.

She could scarcely eat, for mortification and disappointment. She had not had an opportunity of relating the misadventure to her pony, and when, at leaving, the planter solicitously asked how she was going to get home, Herminia replied with forced dignity that she had left her horse tied a little below in the woods.

There was the wood all right, and there was Herminia, but where was the pony? That was the question which Herminia seemed to be asking of the big pine tree when Solistan rode up in such hot haste and flung himself from the saddle as if to reach out for some prize that he had pursued and captured.

"Oh! Solistan! I lef' Ti Démon fasten' yere this mornin'; he couldn' walk; an' now he's gone! Oh! Solistan! Someone mus' 'ave stole' im!"

"Ti Démon is in my lot eatin' co'n fo' all he's worth. The saddle was turned under 'im. I thought you'd got hurt." Solistan wiped his steaming , beaming hace with his bandanna; and Herminia felt at beholding him that she had never been so glad or thankful to see any one in her life. And she could not think of any one whom she would rather have seen at that moment; not even Mr. Prospere. Not even if he had come along and said:

"Allow me the pleasure of escorting you home in my buggy, Herminia!"

Solistan's was a big, broadbacked horse, and Herminia sat very comfortably behind the young man on her way back to the bayou; holding on to his suspenders when the occasion required it.

After they had reached Solistan's home and he had brought forth Ti Démon resaddled and refreshed, the following bit of conversation took place between them. Herminia was mounted, ready to start, and Solistan was still holding the animal's bridle.

"That Ti Démon of yo's is played out, Herminia. He isn't safe, I tell you. He'll play you a mean trick some these days. I been thinkin' you better use that li'l mare I traded with Raul fo' las' spring."

"Oh! Solistan! it would take too much corn to feed 'im. We got Raymond's mule to feed; an' Ti Démon eats fo' three, him-"

"Oh! shoot Ti Démon; his time's over."

"Shoot Ti Démon!" cried the girl, flushing with indignation. "You talkin' like crazy, Solistan. I would soon think o' takin' a gun an' shootin' someone passin' 'long the road."

"I'm jus' talkin'," laughed Solistan, perceiving the impression which his heartless remark had produced. "Ole Démon's good fo' a long time yet. He's plenty good to haul water or tote the children up an' down the bayou road. But don't you ever trus' yo'se'f in the woods with 'im again."

"You c'n be sho' of that, Solistan."

"An' 'bout feedin'," he went on, greatly occupied with the buckle of Ti Démon's bridle, "I could keep on feedin' the ho'se, an' if that plan don't suit you, w'at you think 'bout takin' me long with the ho'se Herminia?"

"Takin' you, Solistan!"

"W'y not? We plenty ole 'nough; you mus' be mos' eighteen, an' I'm goin; on twenty-three, me."

"I better be goin'. We c'n talk 'bout that 'nother time."

"W'en, Herminia! W'en?" implored Solistan holding on to the bridle of her pony, "tonight if I come down yonder? Say, tonight?"

"Oh Solistan, le' me go!"

"An' w'at will you tell me, Herminia?"

"We'll see 'bout that," she laughed over her shoulder as Ti Démon started away with a stiff trot.

But all the joy of life had forever left the breast of Ti Démon. Solistan's sinister remarks had made a deep and painful impression which he could not rid himself of.

When, in the autumn following, the young farmer took Herminia to be his wife, and also took Ti Démon with the benevolent intention of feeding him all the rest of his life, it was then that Ti Démon's days were given over to brooding upon the possible fate which awaited him.

Once in an unguarded moment, Ti Démon walked himself off, across Bayou Derbanne, along the Sabine and away from the haunts which had known him so long.

"If there's goin' to be any shootin'," reflected Ti Démon as he limped along, swishing his tail, "it's time fo' me to be pullin' my freight."

It was during the winter following that Solistan one evening to his wife as she bent over the fire, getting their evening meal. "W'at you think, Herminia? Raul tole me w'en he was drivin' his drove of cattle into Texas las' month, they came 'cross Ti Démon layin' dead in the Bonham road. The li'le rascal mus' a' been on his way to the Indian Nation."

"Oh! Po' Ti Démon!" exclaimed Herminia holding aloft the

huge spoon with which she had been stirring the couche-couche. "He was a good an' faithful ho'se! yes!"

"That's true, Herminia," replied Solistan with philosophic resignation, "but who knows! maybe it is all fo' the best!"

IVAN AND THE CHESTNUT HORSE

RUSSIAN FAIRY TALE

IN A FAR LAND WHERE THEY PAY PEOPLE TO KEEP ITS NAME A PROFOUND secret, there lived an old man who brought up his three sons just exactly in the way they should go. He taught them the three R's, and also showed them what books to read and how to read them. He was particularly careful about their education, for he had learned that to know things was to be able to do things.

At last, when he came to die, he gathered his three sons round his deathbed and cautioned them.

'Do not forget,' he said—'do not forget to come and read the prayers over my grave.'

'We will not forget, father,' they replied.

The two elder brothers were great big, strapping fellows, but the youngest one, Ivan, was a mere stripling. As they all stood around the bed of their dying father, he looked a mere reed compared to his proud, stout, elder brothers. But his eyes were full of fire and spirit, and the firm expression of his mouth showed great determination. And, when the father had breathed his last, and his two elder brothers wept without restraint, Ivan stood silent, his pale face set and his eyes full of the bright wonder of tears that would not melt.

On the day that they buried their father, Ivan returned to the grave in the evening to read prayers over it. He had done so, and was making his way homeward, when there was a great clatter of hoofs behind him; then, as he reached the village square, the horseman pulled up and dismounted quite near to him. After blowing a loud blast on his silver trumpet—for he was the King's messenger—he cried in a loud voice:

'All and every man, woman and child, take notice, in the name of the King. It is the King's will that this proclamation be cried abroad in every town and village where his subjects dwell. The King's daughter, Princess Helena the Fair, has caused to be built for herself a shrine having twelve pillars and twelve rows of beams. And she sits there upon a high throne till the time when the bridegroom of her choice rides by. And this is how she shall know him: with one leap of his steed he reaches the height of the tower, and, in passing, his lips press those of the Princess as she bends from her throne. Wherefore the King has ordered this to be proclaimed throughout the length and breadth of the land, for if any deems himself able so to reach the lips of the Princess and win her, let him try. In the name of the King I have said it!'

The blood of the youth of the nation, wherever this proclamation was issued, took flame and leapt to touch the lips of Princess Helena the Fair. All wondered to whose lot this lucky fate would fall. Some said it would be to the most daring, others contended that it was a matter of the leaping powers of the steed, and yet others that it depended not only on the steed but on the daring skill of the rider also.

When the three brothers had listened to the words of the King's messenger they looked at one another; at least the elder two did, for it was apparent to them that Ivan, the youngest, was quite out of the competition, whereas they, two splendid handsome fellows, were distinctly in it.

'Brothers,' said Ivan at last, 'our first thought must be to fulfil our father's dying wish. But, if you prefer it, we could take it in turns to read the prayers over our father's grave. Let it be the duty of one of us each day to fulfil the duty, morning and evening.'

The elder brothers agreed readily to this, but, when Ivan asked whose turn it should be on the morrow, they both began to make excuses.

The chestnut horse seemed to linger in the air at the top of its leap while that kiss endured.

'As for me,' said the eldest, 'I must go and order the work of the farm my father left me, and that will take seven days.'

'And for me,' said the younger, 'I must see to the estate which is my part of the inheritance, and that also will take seven days.'

'Then,' replied Ivan, 'if I perform the duty for seven days, you will each do your share afterwards?'

His brothers agreed still more readily than before. Then they went their ways, Ivan full of thoughts of his father, and the other two to train their jumping horses, the one on his farm and the other on his estate. And both laughed to themselves, for neither knew the purpose of the other.

How they curled their hair and cleaned their teeth, and practised 'prunes and prisms' with their mouths close to the looking-glass!— so that when, at one bound of their magnificent steeds, they reached the level of the Princess's lips, to aim the kiss that was to win the prize, they would make a brave show, and a conquering one. As for their little brother, they each thought he could go on praying over their father's grave as long as he liked,—it would be the best thing he could do, and it would not interfere with their secret plans, so carefully concealed from each other and from him.

So, for seven days, in their separate districts, they raced about on their horses by day and dreamed of the greatest leaping feats by night. And at the end of the seven days the youngest brother summoned them to keep their agreement, and asked which of them would read the prayers, morning and evening, for the second seven days.

'I have done my part,' he said; 'now it is for you to arrange between you which one shall continue the sacred duty.'

The two elder brothers looked at each other and then at Ivan.

'As for me,' said one, 'I care little who does it, so long as I am free to get on with my business, which is more important.'

'And as for me,' said the other, 'I am in no mind to watch each blade of grass growing on the grave. I cannot really afford the time, I am so busy. You, Ivan,—you are different: you are not a man of affairs; how could you spend your time better than reading prayers over our father's grave?'

'So be it,' replied Ivan. 'You get back to your work and I will attend to the sacred duty for another seven days.'

The two elder brothers went their separate ways, and for seven more days devoted their entire attention to training their horses for the flying leap at the Princess's lips. How they tore like mad about the fields! How they jumped the hedges and ditches! How they curled their hair and dyed their moustaches and practised their lips, not only to 'prunes and prisms,' but to 'peaches of passion' and 'pomegranates,' and 'peripatetic perambulation' and everything they could think of! In fact, they paid so much attention to the lips which were to meet those of the Princess at the top of the flying leap, that they began to neglect their own and their horses' meals. In other words, they were beginning to show signs of over-training.

At the end of the second seven days Ivan again summoned them to a family council, and asked them if either of them could now take up the sacred duty. But no; thinking heavily on horses and lips, and high jumps and kisses, they spoke lightly of fields to be tilled, seed to be sown, and all such things that must be done at once. Their view was—and they got quite friendly over it—that Ivan should be more than delighted to bear this pleasurable burden of reading prayers over his father's grave. Indeed, nothing but the stern call of immediate duty would prevail upon them to relinquish a task so pleasant.

'So be it,' said Ivan; 'I will perform the sacred duty for another seven days.' But as he spoke, he noted his brothers' curled hair and dyed moustaches, and gleaned from this, and from the look of sudden suspicion and jealousy exchanged between them, that they were both in love with the same fair one. But he kept this to himself, and left them to their own concerns.

Again, at the end of seven days, when Ivan had read the prayers devoutly, he summoned his brothers. But they did not come. Both sent messages saying that they were frightfully busy, and would he be so good as to go on with the sacred duty until they could be spared to do their share later on. Ivan accepted their messages, and went on reading the prayers over the father's grave.

Meanwhile each of his brothers prepared for the great flying leap; and each said to himself: 'What about Ivan? He would like to see this great exploit. It might make a man of him. He is altogether lacking in ambition, and to see a great deed done might stir him to try to be a great hero himself. But yet—I fear it would never do. He is so weedy, so insignificant. I feel I should lose by having a brother like that anywhere about. No; he is far better reading prayers over our father's grave.'

So each in his own way resolved to go in alone—apart from the other and apart from Ivan.

The morning of the great day came. The eldest brother had chosen from his horses a magnificent black one with arched neck and flowing mane and tail. The second brother had selected a bay equally splendid. And now, at sunrise, they were, each unknown to the other, combing their well-curled hair, re-dyeing their moustaches, and booting and trapping themselves for the wonderful display of prowess the day was to bring forth. And they did not forget to make sure that their lips were as fit as they were anxious for the 'high kiss.'

At the appointed time they rode into the lists and drew their lots, and neither was altogether surprised at seeing his brother among the host of competitors for the hand of Helena the Fair. Their surprise came later, when Ivan arrived on the scene.

It so happened in this way: that, towards evening, when his two brothers had each had their last try to leap up to the Princess's lips and failed, like every one else, Ivan himself was reading the prayers over his father's grave. Suddenly a great emotion came over him, and he stopped in his reading. He was filled with a longing to look just for once upon the face of Helena the Fair, for whose favour he knew that the most splendid in the land were competing with their wonderful steeds. So strong was this longing that he broke down and, bending over his father's grave, wept bitterly.

And then a strange thing happened. His father heard him in his coffin, and shook himself free from the damp earth, and came out and stood before him.

'Do not weep, Ivan, my son,' he said. And Ivan looked up and was terrified at the sight of him.

'Nay, my son, do not fear me,' his father went on. 'You have fulfilled my dying wish, and I will help you in your trouble. You wish to look upon the face of Helena the Fair, and so it shall be.'

With this he drew himself up, and his aspect was commanding. Then he called in a loud voice, and, as the echoes of his tones began to die away, Ivan heard them change into the far-distant beat of a horse's hoofs. After listening for a while his father called again, and this time the echo was a horse's neigh and galloping hoofs. It seemed beyond the hillside, and Ivan looked up and wondered. A third time his father called, and nearer and nearer came the galloping sound, until at last, with a thundering snort and a ringing neigh, a beautiful chestnut horse appeared, circled round them thrice, and then came to a halt before them, its two forefeet close together and its eyes, ears, and nostrils shooting flames of fire.

Then came a voice, and Ivan knew it was the voice of the chestnut horse with the proudly arched neck and flowing mane:

'What is your will? Command me and I obey!'

The father took Ivan by the hand and led him to the horse's head.

'Enter here at the right ear,' he said, 'and pass through, and make your way out at the left ear. By so doing you will be able to command the horse, and he will do whatever you may wish that a horse should do.'

So Ivan, nothing doubting, passed in at the right ear of the chestnut horse and came out at the left; and immediately there was a wonderful change in him. He was no longer a dreamy youth: he was at once a man of affairs, and the light of a high ambition shone in his eyes.

'Mount! Go, win the Princess Helena the Fair!' said his father, and immediately vanished.

With one spring Ivan was astride the chestnut horse, and, in another moment, they were speeding like lightning towards the shrine of Helena the Fair.

The sun was setting, and the two elder brothers, disconsolate, were about to withdraw from the field, when, startled by the cries of the people, they saw a steed come galloping on, well ridden, and at a terrific pace. They turned to look and they marked how Helena the Fair, disappointed of all others, leaned out to watch the oncoming horseman. And the whole concourse turned and stood to await the possible event.

On came the chestnut horse, his nostrils snorting fire, his hoofs shaking the earth. He neared the shrine, and, to a masterful rein, rose at a flying leap. The daring rider looked up and the Princess leaned down, but he could not reach her lips, ready as they were.

The whole field now stood at gaze as the chestnut horse with its rider circled round and came up again. And this time, with a splendid leap, the brave steed bore its rider aloft so that the fragrant breath of the Princess seemed to meet his nostrils, and yet his lips did not meet hers.

Again they circled round while all stood still and tense. Again the chestnut steed rose to the leap, and, this time, the lips of Ivan met those of the Princess in a long sweet kiss, for the chestnut horse seemed to linger in the air at the top of its leap while that kiss endured.

Then, while the Princess looked after, horse and rider reached the ground and disappeared like lightning.

Instantly the host of onlookers swarmed in.

'Who is he? Where is he?' was the cry on every hand. 'He kissed her on the lips, and she kissed him. Look at her! Is it not true?'

It was true, for Princess Helena the Fair, with a lovelight in her eyes, was leaning down and searching, with all her soul, even for the very dust spurned from the heels of her lover's horse. But she could see nothing, and sank back within her shrine, treasuring the kiss upon her lips; while the people, dissatisfied, but wondering greatly, melted away. Among them went the splendid brothers, seeking how they could sell their well-trained horses to advantage, for they had both been frantically near to the Princess's lips.

Whither had Ivan flown on the chestnut horse? Loosing the

reins—he cared for nothing but the kiss—he let his steed go, and presently it came to a standstill before his father's grave. There he dismounted and turned the horse adrift. As if its errand was completed, it galloped off; a rainbow came down to meet it, and, closing in, seemed to snatch it up in its folds. Ivan was alone before his father's grave.

Once more he bowed himself in prayer. Once more his father appeared before him.

'Thou hast done well, O my son,' he said. 'Thou hast fulfilled my dying wish, but my living wish is yet to be fulfilled. To-morrow Helena the Fair will summon the people and demand her bridegroom. Be thou there, but say nothing.'

With this Ivan found himself alone.

On the following day there was a great gathering at the palace, and, in the midst of it, sat Princess Helena the Fair demanding her bridegroom—the one who had leapt to her lips and won her from all others. Her heart and soul and body were his. The half of her kingdom to come was his. She, herself, was his;—where was he?

Search was made among the highest in the land, but, fearing a demand for the repetition of the leap and the kiss, none came forward. Ivan sat at the back, a humble spectator.

'She is thinking of that leap and that kiss,' said he to himself. 'When she sees me as I am, then let her judge.' But love, though blind, has eyes. The Princess rose from her seat and swept a glance over the people. She saw the two handsome elder brothers and passed them by as so much dirt. Then, by the light of love, she descried, sitting in a corner, where the lights were low, the hero of the chestnut horse,—the one who had leapt high and reached her lips in the first sweet kiss of love.

She knew him at once, and, as all looked on in wonder, she made her way to that dim corner, took him by the hand without a word, and led him up, past the throne of honour, to an antechamber, where, with the joyous cries of the people ringing in their ears, their lips met a second time,—at the summit of a leap of joy.

At that moment the King entered, knowing all.

'What is this?' said he.

Then he smiled, for he understood his daughter, and knew that she had not only chosen her lover, but had won her choice.

'My son,' he added, without waiting for an answer, 'you and yours will reign after me. Look to it! Now let us go to supper.'

THE GOBLIN PONY
FRENCH FOLK TALE

'Don't stir from the fireplace to-night,' said old Peggy, 'for the wind is blowing so violently that the house shakes; besides, this is Hallow-e'en, when the witches are abroad, and the goblins, who are their servants, are wandering about in all sorts of disguises, doing harm to the children of men.'

'Why should I stay here?' said the eldest of the young people. 'No, I must go and see what the daughter of old Jacob, the rope-maker, is doing. She wouldn't close her blue eyes all night if I didn't visit her father before the moon had gone down.'

'I must go and catch lobsters and crabs' said the second, 'and not all the witches and goblins in the world shall hinder me.'

So they all determined to go on their business or pleasure, and scorned the wise advice of old Peggy. Only the youngest child hesitated a minute, when she said to him, 'You stay here, my little Richard, and I will tell you beautiful stories.'

But he wanted to pick a bunch of wild thyme and some blackberries by moonlight, and ran out after the others. When they got outside the house they said: 'The old woman talks of wind and storm, but never was the weather finer or the sky more clear; see how majestically the moon stalks through the transparent clouds!'

Then all of a sudden they noticed a little black pony close beside them.

'Oh, ho!' they said, 'that is old Valentine's pony; it must have escaped from its stable, and is going down to drink at the horse-pond.'

'My pretty little pony,' said the eldest, patting the creature with his hand, 'you mustn't run too far; I'll take you to the pond myself.'

With these words he jumped on the pony's back and was quickly followed by his second brother, then by the third, and so on, till at last they were all astride the little beast, down to the small Richard, who didn't like to be left behind.

On the way to the pond they met several of their companions, and they invited them all to mount the pony, which they did, and the little creature did not seem to mind the extra weight, but trotted merrily along.

The quicker it trotted the more the young people enjoyed the fun; they dug their heels into the pony's sides and called out, 'Gallop, little horse, you have never had such brave riders on your back before!'

In the meantime the wind had risen again, and the waves began to howl; but the pony did not seem to mind the noise, and instead of going to the pond, cantered gaily towards the sea-shore.

Richard began to regret his thyme and blackberries, and the eldest brother seized the pony by the mane and tried to make it turn round, for he remembered the blue eyes of Jacob the rope-maker's daughter. But he tugged and pulled in vain, for the pony galloped straight on into the sea, till the waves met its forefeet. As soon as it felt the water it neighed lustily and capered about with glee, advancing quickly into the foaming billows. When the waves had covered the children's legs they repented their careless behaviour, and cried out: 'The cursed little black pony is bewitched. If we had only listened to old Peggy's advice we shouldn't have been lost.'

The further the pony advanced, the higher rose the sea; at last the waves covered the children's heads and they were all drowned.

Towards morning old Peggy went out, for she was anxious about the fate of her grandchildren. She sought them high and low, but could not find them anywhere. She asked all the neighbours if they had seen the children, but no one knew anything about them, except that the eldest had not been with the blue-eyed daughter of Jacob the rope-maker.

As she was going home, bowed with grief, she saw a little black pony coming towards her, springing and curveting in every direction. When it got quite near her it neighed loudly, and galloped past her so quickly that in a moment it was out of her sight.

RED DUST AND DANCING HORSES
BETH CATO

No horses existed on Mars. Nara could change that.

She stared out the thick-paned window. Tinted dirt sprawled to a horizon, mesas and rock-lipped craters cutting the mottled sky. It almost looked like a scene from somewhere out of the Old West on Earth, like in the two-dimensional movies she studied on her tablet. Mama thought that 20th-century films were the ultimate brain-rotting waste of time, so Nara made sure to see at least two a week. Silver, Trigger, Buttermilk, Rex, Champion—she knew them all. She had spent months picturing just how their hooves would sink into that soft dirt, how their manes would lash in the wind. How her feet needed to rest in the stirrups, heels down, and how the hot curve of a muzzle would fit between her cupped hands.

The terraforming process had come a long way in the two hundred years since mechs established the Martian colonies. Nara didn't need a pressure suit to walk outside, but in her lifetime she'd never breathe on her own outside of her house or the Corcoran Dome. There would never be real horses here, not for hundreds of years, if ever. But a mechanical horse could find its way home in a dust storm, or handle the boggy sand without breaking a leg. She could ride it. Explore. It would be better than nothing. Her forehead bumped against the glass. But to have a real horse with hot skin and silky mane...

"Nara, you're moping again." Mama held a monitor to each window, following the seal along the glass. "No matter how long you stare out the window and sulk, we can't afford to fly you back to Earth just to see horses. They're hard to find as it is. Besides, you know what happened when that simulator came through last year."

Yeah. Each Martian-borne eleven-year-old child had sat in a booth strung with wires and sensors so that they could feel the patter of rain and touch the flaking dryness of eucalyptus bark. Nara smelled the dankness of fertile earth for the very first time. She threw up. The administrators listed her as a category five Martian, needing the longest quarantine time to acclimate to Earth, if she ever made the trip.

"Blast it, another inner seal is weakening," Mama muttered, moving to the next window.

The dull clang of metal echoed down the hall, followed by the soft whir of Papa's mechs. Papa would understand. He would listen.

Her feet tapped down the long tunnel to his workshop. Nara rubbed the rounded edge of the tablet tucked at her waist. Sand pattered against the walls as the wind whistled a familiar melody.

The workshop stood twice as big as the rest of the household, echoing with constantly-clicking gears. The grey dome bowed overhead, the skylight windows showing only red. Papa's legs stuck out from beneath the belly of a mining cart, his server mechs humming as they dismantled the plating on a small trolley alongside him. The workshop was half empty. The basalt mine had received a new load of equipment just two weeks before, and as Papa described it, he'd have a lull before everything decided to break again. Judging by the lack of dents on this cart, the lull was already over.

"Hey, girly. Hand me the tenner," Papa said, a hand thrusting through a gap in the chassis. Nara passed him the tool. "What're you up to?"

"Nothing." Nara slipped open the tablet, expanding the

screen with a tug of her fingers. After a few taps, she accessed the data she wanted: the anatomy of the horse. Her fingers flicked up, removing the layer of skin, then the muscles, leaving the bones. One of the nearby mechs bowed, his knees fluid and graceful as he picked up a tire and conveyed it to a stack on the far side. Nara squinted, looking between the mech and the screen.

"You're never up to nothing," Papa said. "Did Mama kick you out of the house?"

"Not yet. I was wondering something, actually. Think I could use the extra space you have in here to make a project?"

Wheels whined as Papa pushed himself out. "What sort of project?" Grey and red smudges framed the skin around his goggles.

Nara held up the tablet, projecting the images out six inches. Papa chuckled low. "Why am I not surprised?" he asked. "You want to build a horse?"

"I think I can," she said.

"Oh, I know you can, I just didn't think you'd settle for that. Let me see." He held it directly overhead, then grunted as he passed it back. "The leg structure's not that different than the diggers you helped me with last month. Your main issues will be balancing the mass and nailing the AI."

She nodded, her mind already filtering through the possibilities. She had to think of horse breeds, no—she would think of specific horses. Trigger, her favorite. He was tough and fast, with all the grace of a dancer. Oh, how he could dance. His hooves shuffled, his gold skin shimmering and muscles coiling. Nara would watch him, holding her breath. Nothing on Mars could move like that.

"You'll have to use the scrap pile," Papa continued, snapping her out of a reverie. "But if you need anything fresh, you need to order through me, and you'll have to work for it. This isn't going to be cheap."

"Cheaper than a trip to Earth," Mother said from the doorway. "And speaking of expenses, we're going to need inner sealants replaced on three windows as soon as this storm is over. One gap was so big a fiend beetle could almost squeeze through from inside the walls, and God knows what it would cost if one of those got in."

"As if it's ever just one," Papa said, shaking his head. "Well, we're due for a full sealant inspection anyway."

Nara closed the equine anatomy charts, her eyes already taking in the nearest scrap pile and a stout piece of pipe ideal for a femur. Mama and Papa's chatter faded. She tapped her fingers along the tablet, already picturing a horse of her own, programmed to nuzzle her shoulder and whicker in greeting.

Papa was wrong. Balancing the mass would be easy. The artificial intelligence could be adapted from existing programs. Realism was the issue. A glossy hair coat, a trailing mane and tail, the musty smell described in the old books she'd read.

Worst of all, she might never know if she got it right.

NARA'S BOOTS THUDDED ALONG THE ELEVATED BOARDWALK, HER BREATHS rasping through her mask. She couldn't be late for her one day of physical attendance in school for the week. Papa had already threatened to dismantle the horse if her grades dropped again. A fiend beetle crunched underfoot in a muddle of juiciness and grit.

So far, beetles were one of the few things that could survive unaided on the Martian surface. Scientists hailed it as a landmark of the terraforming process. Nara crushed the bugs as a hobby.

Six months of work, and the skeleton was complete, and most of the nerve structure as well. She had stayed up late working on the wiring in the neck and reins and connecting them to the processors in the makeshift brain. The skin would be next on the agenda. Papa had suggested she use a thin alloy, the sort used for biometric floors. That way it could be programmed to respond to heel touches and shifts in weight.

She shoved through several sets of doors to enter the dome. A dozen beetles tried to follow, the floor vents sending them rolling like tumbleweeds in an old movie. The next two doors repeated the process and secured behind her. Nara disengaged the breathing apparatus from her mask and took in a deep inhalation of recycled air. For all the inconvenience of living beyond the dome, she preferred it to the tight confines of the city with its block-stacks of buildings and stale stink.

She slid into her cubicle just as the bell rang. Her friend Chu nodded from the adjoining side. Nara set her tablet in its cradle, and grimaced. Another day wasted in school when she could be working on her horse instead.

Throughout mathematics and mineral sciences, she let her fingers busy themselves while she pondered the wiring system for her horse. It's not as though the school work was difficult. Quiz results came back instantly; she missed two equations. Nara grunted. Perhaps she should focus more.

"As Heritage Month comes to a close, all sixth year students study the contributions of the head financier of the Corcoran Colony, the late Mrs. Florence Corcoran," said the professor from the head of the room. A hologram of Mrs. Corcoran flickered overhead, her face smiling as she posed with an old-fashioned pick-axe over her shoulder.

"As you all know, Mrs. Corcoran believed that Earth's cultural heritage deserved a place on Mars. Your tablets have just received a list of the artifacts of the Corcoran household." The file appeared on Nara's small screen. "During next year's Pioneer Heritage Month, the Corcoran Museum will open. Your task is to choose an object from her archive and write a thousand-word essay on the object's history both on Mars and Earth."

A low groan filled the room.

Nara pursed her lips. She could throw together a thousand-word essay in fifteen minutes. It wouldn't eat up too much of her project time. She opened the file, skimming the list. It dragged on, page after page. The fanciest objects were listed first—the paintings, the jewelry, the clothing. Florence Corcoran had been an obsessive collector of old Earth, especially items pertaining to Texas. All of it dull. Well, the leather belt collection might work as a report subject, especially if Nara could touch or smell the stuff. Importing genuine leather for a saddle and bridle would cost more than all the metal parts of her horse combined. She was going to make do with synthetics.

She scrolled down for an eternity. Early space shuttle detritus, bull horns, an oil derrick, a preserved horse skin. Nara stopped cold.

A horse? She clicked for more information.

Trigger, a rearing palomino horse dating from the mid-20th century, his skin preserved and mounted on a plaster body. Nara's heart threatened to escape her chest. Trigger, her Trigger, was here on Mars? Not only a horse, but one of the most beautiful horses of all time.

"We have passes available so you can all visit the Corcoran household and see the items in person," her teacher continued.

"This is it," Nara murmured.

"What?" Chu whispered.

She ignored him, her mind already analyzing the possibilities. Her prototype horse would take another six months at least. If there was some way to get this skin, maybe she could use it. Mount it on top of the metal frame—well, no, it probably couldn't withstand the sand. But if she could study the texture, it would be easier to mimic. Would the museum sell such an old artifact? Nara fidgeted with the edge of her tablet. Could she steal it?

Maybe a way could be found. Adrenaline zinged through her fingertips. She could see and touch a real horse, and not just any horse—Trigger. Hot tears burned her eyes and pattered against her desk.

This was meant to be.

As Nara entered the grounds of the Corcoran Mansion, she was keenly aware of every security measure scrutinizing her. The cameras on high, glassy lenses glaring. The slight give of the cushioned tile underfoot, implying a biometric measure to contrast her weight coming and going. The slits in the walls that memorized her irises.

Stupid, stupid, stupid. Of course there would be excellent security here. She was day-dreaming to think otherwise. Still, maybe there was a loophole in the system. Trigger's skin had been a low-priority item stuck far back on the list. Centuries old, an archaic artifact that meant nothing to anyone else. It wasn't even scheduled for a berth in the museum.

"Ah. You. Chu's little friend." Her friend's grandfather edged close, his small body straight as a support pillar.

"I didn't know you were working inside the mansion now, Grandfather," Nara said, handing over her tablet with her student pass loaded.

He grunted, the sound a husky echo of Chu. "I have been since the Museum was announced, taking inventory of her treasure trove. You're the first student to take advantage of the pass, you know? No one else seems interested in seeing the works in person. Probably will be the same when the place opens, I'm afraid." He pressed the tablet back into her hands.

"Well, I care." Nara stood a bit straighter.

She had spent the past week re-watching every available movie showing Trigger. Nara knew the sway of his mane, how his hind-quarters bunched as he reared, how his muscles flexed beneath shimmering gold skin. He could kiss girls with his lips flared, rear on command, walk on his hind legs, and perform dozens of other tricks; even if Nara heightened the resolution on the picture, it was difficult to detect Roy Rogers's cues. Trigger wasn't a mere horse—he had to be the smartest horse that ever was.

Trigger's presence on Mars had to be destiny. She was meant to know him in real life, centuries after the fact, long after civilization had forgotten him. Trigger would teach her how to make her horse even more real.

"What artifact do you want to see? Most of the good stuff is here in the house." Chu's grandfather motioned behind him. Down the hall, a large painting of two naked people in a jungle filled the wall, the woman holding an apple outstretched in a pudgy hand.

She tried not to look too disgusted. "No. I want artifact 3046."

"Three-thousand range?" His eyes narrowed. "That will be in the old warehouse. All came in the second colony drop. You sure you want to go there?"

"Absolutely."

She couldn't help but notice his sour expression on their long walk out behind the mansion. The warehouse stretched along the back wall of the dome, the clay brick walls red-tinted and pecked by sandblasts. It had to be a mech-built storage house, dating from before the completion of the dome and human arrival.

Grandfather stood as the iris security scanned him in, grunting for Nara to follow. The floor beneath her feet seemed shiny and new, each step sinking in by millimeters. More security, but not as much as the household.

"Forty-six, forty-six." He muttered as he walked. Metal scaffolding stretched to the high ceiling, the rafters filled with wooden boxes. Nara stroked a box in passing, not even gasping when a splinter snagged her flesh. Mrs. Corcoran had been very wealthy indeed to have so much wood, and for it to be used for mere storage.

"Here." Grandfather stopped. A pink tarp filled the bin space ahead. A device at his waistband beeped. "Damn it all. Another guest and Rorie's not in. Can you behave yourself?"

Her heartbeat raced in hopefulness. He was leaving her here, alone? "Yes."

"It's all junk here, anyway. Just wait and I'll be back to escort you out." He marched away, his steps brisk.

Nara stood there for a moment, taking in the fading echo of his footsteps. That pink tarp... She bit her lip and lifted up the sheet.

Trigger's pale orange coat looked soft to the touch, his ears back. His entire body seemed coiled, ready to strike. An ornate bridle dangled from his face. Oh, his white blaze! Even tinted pink, it was beautiful to behold. Despite the glare of security, Nara couldn't resist reaching up on tiptoe to stroke his muzzle. The prickliness surprised her. It was like she had imagined, and so much more. But Trigger, beautiful, graceful Trigger...

A sob choked in her throat as she stepped back. Trigger had succumbed to death at last.

The pink dust on the tarp had been the first hint. The lower half of his body had been chewed away clear to the blackened plaster below. The old building hadn't sealed out fiend beetles. His saddle had slipped sideways, the girth almost eaten clear through. Only a nub remained of the flared plume of tail. Tatters of skin dangled against the plaster, fragments littering the floor like a poor haircut. Of his powerful dancing legs, nothing remained at all.

Nara lowered herself to the floor, the grey stone chilled beneath her. Trigger was dead. Dead. His skin would crumble if it moved at all. His legs would never waltz again, never leap over cars, never lower in a handsome curtsy.

"I'm sorry. I'm sorry," Nara whispered. "You were so beautiful. You still are." She stood, standing close enough to breathe him in. He stank of Martian dust and degradation, no more. The creamy mane shifted between her fingertips, a tuft coming away in her hand. She curled her fingers into a fist.

Horses didn't belong on Mars. She knew it, but she hadn't wanted to accept it. This horse had survived centuries on Earth: wars, fires, owner after owner, the long journey here, only to be eaten away by ever-hungry bugs brought along for the ride. Trigger deserved better. He deserved to be timeless.

"I still love you, Trigger," she whispered. In her mind, she could see the intelligent gleam in his eyes; hear the rhythmic clatter of his hooves.

Footsteps thudded behind her. Nara swiped an arm against her cheeks and took a steadying breath.

"Oh. You found our half-eaten creature." Chu's grandfather stepped alongside her. Nara clutched her fists tighter. "It's a shame. Some of these crates hold old masters--Rodan, Picasso. The fiend beetles had a feast. As it is now, the leather around this thing's belly is the only thing worth keeping, and that's just scrap. If someone broke in here, they'd want to steal the security system."

Chu's grandfather didn't even know the proper name for a saddle. Nara swallowed, choking as if on a handful of sand. "Is he really going to be thrown out?"

He scratched at his smooth chin. "Eventually. They plan on tearing this structure down before the museum opens. Things like that won't survive the move." He motioned to the floor and the scattered bits of hair and skin and degrading plaster.

"If that happens... can you let me know? I mean..."

Grandfather shook his head, chuckling. "Ah yes. Chu told me you have a thing for horses. That's what this is, right? Smaller than I expected. But yes, I can tell you when this row comes up for disposal. I hate to think what your mother would say."

Nara looked away. "I know what she'll say."

Trigger was only a thing to him. No one here knew about horses. No one cared. Trigger had been more than a horse. He'd been loved in his lifetime, adored by thousands and thousands. Maybe he could be loved again, and not just by her.

They headed out of the warehouse. Nara released her breath before she stepped across the biometric steps, expelling every bit of air in her lungs. No alarms rang. The presence of a few useless hairs hadn't even registered. She sucked in a breath of refreshing stale air, the strands of mane a moist web in her palm.

PAPA HAD GUIDED HER WORK ON THE FORGE. NARA POUNDED AND SHAPED her own horseshoes, and then nailed them to her horse's hooves. The first hoof prints marring Martian soil looked as they should on Earth: deep and almost circular crescents, a spray of dirt disturbed with each ambling step.

Trigger's alloy skin glowed in glossy gold, a version of palomino for a new world. A white blaze filled the length of his face and curved around into wide nostrils. He snorted, the sound tinny. It could be adjusted later. This was a test run, no more.

"You ready?" Papa asked, the words thick in his mask.

Nara nodded. Papa's broad, gloved hand gave her a boost up into the makeshift saddle woven of rags and polyvinyl chloride belts. She sat high, taking in the jagged red terrain and marbled sky from a new vantage point. The brim of her hardhat cut the afternoon glare. Angling her heels down, she tapped Trigger's ribcage and then engaged the reins. He snorted and moved forward. Gears cranked, soft and whirring, but his gait was lolling and smooth, ears attentive.

Just above his withers, a knot of long, white hairs dangled down and brushed the backs of her gloves. Nara closed her eyes for an instant, imagining an intact mane, a green horizon, the warmth of pumping blood beneath her and not an engine. Trigger couldn't come to life again, not truly, but she could grant him a different sort of immortality.

"The whole colony will learn all about horses, and you," she whispered within her mask, guiding him towards the nearest ridge.

"I'll start programming your tricks in the next few weeks. Everyone will laugh and cheer when you blow kisses and dance. You'll be loved again, Trigger. Remembered." She laid a hand against his chilled neck.

The sun glowed fierce yellow overhead. Nara glanced over her shoulder and smiled at the deep cut of hoof prints leading back towards home.

THE DUN HORSE
PAWNEE FOLK TALE

MANY YEARS AGO THERE LIVED IN THE PAWNEE TRIBE AN OLD WOMAN and her grandson a boy about sixteen years old. These people had no relations and were very poor. They were so poor that they were despised by the rest of the tribe. They had nothing of their own; and always, after the village started to move the camp from one place to another, these two would stay behind the rest, to look over the old camp and pick up anything that the other Indians had thrown away as worn out or useless. In this way they would sometimes get pieces of robes, wornout moccasins with holes in them, and bits of meat.

Now, it happened one day, after the tribe had moved away from the camp, that this old woman and her boy were following along the trail behind the rest, when they came to a miserable old wornout dun horse, which they supposed had been abandoned by some Indians. He was thin and exhausted, was blind of one eye, had a bad sore back, and one of his forelegs was very much swollen. In fact, he was so worthless that none of the Pawnees had been willing to take the trouble to try to drive him along with them. But when the old woman and her boy came along, the boy said, "Come now, we will take this old horse, for we can make him carry our pack." So the old woman put her pack on the horse, and drove him along, but he limped and could only go very slowly.

II

THE TRIBE MOVED UP ON THE NORTH PLATTE, UNTIL THEY CAME TO Court House Rock. The two poor Indians followed them, and camped with the others. One day while they were here, the young men who had been sent out to look for buffalo, came hurrying into camp and told the chiefs that a large herd of buffalo were near, and that among them was a spotted calf.

The Head Chief of the Pawnees had a very beautiful daughter, and when he heard about the spotted calf, he ordered his old crier to go about through the village and call out that the man who killed the spotted calf should have his daughter for his wife. For a spotted robe is ti-war'-uks-ti—big medicine.

The buffalo were feeding about four miles from the village, and the chiefs decided that the charge should be made from there. In this way, the man who had the fastest horse would be the most likely to kill the calf. Then all the warriors and the young men picked out their best and fastest horses, and made ready to start. Among those who prepared for the charge was the poor boy on the old dun horse. But when they saw him, all the rich young braves on their fast horses pointed at him and said, "Oh, see; there is the horse that is going to catch the spotted calf;" and they laughed at him, so that the poor boy was ashamed, and rode off to one side of the crowd, where he could not hear their jokes and laughter.

When he had ridden off some little way the horse stopped and turned his head round, and spoke to the boy. He said, "Take me down the creek, and plaster me all over with mud. Cover my head and neck and body and legs." When the boy heard the horse speak, he was afraid; but he did as he was told. Then the horse said, "Now mount, but do not ride back to the warriors, who laugh at you because you have such a poor horse. Stay right here until the word is given to charge." So the boy stayed there.

And presently all the fine horses were drawn up in line and

pranced about, and were so eager to go that their riders could hardly
hold them in; and at last the old crier gave the word, Loo-ah! —Go!
Then the Pawnees all leaned forward on their horses and yelled,
and away they went. Suddenly, away off to the right, was seen the
old dun horse. He did not seem to run. He seemed to sail along like
a bird. He passed all the fastest horses, and in a moment he was
among the buffalo. First he picked out the spotted calf, and charging
up alongside of it, U-ra-rish! Straight flew the arrow. The calf fell.
The boy drew another arrow, and killed a fat cow that was running
by. Then he dismounted and began to skin the calf, before any of
the other warriors had come up. But when the rider got off the old
dun horse, how changed he was! He pranced about and would hardly stand still near the dead buffalo. His back was all right again; his
legs were well and fine; and both his eyes were clear and bright.

The boy skinned the calf and the cow that he had killed, and
then he packed all the meat on the horse, and put the spotted robe
on top of the load, and started back to the camp on foot, leading the
dun horse. But even with this heavy load the horse pranced all the
time, and was scared at everything he saw. On the way to camp, one
of the rich young chiefs of the tribe rode up by the boy and offered
him twelve good horses for the spotted robe, so that he could marry
the Head Chief's beautiful daughter; but the boy laughed at him and
would not sell the robe.

Now, while the boy walked to the camp leading the dun horse,
most of the warriors rode back, and one of those that came first to
the village went to the old woman and said to her, "Your grandson
has killed the spotted calf." And the old woman said, "Why do you
come to tell me this? You ought to be ashamed to make fun of my
boy, because he is poor." The warrior said, "What I have told you is
true," and then he rode away. After a little while another brave rode
up to the old woman, and said to her, "Your grandson has killed the
spotted calf." Then the old woman began to cry, she felt so badly
because every one made fun of her boy, because he was poor.

Pretty soon the boy came along, leading the horse up to the
lodge where he and his grandmother lived. It was a little lodge, just
big enough for two, and was made of old pieces of skin that the old

woman had picked up, and was tied together with strings of rawhide and sinew. It was the meanest and worst lodge in the village. When the old woman saw her boy leading the dun horse with the load of meat and the robes on it, she was very surprised. The boy said to her, "Here, I have brought you plenty of meat to eat, and here is a robe, that you may have for yourself. Take the meat off the horse." Then the old woman laughed, for her heart was glad. But when she went to take the meat from the horse's back, he snorted and jumped about, and acted like a wild horse. The old woman looked at him in wonder, and could hardly believe that it was the same horse. So the boy had to take off the meat, for the horse would not let the old woman come near him.

III

THAT NIGHT THE HORSE SPOKE AGAIN TO THE BOY AND SAID, "WA-TI-HES Chah'-ra-rat wa-ta. Tomorrow the Sioux are coming—a large war party. They will attack the village, and you will have a great battle. Now, when the Sioux are all drawn up in line of battle, and are all ready to fight, you jump on to me, and ride as hard as you can, right into the middle of the Sioux, and up to their Head Chief, their greatest warrior, and count coup on him, and kill him, and then ride back. Do this four times, and count coup on four of the bravest Sioux, and kill them, but don't go again. If you go the fifth time, maybe you will be killed, or else you will lose me. La-ku'-ta-chix—remember." So the boy promised.

The next day it happened as the horse had said, and the Sioux came down and formed in line of battle. Then the boy took his bow and arrows, and jumped on the dun horse, and charged into the midst of them. And when the Sioux saw that he was going to strike their Head Chief, they all shot their arrows at him, and the arrows flew so thickly across each other that they darkened the sky, but none of them hit the boy. And he counted coup on the Chief, and killed him, and then rode back. After that he charged again among the Sioux, where they were gathered thickest, and counted coup on their bravest warrior, and killed him. And then twice more, until he had gone four times as the horse had told him.

But the Sioux and the Pawnees kept on fighting, and the boy stood around and watched the battle. And at last he said to himself, "I have been four times and have killed four Sioux, and I am all right, I am not hurt anywhere; why may I not go again?" So he jumped on the dun horse, and charged again. But when he got among the Sioux, one Sioux warrior drew an arrow and shot. The arrow struck the dun horse behind the forelegs and pierced him through. And the horse fell down dead. But the boy jumped off, and fought his way through the Sioux, and ran away as fast as he could to the Pawnees.

Now, as soon as the horse was killed, the Sioux said to each other: "This horse was like a man. He was brave. He was not like a horse." And they took their knives and hatchets, and hacked the dun horse and gashed his flesh, and cut him into small pieces.

The Pawnees and Sioux fought all day long, but toward night the Sioux broke and fled.

IV

THE BOY FELT VERY BADLY THAT HE HAD LOST HIS HORSE; AND, AFTER THE fight was over, he went out from the village to where it had taken place, to mourn for his horse. He went to the spot where the horse lay, and gathered up all the pieces of flesh, which the Sioux had cut off, and the legs and the hoofs, and put them all together in a pile. Then he went off to the top of a hill near by, and sat down and drew his robe over his head, and began to mourn for his horse.

As he sat there, he heard a great wind-storm coming up, and it passed over him with a loud rushing sound, and after the wind came a rain. The boy looked down from where he sat to the pile of flesh and bones, which was all that was left of his horse, and he could just see it through the rain. And the rain passed by, and his heart was very heavy, and he kept on mourning.

And pretty soon came another rushing wind, and after it a rain; and as he looked through the driving rain toward the spot where the pieces lay, he thought that they seemed to come together and take shape, and that the pile looked like a horse lying down, but he could not see well for the thick rain.

After this came a third storm like the others; and now when he looked toward the horse he thought he saw its tail move from side to side two or three times, and that it lifted its head from the ground. The boy was afraid, and wanted to run away, but he stayed.

And as he waited, there came another storm. And while the rain fell, looking through the rain, the boy saw the horse raise himself up on his forelegs and look about. Then the dun horse stood up.

V

THE BOY LEFT THE PLACE WHERE HE HAD BEEN SITTING ON THE HILLTOP, and went down to him. When the boy had come near to him, the horse spoke and said: "You have seen how it has been this day; and from this you may know how it will be after this. But Ti-ra'-wa has been good, and has let me come back to you. After this, do what I tell you; not any more, not any less." Then the horse said: "Now lead me off, far away from the camp, behind that big hill, and leave me there to-night, and in the morning come for me;" and the boy did as he was told.

And when he went for the horse in the morning, he found with him a beautiful white gelding, much more handsome than any horse in the tribe. That night the dun horse told the boy to take him again to the place behind the big hill, and to come for him the next morning; and when the boy went for him again, he found with him a beautiful black gelding. And so for ten nights, he left the horse among the hills, and each morning he found a different coloured horse, a bay, a roan, a gray, a blue, a spotted horse, and all of them finer than any horses that the Pawnees had ever had in their tribe before.

Now the boy was rich, and he married the beautiful daughter of the Head Chief, and when he became older he was made Head Chief himself. He had many children by his beautiful wife, and one day when his oldest boy died, he wrapped him in the spotted calf robe and buried him in it. He always took good care of his old grandmother, and kept her in his own lodge until she died. The dun horse was never ridden except at feasts, and when they were going to have a doctors' dance, but he was always led about with the Chief wherever he went. The horse lived in the village for many years, until he became very old. And at last he died.

THE MAGICIAN'S HORSE
GREEK FAIRY TALE

ONCE UPON A TIME, THERE WAS A KING WHO HAD THREE SONS. NOW IT happened that one day the three princes went out hunting in a large forest at some distance from their father's palace, and the youngest prince lost his way, so his brothers had to return home without him.

For four days the prince wandered through the glades of the forest, sleeping on moss beneath the stars at night, and by day living on roots and wild berries. At last, on the morning of the fifth day, he came to a large open space in the middle of the forest, and here stood a stately palace; but neither within nor without was there a trace of human life. The prince entered the open door and wandered through the deserted rooms without seeing a living soul. At last he came on a great hall, and in the centre of the hall was a table spread with dainty dishes and choice wines. The prince sat down, and satisfied his hunger and thirst, and immediately afterwards the table disappeared from his sight. This struck the prince as very strange; but though he continued his search through all the rooms, upstairs and down, he could find no one to speak to. At last, just as it was beginning to get dark, he heard steps in the distance and he saw an old man coming towards him up the stairs.

'What are you doing wandering about my castle?' asked the old man.

To whom the prince replied: 'I lost my way hunting in the forest. If you will take me into your service, I should like to stay with you, and will serve you faithfully.'

'Very well,' said the old man. 'You may enter my service. You will have to keep the stove always lit, you will have to fetch the wood for it from the forest, and you will have the charge of the black horse in the stables. I will pay you a florin a day, and at meal times you will always find the table in the hall spread with food and wine, and you can eat and drink as much as you require.'

The prince was satisfied, and he entered the old man's service, and promised to see that there was always wood on the stove, so that the fire should never die out. Now, though he did not know it, his new master was a magician, and the flame of the stove was a magic fire, and if it had gone out the magician would have lost a great part of his power.

One day the prince forgot, and let the fire burn so low that it very nearly burnt out. Just as the flame was flickering the old man stormed into the room.

'What do you mean by letting the fire burn so low?' he growled. 'I have only arrived in the nick of time.' And while the prince hastily threw a log on the stove and blew on the ashes to kindle a glow, his master gave him a severe box on the ear, and warned him that if ever it happened again it would fare badly with him.

One day the prince was sitting disconsolate in the stables when, to his surprise, the black horse spoke to him.

'Come into my stall,' it said, 'I have something to say to you. Fetch my bridle and saddle from that cupboard and put them on me. Take the bottle that is beside them; it contains an ointment which will make your hair shine like pure gold; then put all the wood you can gather together on to the stove, till it is piled quite high up.'

So the prince did what the horse told him; he saddled and bridled the horse, he put the ointment on his hair till it shone like gold, and he made such a big fire in the stove that the flames sprang up and set fire to the roof, and in a few minutes the palace was burning like a huge bonfire.

Then he hurried back to the stables, and the horse said to him: 'There is one thing more you must do. In the cupboard you will find a looking-glass, a brush and a riding-whip. Bring them with you, mount on my back, and ride as hard as you can, for now the house is burning merrily.'

The prince did as the horse bade him. Scarcely had he got into the saddle than the horse was off and away, galloping at such a pace that, in a short time, the forest and all the country belonging to the magician lay far behind them.

In the meantime the magician returned to his palace, which he found in smouldering ruins. In vain he called for his servant. At last he went to look for him in the stables, and when he discovered that the black horse had disappeared too, he at once suspected that they had gone together; so he mounted a roan horse that was in the next stall, and set out in pursuit.

As the prince rode, the quick ears of his horse heard the sound of pursuing feet.

'Look behind you,' he said, 'and see if the old man is following.' And the prince turned in his saddle and saw a cloud like smoke or dust in the distance.

'We must hurry,' said the horse.

After they had galloped for some time, the horse said again: 'Look behind, and see if he is still at some distance.'

'He is quite close,' answered the prince.

'Then throw the looking-glass on the ground,' said the horse. So the prince threw it; and when the magician came up, the roan horse stepped on the mirror, and crash! his foot went through the glass, and he stumbled and fell, cutting his feet so badly that there was nothing for the old man to do but to go slowly back with him to the stables, and put new shoes on his feet. Then they started once more in pursuit of the prince, for the magician set great value on the horse, and was determined not to lose it.

In the meanwhile the prince had gone a great distance; but the quick ears of the black horse detected the sound of following feet from afar.

'Dismount,' he said to the prince; 'put your ear to the ground, and tell me if you do not hear a sound.'

So the prince dismounted and listened. 'I seem to hear the earth tremble,' he said; 'I think he cannot be very far off.'

'Mount me at once,' answered the horse, 'and I will gallop as fast as I can.' And he set off so fast that the earth seemed to fly from under his hoofs.

'Look back once more,' he said, after a short time, 'and see if he is in sight.'

'I see a cloud and a flame,' answered the prince; 'but a long way off.'

'We must make haste,' said the horse. And shortly after he said: 'Look back again; he can't be far off now.'

The prince turned in his saddle, and exclaimed: 'He is close behind us, in a minute the flame from his horse's nostrils will reach us.'

'Then throw the brush on the ground,' said the horse.

And the prince threw it, and in an instant the brush was changed into such a thick wood that even a bird could not have got through it, and when the old man got up to it the roan horse came suddenly to a stand-still, not able to advance a step into the thick tangle. So there was nothing for the magician to do but to retrace his steps, to fetch an axe, with which he cut himself a way through the wood. But it took him some time, during which the prince and the black horse got on well ahead.

But once more they heard the sound of pursuing feet. 'Look back,' said the black horse, 'and see if he is following.'

'Yes,' answered the prince, 'this time I hear him distinctly.'

'Let us hurry on,' said the horse. And a little later he said: 'Look back now, and see if he is in sight.'

'Yes,' said the prince, turning round, 'I see the flame; he is close behind us.'

'Then you must throw down the whip,' answered the horse.' And in the twinkling of an eye the whip was changed into a broad river. When the old man got up to it he urged the roan horse into the water, but as the water mounted higher and higher, the magic flame which gave the magician all his power grew smaller and smaller, till, with a fizz, it went out, and the old man and the roan horse sank in the river and disappeared. When the prince looked round they were no longer to be seen.

'Now,' said the horse, 'you may dismount; there is nothing more to fear, for the magician is dead. Beside that brook you will find a willow wand. Gather it, and strike the earth with it, and it will open and you will see a door at your feet.'

When the prince had struck the earth with the wand a door appeared, and opened into a large vaulted stone hall.

'Lead me into that hall,' said the horse, 'I will stay there; but you must go through the fields till you reach a garden, in the midst of which is a king's palace. When you get there you must ask to be taken into the king's service. Good-bye, and don't forget me.'

So they parted; but first the horse made the prince promise not to let anyone in the palace see his golden hair. So he bound a scarf round it, like a turban, and the prince set out through the fields, till he reached a beautiful garden, and beyond the garden he saw the walls and towers of a stately palace. At the garden gate he met the gardener, who asked him what he wanted.

'I want to take service with the king,' replied the prince.

'Well, you may stay and work under me in the garden,' said the man; for as the prince was dressed like a poor man, he could not tell that he was a king's son. 'I need someone to weed the ground and to sweep the dead leaves from the paths. You shall have a florin a day, a horse to help you to cart the leaves away, and food and drink.'

So the prince consented, and set about his work. But when his food was given to him he only ate half of it; the rest he carried to the vaulted hall beside the brook, and gave to the black horse. And this he did every day, and the horse thanked him for his faithful friendship.

One evening, as they were together, after his work in the garden was over, the horse said to him: 'To-morrow a large company of princes and great lords are coming to your king's palace. They are coming from far and near, as wooers for the three princesses. They will all stand in a row in the courtyard of the palace, and the three princesses will come out, and each will carry a diamond apple in her hand, which she will throw into the air. At whosesoever feet the apple falls he will be the bridegroom of that princess. You must be close by in the garden at your work. The apple of the youngest princess, who is much the most beautiful of the sisters, will roll past the wooers and stop in front of you. Pick it up at once and put it in your pocket.'

The next day, when the wooers were all assembled in the courtyard of the castle, everything happened just as the horse had said. The princesses threw the apples into the air, and the diamond apple of the youngest princess rolled past all the wooers, out on to the garden, and stopped at the feet of the young gardener, who was busy sweeping the leaves away. In a moment he had stooped down, picked up the apple and put it in his pocket. As he stooped the scarf round his head slipped a little to one side, and the princess caught sight of his golden hair, and loved him from that moment.

But the king was very sad, for his youngest daughter was the one he loved best. But there was no help for it; and the next day a threefold wedding was celebrated at the palace, and after the wedding the youngest princess returned with her husband to the small hut in the garden where he lived.

Some time after this the people of a neighbouring country went to war with the king, and he set out to battle, accompanied by the husbands of his two eldest daughters mounted on stately steeds. But the husband of the youngest daughter had nothing but the old broken-down horse which helped him in his garden work; and the king, who was ashamed of this son-in-law, refused to give him any other.

So as he was determined not to be left behind, he went into the garden, mounted the sorry nag, and set out. But scarcely had he ridden a few yards before the horse stumbled and fell. So he dismounted and went down to the brook, to where the black horse lived in the vaulted hall. And the horse said to him: 'Saddle and bridle me, and then go into the next room and you will find a suit of armour and a sword. Put them on, and we will ride forth together to battle.'

And the prince did as he was told; and when he had mounted the horse his armour glittered in the sun, and he looked so brave and handsome, that no one would have recognised him as the gardener who swept away the dead leaves from the paths. The horse bore him away at a great pace, and when they reached the battle-field they saw that the king was losing the day, so many of his warriors had been slain. But when the warrior on his black charger and in glittering armour appeared on the scene, hewing right and left with his sword, the enemy were dismayed and fled in all directions, leaving the king master of the field. Then the king and his two sons-in-law, when they saw their deliverer, shouted, and all that was left of the army joined in the cry: 'A god has come to our rescue!' And they would have surrounded him, but his black horse rose in the air and bore him out of their sight.

Soon after this, part of the country rose in rebellion against the king, and once more he and his two sons-in-law had to fare forth to battle. And the son-in-law who was disguised as a gardener wanted to fight too. So he came to the king and said: 'Dear father, let me ride with you to fight your enemies.'

'I don't want a blockhead like you to fight for me,' answered the king. 'Besides, I haven't got a horse fit for you. But see, there is a carter on the road carting hay; you may take his horse.'

So the prince took the carter's horse, but the poor beast was old and tired, and after it had gone a few yards it stumbled and fell. So the prince returned sadly to the garden and watched the king ride forth at the head of the army accompanied by his two sons-in-law. When they were out of sight the prince betook himself to the vaulted chamber by the brook-side, and having taken counsel of the faithful black horse, he put on the glittering suit of armour, and was borne on the back of the horse through the air, to where the battle was being fought. And once more he routed the king's enemies, hacking to right and left with his sword. And again they all cried: 'A god has come to our rescue!' But when they tried to detain him the black horse rose in the air and bore him out of their sight.

When the king and his sons-in-law returned home they could talk of nothing but the hero who had fought for them, and all wondered who he could be.

Shortly afterwards the king of a neighbouring country de-

clared war, and once more the king and his sons-in-law and his subjects had to prepare themselves for battle, and once more the prince
begged to ride with them, but the king said he had no horse to spare
for him. 'But,' he added, 'you may take the horse of the woodman
who brings the wood from the forest, it is good enough for you.'

So the prince took the woodman's horse, but it was so old
and useless that it could not carry him beyond the castle gates. So
he betook himself once more to the vaulted hall, where the black
horse had prepared a still more magnificent suit of armour for him
than the one he had worn on the previous occasions, and when he
had put it on, and mounted on the back of the horse, he bore him
straight to the battle-field, and once more he scattered the king's
enemies, fighting single-handed in their ranks, and they fled in all
directions. But it happened that one of the enemy struck with his
sword and wounded the prince in the leg. And the king took his own
pocket-handkerchief, with his name and crown embroidered on it,
and bound it round the wounded leg. And the king would fain have
compelled him to mount in a litter and be carried straight to the
palace, and two of his knights were to lead the black charger to the
royal stables. But the prince put his hand on the mane of his faithful
horse, and managed to pull himself up into the saddle, and the horse
mounted into the air with him. Then they all shouted and cried:
'The warrior who has fought for us is a god! He must be a god.'

And throughout all the kingdom nothing else was spoken
about, and all the people said: 'Who can the hero be who has fought
for us in so many battles? He cannot be a man, he must be a god.'

And the king said: 'If only I could see him once more, and if it
turned out that after all he was a man and not a god, I would reward
him with half my kingdom.'

Now when the prince reached his home—the gardener's hut
where he lived with his wife—he was weary, and he lay down on
his bed and slept. And his wife noticed the handkerchief bound
round his wounded leg, and she wondered what it could be. Then
she looked at it more closely and saw in the corner that it was embroidered with her father's name and the royal crown. So she ran
straight to the palace and told her father. And he and his two sons-

in-law followed her back to her house, and there the gardener lay asleep on his bed. And the scarf that he always wore bound round his head had slipped off, and his golden hair gleamed on the pillow. And they all recognised that this was the hero who had fought and won so many battles for them.

Then there was great rejoicing throughout the land, and the king rewarded his son-in-law with half of his kingdom, and he and his wife reigned happily over it.

THE DEVIL AND TOM WALKER
WASHINGTON IRVING

A FEW MILES FROM BOSTON IN MASSACHUSETTS, THERE IS A DEEP INLET, winding several miles into the interior of the country from Charles Bay, and terminating in a thickly-wooded swamp or morass. On one side of this inlet is a beautiful dark grove; on the opposite side the land rises abruptly from the water's edge into a high ridge, on which grow a few scattered oaks of great age and immense size. Under one of these gigantic trees, according to old stories, there was a great amount of treasure buried by Kidd the pirate. The inlet allowed a facility to bring the money in a boat secretly and at night to the very foot of the hill; the elevation of the place permitted a good look-out to be kept that no one was at hand; while the remarkable trees formed good landmarks by which the place might easily be found again. The old stories add, moreover, that the devil presided at the hiding of the money, and took it under his guardianship; but this, it is well known, he always does with buried treasure, particularly when it has been ill-gotten. Be that as it may, Kidd never returned to recover his wealth; being shortly after seized at Boston, sent out to England, and there hanged for a pirate.

About the year 1727, just at the time that earthquakes were

prevalent in New England, and shook many tall sinners down upon their knees, there lived near this place a meagre, miserly fellow, of the name of Tom Walker. He had a wife as miserly as himself: they were so miserly that they even conspired to cheat each other. Whatever the woman could lay hands on, she hid away; a hen could not cackle but she was on the alert to secure the new-laid egg. Her husband was continually prying about to detect her secret hoards, and many and fierce were the conflicts that took place about what ought to have been common property. They lived in a forlorn-looking house that stood alone, and had an air of starvation. A few straggling savin-trees, emblems of sterility, grew near it; no smoke ever curled from its chimney; no traveller stopped at its door. A miserable horse, whose ribs were as articulate as the bars of a gridiron, stalked about a field, where a thin carpet of moss, scarcely covering the ragged beds of pudding-stone, tantalized and balked his hunger; and sometimes he would lean his head over the fence, look piteously at the passer-by, and seem to petition deliverance from this land of famine.

The house and its inmates had altogether a bad name. Tom's wife was a tall termagant, fierce of temper, loud of tongue, and strong of arm. Her voice was often heard in wordy warfare with her husband; and his face sometimes showed signs that their conflicts were not confined to words. No one ventured, however, to interfere between them. The lonely wayfarer shrunk within himself at the horrid clamour and clapper-clawing; eyed the den of discord askance; and hurried on his way, rejoicing, if a bachelor, in his celibacy.

One day that Tom Walker had been to a distant part of the neighbourhood, he took what he considered a short cut homeward, through the swamp. Like most short cuts, it was an ill-chosen route. The swamp was thickly grown with great gloomy pines and hemlocks, some of them ninety feet high, which made it dark at noonday, and a retreat for all the owls of the neighbourhood. It was full of pits and quagmires, partly covered with weeds and mosses, where the green surface often betrayed the traveller into a gulf of black, smothering mud: there were also dark and stagnant pools, the abodes of the tadpole, the bull-frog, and the water-snake; where the trunks of pines and hemlocks lay half-drowned, half-rotting, looking like alligators sleeping in the mire.

Tom had long been picking his way cautiously through this treacherous forest; stepping from tuft to tuft of rushes and roots, which afforded precarious footholds among deep sloughs; or pacing carefully, like a cat, along the prostrate trunks of trees; startled now and then by the sudden screaming of the bittern, or the quacking of a wild duck rising on the wing from some solitary pool. At length he arrived at a firm piece of ground, which ran out like a peninsula into the deep bosom of the swamp. It had been one of the strongholds of the Indians during their wars with the first colonists. Here they had thrown up a kind of fort, which they had looked upon as almost impregnable, and had used as a place of refuge for their squaws and children. Nothing remained of the old Indian fort but a few embankments, gradually sinking to the level of the surrounding earth, and already overgrown in part by oaks and other forest trees, the foliage of which formed a contrast to the dark pines and hemlocks of the swamp.

It was late in the dusk of evening when Tom Walker reached the old fort, and he paused there awhile to rest himself. Any one but he would have felt unwilling to linger in this lonely, melancholy place, for the common people had a bad opinion of it, from the stories handed down from the time of the Indian wars; when it was asserted that the savages held incantations here, and made sacrifices to the evil spirit.

Tom Walker, however, was not a man to be troubled with any fears of the kind. He reposed himself for some time on the trunk of a fallen hemlock, listening to the boding cry of the tree-toad, and delving with his walking-staff into a mound of black mould at his feet. As he turned up the soil unconsciously, his staff struck against something hard. He raked it out of the vegetable mould, and lo! a cloven skull, with an Indian tomahawk buried deep in it, lay before him. The rust on the weapon showed the time that had elapsed since this death-blow had been given. It was a dreary memento of the fierce struggle that had taken place in this last foothold of the Indian warriors.

"Humph!" said Tom Walker, as he gave it a kick to shake the dirt from it.

"Let that skull alone!" said a gruff voice. Tom lifted up his eyes, and beheld a great black man seated directly opposite him, on the stump of a tree. He was exceedingly surprised, having neither heard nor seen any one approach; and he was still more perplexed on observing, as well as the gathering gloom would permit, that the stranger was neither negro nor Indian. It is true he was dressed in a rude half Indian garb, and had a red belt or sash swathed round his body; but his face was neither black nor copper-colour, but swarthy and dingy, and begrimed with soot, as if he had been accustomed to toil among fires and forges. He had a shock of coarse black hair, that stood out from his head in all directions, and bore an ax on his shoulder.

He scowled for a moment at Tom with a pair of great red eyes.

"What are you doing on my grounds?" said the black man, with a hoarse growling voice.

"Your grounds!" said Tom, with a sneer, "no more your grounds than mine; they belong to Deacon Peabody."

"Deacon Peabody be d—d," said the stranger, "as I flatter myself he will be, if he does not look more to his own sins and less to those of his neighbours. Look yonder, and see how Deacon Peabody is faring."

Tom looked in the direction that the stranger pointed, and beheld one of the great trees, fair and flourishing without, but rotten at the core, and saw that it had been nearly hewn through, so that the first high wind was likely to blow it down. On the bark of the tree was scored the name of Deacon Peabody, an eminent man, who had waxed wealthy by driving shrewd bargains with the Indians. He now looked around, and found most of the tall trees marked with the name of some great man of the colony, and all more or less scored by the ax. The one on which he had been seated, and which had evidently just been hewn down, bore the name of Crowninshield; and he recollected a mighty rich man of that name, who made a vulgar display of wealth, which it was whispered he had acquired by buccaneering.

"He's just ready for burning!" said the black man, with a growl of triumph. "You see I am likely to have a good stock of firewood for winter."

"But what right have you," said Tom, "to cut down Deacon Peabody's timber?"

"The right of a prior claim," said the other. "This woodland belonged to me long before one of your whitefaced race put foot upon the soil."

"And pray, who are you, if I may be so bold?" said Tom.

"Oh, I go by various names. I am the wild huntsman in some countries; the black miner in others. In this neighbourhood I am known by the name of the black woodsman. I am he to whom the red men consecrated this spot, and in honour of whom they now and then roasted a white man, by way of sweet-smelling sacrifice. Since the red men have been exterminated by you white savages, I amuse myself by presiding at the persecutions of Quakers and Anabaptists; I am the great patron and prompter of slave-dealers, and the grand-master of the Salem witches."

"The upshot of all which is, that, if I mistake not," said Tom, sturdily, "you are he commonly called Old Scratch."

"The same, at your service!" replied the black man, with a half civil nod.

Such was the opening of this interview, according to the old story; though it has almost too familiar an air to be credited. One would think that to meet with such a singular personage, in this wild, lonely place, would have shaken any man's nerves; but Tom was a hard-minded fellow, not easily daunted, and he had lived so long with a termagant wife, that he did not even fear the devil.

It is said that after this commencement they had a long and earnest conversation together, as Tom returned homeward. The black man told him of great sums of money buried by Kidd the pirate, under the oak-trees on the high ridge, not far from the morass. All these were under his command, and protected by his power, so that none could find them but such as propitiated his favour. These he offered to place within Tom Walker's reach, having conceived an especial kindness for him; but they were to be had only on certain conditions. What these conditions were may be easily surmised, though Tom never disclosed them publicly. They must have been very hard, for he required time to think of them, and he was not a man to stick at trifles when money was in view. When they had reached the edge of the swamp, the stranger paused. "What proof have I that all you have been telling me is true?" said Tom. "There's my signature," said the black man, pressing his finger on Tom's forehead. So saying, he turned off among the thickets of the swamp, and seemed, as Tom said, to go down, down, down, into the earth, until nothing but his head and shoulders could be seen, and so on, until he totally disappeared.

When Tom reached home, he found the black print of a finger burnt, as it were, into his forehead, which nothing could obliterate.

The first news his wife had to tell him was the sudden death of Absalom Crowninshield, the rich buccaneer. It was announced in the papers with the usual flourish, that "A great man had fallen in Israel."

Tom recollected the tree which his black friend had just hewn down, and which was ready for burning. "Let the freebooter roast," said Tom, "who cares!" He now felt convinced that all he had heard and seen was no illusion.

He was not prone to let his wife into his confidence; but as this was an uneasy secret, he willingly shared it with her. All her avarice was awakened at the mention of hidden gold, and she urged her husband to comply with the black man's terms, and secure what would make them wealthy for life. However Tom might have felt disposed to sell himself to the Devil, he was determined not to do so to oblige his wife; so he flatly refused, out of the mere spirit of contradiction. Many and bitter were the quarrels they had on the subject; but the more she talked, the more resolute was Tom not to be damned to please her.

At length she determined to drive the bargain on her own account, and if she succeeded, to keep all the gain to herself. Being of the same fearless temper as her husband, she set off for the old Indian fort towards the close of a summer's day. She was many hours absent. When she came back, she was reserved and sullen in her replies. She spoke something of a black man, whom she had met about twilight hewing at the root of a tall tree. He was sulky, however, and would not come to terms: she was to go again with a propitiatory offering, but what it was she forbore to say.

The next evening she set off again for the swamp, with her apron heavily laden. Tom waited and waited for her, but in vain; midnight came, but she did not make her appearance: morning, noon, night returned, but still she did not come. Tom now grew uneasy for her safety, especially as he found she had carried off in her apron the silver tea-pot and spoons, and every portable article of value. Another night elapsed, another morning came; but no wife. In a word, she was never heard of more.

What was her real fate nobody knows, in consequence of so many pretending to know. It is one of those facts which have become confounded by a variety of historians. Some asserted that she lost her way among the tangled mazes of the swamp, and sank into some pit or slough; others, more charitable, hinted that she had eloped with the household booty, and made off to some other province; while others surmised that the tempter had decoyed her into a dismal quagmire, on the top of which her hat was found lying. In confirmation of this, it was said a great black man, with an ax on his shoulder, was seen late that very evening coming out of the swamp, carrying a bundle tied in a check apron, with an air of surly triumph.

The most current and probable story, however, observes, that Tom Walker grew so anxious about the fate of his wife and his property, that he set out at length to seek them both at the Indian fort. During a long summer's afternoon he searched about the gloomy place, but no wife was to be seen. He called her name repeatedly, but she was nowhere to be heard. The bittern alone responded to his voice, as he flew screaming by; or the bull-frog croaked dolefully from a neighbouring pool. At length, it is said, just in the brown hour of twilight, when the owls began to hoot, and the bats to flit about, his attention was attracted by the clamour of carrion crows hovering about a cypress-tree. He looked up, and beheld a bundle tied in a check apron, and hanging in the branches of the tree, with a great vulture perched hard by, as if keeping watch upon it. He leaped with joy; for he recognized his wife's apron, and supposed it to contain the household valuables.

"Let us get hold of the property," said he, consolingly to himself, "and we will endeavour to do without the woman."

As he scrambled up the tree, the vulture spread its wide wings, and sailed off, screaming, into the deep shadows of the forest. Tom seized the checked apron, but, woeful sight! found nothing but a heart and liver tied up in it!

Such, according to this most authentic old story, was all that was to be found of Tom's wife. She had probably attempted to deal with the black man as she had been accustomed to deal with her husband; but though a female scold is generally considered a match for the devil, yet in this instance she appears to have had the worst of it. She must have died game, however; for it is said Tom noticed many prints of cloven feet deeply stamped about the tree, and found handfuls of hair, that looked as if they had been plucked from the coarse black shock of the woodman. Tom knew his wife's prowess by experience. He shrugged his shoulders, as he looked at the signs of a fierce clapper-clawing. "Egad," said he to himself, "Old Scratch must have had a tough time of it!"

Tom consoled himself for the loss of his property, with the loss of his wife, for he was a man of fortitude. He even felt something like gratitude towards the black woodman, who, he considered, had done him a kindness. He sought, therefore, to cultivate a further acquaintance with him, but for some time without success; the old black-legs played shy, for whatever people may think, he is not always to be had for calling for: he knows how to play his cards when pretty sure of his game.

At length, it is said, when delay had whetted Tom's eagerness to the quick, and prepared him to agree to anything rather than not gain the promised treasure, he met the black man one evening in his usual woodman's dress, with his ax on his shoulder, sauntering along the swamp, and humming a tune. He affected to receive Tom's advances with great indifference, made brief replies, and went on humming his tune.

By degrees, however, Tom brought him to business, and they began to haggle about the terms on which the former was to have the pirate's treasure. There was one condition which need not be mentioned, being generally understood in all cases where the devil grants favours; but there were others about which, though of less importance, he was inflexibly obstinate. He insisted that the money found through his means should be employed in his service. He proposed, therefore, that Tom should employ it in the black traffic; that is to say, that he should fit out a slave-ship. This, however, Tom resolutely refused: he was bad enough in all conscience; but the devil himself could not tempt him to turn slave-trader.

Finding Tom so squeamish on this point, he did not insist upon it, but proposed, instead, that he should turn usurer; the devil being extremely anxious for the increase of usurers, looking upon them as his peculiar people.

To this no objections were made, for it was just to Tom's taste.

"You shall open a broker's shop in Boston next month," said the black man.

"I'll do it tomorrow, if you wish," said Tom Walker.

"You shall lend money at two per cent. a month."

"Egad, I'll charge four!" replied Tom Walker.

"You shall extort bonds, foreclose mortgages, drive the merchants to bankruptcy"—

"I'll drive them to the d—l," cried Tom Walker.

"You are the usurer for my money!" said black-legs with delight. "When will you want the rhino?"

"This very night."

"Done!" said the devil.

"Done!" said Tom Walker.—So they shook hands and struck a bargain.

A few days' time saw Tom Walker seated behind his desk in a counting-house in Boston.

His reputation for a ready-moneyed man, who would lend money out for a good consideration, soon spread abroad. Everybody remembers the time of Governor Belcher, when money was particularly scarce. It was a time of paper credit. The country had been deluged with government bills, the famous Land Bank had been established; there had been a rage for speculating; the people had run mad with schemes for new settlements; for building cities in the wilderness; land-jobbers went about with maps of grants, and townships, and Eldorados, lying nobody knew where, but which everybody was ready to purchase. In a word, the great speculating fever which breaks out every now and then in the country, had raged to an alarming degree, and everybody was dreaming of making sudden fortunes from nothing. As usual the fever had subsided; the dream had gone off, and the imaginary fortunes with it; the patients were left in doleful plight, and the whole country resounded with the consequent cry of "hard times."

At this propitious time of public distress did Tom Walker set up as usurer in Boston. His door was soon thronged by customers. The needy and adventurous; the gambling speculator; the dreaming land-jobber; the thriftless tradesman; the merchant with cracked credit; in short, every one driven to raise money by desperate means and desperate sacrifices, hurried to Tom Walker.

Thus Tom was the universal friend of the needy, and acted like a "friend in need"; that is to say, he always exacted good pay and good security. In proportion to the distress of the applicant was the hardness of his terms. He accumulated bonds and mortgages; gradually squeezed his customers closer and closer: and sent them at length, dry as a sponge, from his door.

In this way he made money hand over hand; became a rich and mighty man, and exalted his cocked hat upon 'Change. He built himself, as usual, a vast house, out of ostentation; but left the greater part of it unfinished and unfurnished, out of parsimony. He even set up a carriage in the fulness of his vainglory, though he nearly starved the horses which drew it; and as the ungreased wheels groaned and screeched on the axle-trees, you would have thought you heard the souls of the poor debtors he was squeezing.

As Tom waxed old, however, he grew thoughtful. Having secured the good things of this world, he began to feel anxious about those of the next. He thought with regret on the bargain he had made with his black friend, and set his wits to work to cheat him out of the conditions. He became, therefore, all of a sudden, a violent church-goer. He prayed loudly and strenuously, as if heaven were to be taken by force of lungs. Indeed, one might always tell when he had sinned most during the week, by the clamour of his Sunday devotion. The quiet Christians who had been modestly and stead-fastly travelling Zionward, were struck with self-reproach at see-ing themselves so suddenly outstripped in their career by this new-made convert. Tom was as rigid in religious as in money matters; he was a stern supervisor and censurer of his neighbours, and seemed to think every sin entered up to their account became a credit on his own side of the page. He even talked of the expediency of reviving the persecution of Quakers and Anabaptists. In a word, Tom's zeal became as notorious as his riches.

Still, in spite of all this strenuous attention to forms, Tom had a lurking dread that the devil, after all, would have his due. That he might not be taken unawares, therefore, it is said he always carried a small Bible in his coat-pocket. He had also a great folio Bible on his counting-house desk, and would frequently be found reading it when people called on business; on such occasions he would lay his green spectacles in the book, to mark the place, while he turned round to drive some usurious bargain.

Some say that Tom grew a little crack-brained in his old days, and that, fancying his end approaching, he had his horse new shod, saddled and bridled, and buried with his feet uppermost; because he supposed that at the last day the world would be turned upside down; in which case he should find his horse standing ready for mounting, and he was determined at the worst to give his old friend a run for it. This, however, is probably a mere old wives' fable. If he really did take such a precaution, it was totally superfluous; at least so says the authentic old legend; which closes his story in the fol-lowing manner.

One hot summer afternoon in the dog-days, just as a terrible black thunder-gust was coming up, Tom sat in his counting-house, in his white linen cap and India silk morning-gown. He was on the point of foreclosing a mortgage, by which he would complete the ruin of an unlucky land-speculator for whom he had professed the greatest friendship. The poor land-jobber begged him to grant a few months' indulgence. Tom had grown testy and irritated, and refused another day.

"My family will be ruined, and brought upon the parish," said the land-jobber. "Charity begins at home," replied Tom; "I must take care of myself in these hard times."

"You have made so much money out of me," said the speculator.

Tom lost his patience and his piety. "The devil take me," said he, "if I have made a farthing!"

Just then there were three loud knocks at the street-door. He stepped out to see who was there. A black man was holding a black horse, which neighed and stamped with impatience.

"Tom, you're come for," said the black fellow, gruffly. Tom shrank back, but too late. He had left his little Bible at the bottom of his coat-pocket, and his big Bible on the desk buried under the mortgage he was about to foreclose: never was sinner taken more unawares. The black man whisked him like a child into the saddle, gave the horse the lash, and away he galloped, with Tom on his back, in the midst of the thunder-storm. The clerks stuck their pens behind their ears, and stared after him from the windows. Away went Tom Walker, dashing down the street; his white cap bobbing up and down; his morning-gown fluttering in the wind, and his steed striking fire out of the pavement at every bound. When the clerks turned to look for the black man, he had disappeared.

Tom Walker never returned to foreclose the mortgage. A countryman, who lived on the border of the swamp, reported that in the height of the thunder-gust he had heard a great clattering of hoofs and a howling along the road, and running to the window caught sight of a figure, such as I have described, on a horse that galloped like mad across the fields, over the hills, and down into the black hemlock swamp towards the old Indian fort; and that shortly after a thunder-bolt falling in that direction seemed to set the whole forest in a blaze.

The good people of Boston shook their heads and shrugged

their shoulders, but had been so much accustomed to witches and goblins, and tricks of the devil, in all kinds of shapes, from the first settlement of the colony, that they were not so much horror-struck as might have been expected. Trustees were appointed to take charge of Tom's effects. There was nothing, however, to administer upon. On searching his coffers, all his bonds and mortgages were found reduced to cinders. In place of gold and silver, his iron chest was filled with chips and shavings; two skeletons lay in his stable instead of his half-starved horses, and the very next day his great house took fire and was burnt to the ground.

Such was the end of Tom Walker and his ill-gotten wealth. Let all griping money-brokers lay this story to heart. The truth of it is not to be doubted. The very hole under the oak-trees, whence he dug Kidd's money, is to be seen to this day; and the neighbouring swamp and old Indian fort are often haunted in stormy nights by a figure on horseback, in morning-gown and white cap, which is doubtless the troubled spirit of the usurer. In fact, the story has resolved itself into a proverb, and is the origin of that popular saying, so prevalent throughout New England, of "The Devil and Tom Walker."

THE HERO OF ABARXIA
DEBORAH J. ROSS

WHEN WORD ARRIVED THAT THE WAR WAS OVER, THE KINGDOM WENT mad with joy. The enemy had been soundly defeated at the Vale of Abarxia and their Prince-general, Jarez, had been slain. Each report was more extravagant in its praise of Prince Givors than the one before. Surely, everyone said, he was the bravest of men and the most shrewd and resourceful of military leaders.

The triumphal procession made its way into the capital city and down the broad, straight avenue festooned with pennons of crimson and silver-edged blue. Unmistakable by his golden hair and the noble carriage, Givors rode at the head of his company where all the city could see him and feel themselves part of his glory.

King Mornand watched from the balcony of the Hall of Justice. His chest had been paining him more than usual, his breath failed him with even the smallest exertion, and so he had taken advantage of an old man's privilege and waited for his son to come to him. If his hopes had been fulfilled, then he would soon be able to rest, knowing the kingdom was at last in good hands.

The cortege advanced a little further and now, even with his aged eyes, Mornand saw that Givors no longer rode the heavy-crested black stallion that was the best warhorse within living memory. No, this steed was tall and slender, and its hide caught the light like a shimmering pearl, cream and blue and polished silver. Mornand murmured under his breath, praising all the gods that had ever graced his realm, for this must be one of the legendary aswa horses of the Sahael Desert, famed not only for their speed and beauty but for their fierce loyalty to their masters. He had never heard of one allowing any other than its beloved to ride it, but clearly his son had inspired this one to accept him. It was said that battle tempered men like steel, and what greater proof could there be that Givors had at last risen to the greatness of his heritage?

How Mornand wished he could have been there to witness the final moments of the battle—to see the fall of the enemy and the red flags of victory. To watch Givors raise the victory cup and drain it, the wine overflowing and running in rivulets down his chest—such a sight as had never been seen in all his days. In his younger days, Mornand himself had led his armies and ridden at the head of his horsemen but in all that time, the cup had remained tied to his belt, empty despite his best efforts. All he'd achieved had been an uneasy stalemate that drained vitality from land and men alike. A few deaths here, a few fields overridden there, were followed by funeral pyres and skirmishing back and forth across the trampled land until no crops grew there. And now the son had done accomplished what father and grandfather could not.

Mornand's joy mounted as the parade approached, so much so that he barely noticed how Givors displayed the horse's paces. He saw only the radiance of his son's face and the light that seemed to emanate from his entire body, as if the gods had truly blessed this moment. The prince dismounted, threw the reins to a waiting aide, and bounded up the stairs. A few moments later, he reached the balcony. Tears blurring his sight, Mornand wrapped his son in his arms. The resulting sounds of rejoicing must surely have deafened the heavens.

Then came the necessary pageantry of victory, during which Mornand had scarcely two consecutive private moments in his son's company. On the rare occasions when Givors presented himself to Mornand's chambers, he seemed unable to sit still. He moved about restlessly, gazing out the window or twisting a stray lock in his fingers and then dropping the tangle of hairs on the carpet. Afterward, Mornand gathered up the hairs, fine and gleaming as golden wire, coiled them tenderly, and placed them in a keepsake box.

I entrusted this command to him, Mornand thought, that he might prove himself. Now that he has returned victorious, now that my kingdom will be safe and well-governed, what more can I desire?

This eclipse of a father by his heir was a good thing, a triumphal thing, and if Mornand the man felt a little wistful at times, he was too sage a monarch to complain.

At last came the night of the victory feast. The royal stewards and chefs, the entertainers and musicians, and the wine-sellers and pastry-makers outdid themselves for the feast. Garlands of the finest hothouse roses and ribbons stitched with silver thread adorned the hall, and the tables had been so arranged that the entire assembly had a clear view of the prince. Mornand took his seat and bade the revelers rise from where they knelt. Then a fanfare, composed especially for the occasion, shivered through the air, phrase upon rising phrase of wordless acclaim. When Givors entered through the royal door, the people did not bow as they had to Mornand. They leapt to their feet, cheering and waving, practically dancing in the extremity of their rejoicing. Even as a boy, Givors had always had an instinct for the theatrical gesture, the heroic pose, and now his talents were put to their proper use in generating inspiration and hope.

The feast proceeded with one delicacy following the next, with music and laugher and free-flowing wine. Afterward, there was dancing. Mornand did not lead out the first promenade, leaving that honor to Givors, who selected the loveliest noble-born lady as his partner. Rumors would doubtless spread like wildfire, but the prince went from one lady to the next, always choosing those beauties whose families were rich and powerful. He must wed and he clearly intended to do so advantageously. Mornand had not married for love, for what king had that luxury? Givors had every right to indulge himself with beauty and charm while he could. At one point, Mornand noticed his son's old nurse, who had been granted the favor of a place in the corner, watching the dancing. It was just as well the prince did not notice her, lest even a moment of regret mar the evening.

Mornand retired early, as had become his wont in recent months, with the command that the revelers should continue enjoying themselves, for how many such occasions would any of them see in their lives? He dismissed his usual retinue, save only his oldest and most faithful body-servant and two ceremonial guards. They passed through the royal entrance and into the private corridor that would take them to the king's suite. As the door closed behind them, the sounds of the merry-making dimmed. The light from the fine beeswax candles seemed subdued and they gave off no scent. A man waited beside one of the side doors, shifting from one foot to the other. Mornand knew him, one of the under-stewards.

"Yes, yes, what is it?" Mornand heard the snappishness in his own voice. His joints ached and his heart labored in his chest.

"Your Majesty, I am sorry to—"

"Just say what it is." And get it over with.

"The groom, sire. The one who looks after the prince's horses. He says—it's about the aswa stallion. There's something wrong with the horse, he says. It's languishing."

Of course the horse would languish, if it were as steadfast in devotion as the tales said. For a moment, Mornand felt annoyed at being plagued with such a triviality. And yet, he reflected more soberly, it would not do for the beast to pine away, simply because its new master had other responsibilities. "My own head groom will attend to it," he said, and went on his way.

The next morning, at an appropriate hour and at the appropriate place, the royal groom presented himself, and Mornand knew at first glance that all was not well. The groom's report carried a hint of alarm. The horse was indeed languishing, but not from any physical cause. It might be grief or it might be due to some malign supernatural influence. Would His Majesty care to observe the horse for himself?

His Majesty would not, nor did it please him to diminish the prince's enjoyment of his triumph. Besides, what was the welfare of an animal, even one as rare and noble as this one, compared to the happiness of the heir to the realm and the conqueror of the enemy? The court sorcerer, sojourning these twenty years from his own far-off mountainous land, long noted for arcane arts, would surely know what to do.

Two days later, days in which Mornand had forgotten about the matter, the court sorcerer begged a private audience. For the man, normally so stern and distant, to beg anything was extraordinary. With trepidation, Mornand received the sorcerer in the smallest of his chambers.

It was customary to remain standing in the presence of the king. The sorcerer sat. "As best I can determine, the malady is of the soul, not of the body."

"Horses have souls?"

Dusky brows furrowed. "All that lives partakes of spirit, to a greater or lesser degree. Thus are we joined to all other beings."

Mornand had never felt joined to anyone or anything. Normally, he had no taste for philosophy. Yet the idea intrigued him enough to ignore the sorcerer's lack of respectful address. "Go on."

"Something happened to this horse, most likely during or directly following the climactic battle. Perhaps it witnessed the death of its former master. Without further investigation, I cannot say."

"What form might this investigation take?"

"It is possible—although not entirely without risk—to witness what the horse experienced."

The battle...the moment of victory...Givors dealing the fatal blow to the enemy, Prince Jarez...Givors lifting the victor's cup and draining it... All the things Mornand wished he could have seen for himself.

"You can do this?" Mornand asked, his voice roughened with the intensity of his yearning.

"No, not I. I cannot be both witness and conduit. Some other must undertake the role. Perhaps the head groom?"

Caught by the implications, Mornand ignored the suggestion.

"To be party to the memories of another? Why have you not informed me of such a capability? What an asset that would be, to be able to read the mind of another man—to ascertain his loyalty, his motives! Who could conspire or engage in treachery were such a method to be used?"

"Who indeed?" the sorcerer replied, frowning. "Upon a little reflection, it will become clear why knowing another man's thoughts is to be shunned, not sought. In any event, it is not possible. My order has essayed such an exchange for more than two hundred years, with naught beyond the most humiliating of deaths as a result. The exchange can occur only between beast and man."

"Exchange, you said?"

The sorcerer looked as if he were restraining a sigh of impatience, or perhaps remembering the many times he had attempted to interest Mornand in metaphysical study, and failed. "Two beings cannot share the same memories, the same thoughts, the same consciousness."

"So whoever participated in this enterprise would go into the horse's body, and the horse's mind into his?"

"That is the general idea." The sorcerer seemed to take heart from Mornand's expression of interest. "Precautions would be necessary to ensure that neither physical body is injured. It would be best to sedate the man and place him under restraint, although the horse might merely be confined to a comfortable box stall. There is no need for close physical proximity, once the proper preparation is made."

To see Givors in his finest hour...

"I will undertake this foray into the mind of the aswa horse myself."

For the first time, the sorcerer's calm demeanor wavered. "Your Majesty, you cannot—the risk—that is, it would not be seemly." Visibly, he remembered his position as a foreign courtier, dependent on the king's favor. "For a man of your royal position."

"People have been telling me that since my older brother, who would have been king, died a-hunting when I was five," Mornand snapped. "I must not do this and it is not seemly to do that. I am old enough to know my own wishes, and when last I looked, I still wore the crown. You say that it is possible to witness my son's victory, though it happened a month ago and two hundred leagues away. I say that no man shall have that privilege but myself."

THERE WAS NO NEED AT ALL FOR HIM TO SEE THE HORSE, BUT HE COULD not imagine such an intimate encounter without first acquainting himself with this particular animal. Perhaps, in his heart he knew he ought to ask permission. That, or forgiveness.

The aswa stallion had been housed in the most luxurious portion of the stables. The posts and railings of the box stall were carved with the royal crest. Mornand lifted the latch and the door swung open, silent on its well-oiled hinges. Inside, the bedding was scrupulously clean. The smell of sweet fresh hay overlay something unsettling, not the sour reek of disease but something more insidious.

The stallion stood near the far wall, head lowered, muzzle almost resting on the straw. He did not move when Mornand stepped inside, not even a flicker of those perfectly shaped ears. The brightness of his coat seemed quenched in the diffuse light.

Mornand was not an expert horseman; he could ride well enough, although he had never had to look after his own horses. As a boy he'd loved them, their power and grace and the joy of their speed, the exhilaration of seeing the world from their backs. He knew enough to realize that he now looked upon a horse so sunk in despair as to welcome death. That would be a shame, to be seen as taking such poor care of a rare and priceless steed, not to mention a pity, now that he saw the horse. As he drew closer and laid his hand on the horse's neck, he became aware of the intelligence in the eyes. The gold was dulled, to be sure, but the misery reflected there struck him as unusual, as if the animal were considering his plight in some deep and complex fashion.

He had issued his orders out of purely selfish motives, his own desire to see the battle he himself had never won. The welfare of the horse had been of lesser concern, although as a symbol of his son's greatness, the beast must be seen to flourish. Now it occurred to him that surely this horse, however dim the awareness or misguided the former devotion might have been, was in himself worthy of compassion. Having transferred his loyalty to Givors, the horse might well be suffering the prince's absence. That, too, could not be helped. The demands of royalty and the welfare of the kingdom, as Mornand knew all too well, took precedence over personal concerns.

He ran his hands over the horse's mane and came away with three long coarse hairs, the exact number required for the transfer spell. The hairs shimmered a little, as if some costly metal—white gold or platinum—had been spun into them. These would be knotted with his own in a particular pattern and accompanied by esoteric incantations.

A short time later, when Mornand arranged himself on his bed, his thoughts were already leaping ahead, so eager was he to witness the pivotal and glorious event. The sorcerer wove the hairs, human and horse, together with multicolored strands of vegetable fibers and a few other stringy things Mornand didn't inquire about, and then placed them in a silver box.

"Rest assured, I will guard these with utmost care," the sorcerer said, "for they open the gateway in both directions."

"You mean the horse will enter my mind as well as I enter his?" Mornand asked.

"That. But also for each of you to return."

Instead of the foul-tasting brew Mornand expected, the sorcerer offered a warm drink, pleasantly sweetened with honey and smelling of ripe apples. Surely, nothing but good could come of such an appealing rite.

The potion took hold and he found himself drifting.

HIS FIRST IMPRESSION WAS THAT THE WORLD HAD CHANGED IN HUE, AS IF he had suddenly gone color-blind, and turned very bright. He could see nearly completely around his body without moving his head, and everything smelled and sounded more vivid than he remembered. The effect was so disorienting that he responded without thinking. His muscles tightened for flight. Walls loomed on every side, penning him in. A strange cry shuddered from his mouth. The next moment, several men rushed into the stall and grabbed the straps around his head. They reeked of dead flesh. He tried to pull away, but his rump slammed into the wooden wall and there wasn't enough space to kick. Dimly he realized that the hands and voices were meant to soothe, but he was in too great a panic to control himself. Then, as if the world had given itself a little shake, everything settled into a neat order. He heard a reassuring nicker from the other side of the wall, but it was from one horse to another, and he was not a horse. Or, not entirely.

With that, he stopped fighting the grooms and allowed himself to be walked up and down the neatly-swept dirt aisle until he'd stopped sweating. He relaxed enough to let the horse's own training and instincts take over, so much so that when he was once more returned to the box stall, he thrust his muzzle into the bucket of clean water, drank noisily, and then urinated in the opposite corner. The stall smelled of fresh straw, sweet hay, and the horse's own waste. By this time, he had become accustomed to the animal's thoughts, such as they were.

Remember... he nudged the horse's mind.

The horse's initial response was a wordless version of *Now is all there is.* With a little experimentation, Mornand discovered that what he sought lay not in the horse's present consciousness. He suggested sleep, and the horse folded his legs and lowered himself to the thick padding of straw. Drowsiness came in waves, and through them Mornand inserted his own thoughts, swift and sure like a hawk on the hunt.

As if from afar, he heard the muted sounds of fighting. They came nearer, and with them came vision—vignettes of motion rather than form—and smells. His nostrils filled with the familiar scents of silk and leather, the whiff of sandalwood and clove that perfumed his rider's skin. Try as he might, Mornand could not follow the progress of the battle, although he discerned the shape of his rider's curved sword as it slashed downward and the knots of rapid movement to either side. For long stretches of time, it seemed the horse was either too excited or rushing about too fast to comprehend what was happening. On occasion, he stood with other horses and their riders while his master issued orders and stroked his neck to calm him. During these moments, Mornand felt a pulse of such fierce tenderness, such a sympathy of spirit, that he thought he would be willing to risk any peril, to gallop through walls of fire or swim through lakes of blood, were his master to ask.

I must observe carefully, Mornand remarked to himself, or the horse's animal nature will distort what comes next. His son deserved such a steed, as Prince Jarez surely had not.

The battle settled into a rhythm like the waves on a shore, noise and smells rushing toward the-horse-that-was and then receding, times of movement and of stillness. Always Mornand felt the steadying presence of his rider, the bonds of trust, the response to the occasional stroke of his sweating neck, the gentle pressure of knee or rein. Prince Jarez did not use spurs, nor did he need any. Now and again, Mornand sensed the prince's dismay at the death of his comrades, the flash of hope as the forces of Givors receded, the drenching wash of adrenaline. He heard the screams of men and horses, smelled blood and dust and terror.

The horse advanced, surrounded by the mounted royal guard, prancing with excitement while his rider shouted out orders. Moment by moment, a few strides at a time, they made their way across a field of bodies. Horses stumbled about aimlessly or thrashed where they lay. Here and there, a man sobbed in agony, but many more of them lay motionless. The horse's instinctive revulsion urged him to flee, but the steadfast resoluteness of Prince Jarez calmed his fears.

The racket of fighting diminished as the clash of steel and the shouting of battle cries became distant and scattered. A party of strange horses approached under a ripple of banners. Prince Jarez nudged the horse forward, for a time in the middle of a circle of companions, then alone. From the other party a single rider advanced, mounted on a black stallion. An ordinary horse, sweating with excitement, the black jigged sideways and fought the bit. Ropes of blood-flecked saliva dripped from his jaws.

The two riders went apart from the others, and the aswa horse felt a pulse of brightness from his rider, a flare of anticipation like the first scent of spring green. With a shift of weight, Jarez slipped lightly to the ground. He advanced toward the opposing rider, who dismounted likewise, and although he did not take hold of the reins, the aswa horse came with him. All was as it should be, horse and man bound by a living river of light.

The horse did not understand human speech, but his memory was keen, rendering every moment so vivid that Mornand could follow snatches of the exchange. Out of hearing of the other riders, the two princes were discussing a truce, and now Mornand saw that the flags were white as well as the silver-edged blue Givors used as his personal emblem. A tendril of puzzlement crept through Mornand's thoughts. Until this moment, he had not known of a truce. Givors had reported nothing of it, only of the battle and the vanquishing of his enemy. Perhaps Jarez would now reject the offered terms and storm away. Perhaps—and Mornand in the horse's mind quailed at the thought—perhaps Jarez had violated the traditions of the parley. But the horse felt no trace of alarm, and he would have sensed the flare of anger in his master.

Now the words were harder to understand as the tone of the men's voices became strident. The horse bent his head and touched his muzzle to Jarez's shoulder. Mornand felt the reassurance offered and sought, the memory of the thousand times the gesture had previously united the two. He felt the answering warmth and saw the smile as Jarez turned to stroke the horse's neck.

And watched, through the wide-sweeping vision of the horse, as Givors drew the dagger at his belt and plunged it into Jarez's heart.

The world fractured into chaotic shards, a jagged whirl of color and sound, the strange man—Givors!—shouting, "Treachery! Treachery!" and swinging up on the black horse, wheeling him, digging spurs into his sides...

"To me! To me! Strike them down!"

...the black stallion whirling, trampling Jarez's fallen body...

...the aswa horse himself in a convulsion of rage and madness, hooves flailing, striking flesh and smashing through bone...

...the reek of blood—horse and human—drenching the air, the black horse falling, the rider leaping free...

...a rope, no three, no ten, pinning him to the earth...the strange rider on his back, raking his sides with spurs, his mouth torn by a savage bit...

...loss wailing through the chambers of his mind as if through a desert...

...the slow sinking into darkness...trudging through an eternity of unchanging misery...

...endless...

The land changed and the dust beneath his hooves changed and the harsh, sterile voices of the men changed, and the grief that numbed his spirit die not change...

...endless...

AND THEN IT CAME TO AN END, AND MORNAND SAT UP.

His mouth was dry and his heart felt as if he had wept for a month. He stared at his surroundings, for a moment alarmed that he recognized nothing. With painful slowness, memory returned. He knew where he was—in his own bed, in his own body. Part of him knew who he was—sovereign, father, an old man not far from his own death. He nonetheless grieved for the master he had lost, and also for the son he had never had. Sending Givors to war had not changed him.

His joints protested when he attempted to free himself from the bedcovers and swing his legs over the side. He could have sworn he'd been gone for longer than a single night. By the light slanting through the eastern windows, it was still early in the day. A moment later, a single body servant instead of the usual bevy presented himself, inquired whether the king required his services, and departed with a bow when Mornand declared he wanted to be left alone. The impression of change and the passage of time increased when Mornand, having washed and dressed himself, ventured into his sitting chamber to find a table laid with a simple meal of brown bread, sliced apples, and cold mint-tea. He went to the door, spied a guard not directly outside but a short ways down the hallway, and demanded to see the sorcerer without delay.

Once they were alone behind two sets of closed doors, Mornand confronted the sorcerer. "How long have I been—" despite the impossibility of being overheard, he lowered his voice, "—a horse?"

"A month."

"A month?"

The sorcerer folded his arms over his chest, his brows knotted in a scowl. "I informed you of the risks."

"You did not tell me I'd be lost in that horse's slough of grief for a month!"

"Hmmm."

Mornand heaved himself to his feet and began to pace in order to compose his thoughts. The sorcerer watched, apparently assessing Mornand's mobility and perhaps his soundness of mind as well. With a sigh of resignation, Mornand eased himself into one of the many chairs and schooled his features into civility.

"I have no reason to be angry with you. You did indeed warn me. As was pointed out, the horse had been languishing. I suppose I should be grateful I myself did not languish any longer."

"Indeed," the sorcerer replied with a grunt that indicated he had accepted the apology. "It could have been indefinitely."

Mornand closed his eyes, offering a silent prayer to whatever god had been watching over him. "So tell me what has been happening."

"You may suspect from your physical condition that you did not simply lie abed." Now the sorcerer's expression lightened. "You've been busy."

Mornand thought acerbically that he had indeed, but not in the way the sorcerer meant. He'd been discovering things he would rather not have known. He gestured for the sorcerer to continue.

"You've arranged a peace treaty with Prince Jarez's heir, offering surprisingly compassionate terms. You've given food and medicine to the returning soldiers and made exceptional provision for the families of those who did not return."

Foals must be protected. Once an enemy stallion has submitted, the battle ends. There is enough grass for all.

"You've flatly refused to authorize any new taxes to pay for the rather extravagant festivities in the honor of Prince Givors. In fact, you cut his allowance and reassigned most of his personal retinue to help with the charitable distributions."

"I have? I wonder what Givors said to that."

"The shouting could be heard throughout this wing of the palace. It recurred at even higher volume when you pardoned all thirty men the prince had sentenced to death for sedition, and then removed the prince from his seat on the courts. Shall I go on? I'm sure your own secretary can supply the details of your other decisions."

"I have a secretary?"

Something glinted in the sorcerer's eyes. "I believe Your Majesty set a great many things in order."

Mornand sat in silent amazement. He had done nothing, as the sorcerer well knew. What could a horse know of mercy or justice or the orderly running of a kingdom? Even one of the aswa breed, renowned for loyalty and selfless devotion?

How could a horse in a man's body even talk? The magic must be powerful indeed, or perhaps Mornand's human mind had remembered, even as the aswa horse's mind had done.

Now that he was back in his right body, he must strive to continue what had been so well begun. Yet even as he vowed to himself to be steadfast, he knew that he would fail. He had never been able to deny his son's wishes, not since Givors had been a small boy. It was his failure as both father and king. Had he been able to enforce a healthy discipline, to teach the principles of service, then Givors might have turned out a different man.

How had it all gone wrong? Givors wasn't inherently bad, was he? Mornand remembered the toddler in his lace-trimmed cloak, his hair like flax, flailing about with his tiny bejeweled sword…his face red with fury after he'd slid off the rounded back of his pony, clambering back on, digging in with his spurs and jerking the reins until blood stained the froth from the pony's mouth…

…Givors older now, with a sly tautness around his eyes that smoothed into innocence when he lifted his gaze to his father's… the way the other noble boys would grow silent and hunch their shoulders at his approach…the fuss about the little maid who threw herself from the tower…

Blood rushed to Mornand's head. He felt faint with it, breathless. Chilled. It came to him that the aswa shared some human feelings—

loyalty, certainly, and grief—but not this paralyzing fear. The beast had been numb with grief when Mornand had first entered his mind, but the horse had not remained there. Through Mornand's own body, he had dispensed mercy and kindness.

Protect the foals. Respect the older mares. Defend the weaker members of the herd...

Fear shook Mornand, not only at his own failings but at how little time he had to set things right. He could ask the sorcerer to send him back, to give the aswa a small measure of additional time, but it would not last long. He was an old man who had a few years at most to live, perhaps only months.

No, he thought as he felt an ominous sense of pressure behind his breastbone. Not even that long.

And then Givors would take the throne, without even the ineffectual restraining influence of his father.

Mornand's gaze, which had drifted unseeing about the room, now fixed on the table bearing his private keepsake box. He remembered his own sense of grief that although he and his son might be in each other's physical presence, all pretense of intimacy had long been forsaken. As if the spirit of the aswa horse animated his limbs once more, he went to the box, opened it, and removed the coil of gleaming golden hairs.

His hand did not tremble as he turned to the sorcerer. "Could you make a second charm...with this?"

The sorcerer's black eyes narrowed. "Without the consent of the other party?"

"At the command of his king." Who has too long neglected his duties to his people and his heir.

When it was done, the potion delivered to Prince Givors and all else accomplished, Mornand bade the sorcerer to leave behind the bundle of hairs and dried plants. For long moments, he studied the intricate knots, so like the way the lives of people...and of steeds... might be woven together. As if in the most solemn ritual of office, he carried the bundle to the fire and let it fall into the flames. With that, the power that had sustained him failed and he sank into the nearest chair.

He was dozing when a servant—he could no longer concentrate enough to remember which one—brought a message that Prince Givors requested an audience.

Givors?

The prince entered, not with his usual swagger but lightly, as if he danced over the earth. Just inside the door, he halted and bowed deeply, waiting to be recognized.

"Come closer, my son. My sight is failing."

Before Mornand could draw another breath, Givors knelt before him. Or was it Givors? Mornand could not think clearly. There was some reason why it might not be. But no, the hair like a crown of spun gold was the same, the eyes like the sky on a clear summer's day.

But what was this? Tears? From Givors, who never cried?

Or Givors as he should have been?

"I leave my…" he could not say kingdom, for what meaning did that have for this Givors? "…my herd in your care."

Protect the foals. Respect the older mares. Fight only when you must.

The chin lifted and a ray of light lit the eyes that were so familiar, and for a moment Mornand could not tell to whom he had been speaking. Then it came to him, as the hero of Abarxia bent to kiss his hands, oh so tenderly, oh so surely, that it did not matter.

ABOUT THE EDITOR EVEY BRETT

Evey Brett lives in Southern Arizona with two cats, a snake and her Lipizzan mare, Carrma, who has a habit of arranging the universe to her liking. Evey has attended the Clarion Writer's Workshop for SF/F, The Taos Toolbox workshop, the Lambda Literary Retreat for Emerging LGBT Authors and has an MA in Writing Popular Fiction from Seton Hill University. Published by Lethe Press, Cleis Press, Loose Id, Ellora's Cave and elsewhere, Evey is the author of numerous paranormal and fantasy stories under this name and two others, many of which involve magical horses. "Rafael" is an original story that features characters from her books *Capriole* and *Levade.*

Visit her online at
http://www.eveybrett.wordpress.com

ABOUT THE CONTRIBUTORS

Renee Carter Hall's short fiction has appeared in a variety of publications, including *Strange Horizons, Daily Science Fiction,* and the Anthro Dreams podcast. She lives in West Virginia with her husband, their cat, and a ridiculous number of creative works-in-progress. Readers can find her online at www.reneecarterhall.com and on Twitter as @RCarterHall

Beth Cato is the author of *The Clockwork Dagger,* a steampunk fantasy novel from Harper Voyager. Her short fiction is in *InterGalactic Medicine Show, Beneath Ceaseless Skies,* and *Daily Science Fiction.* She's a Hanford, California native transplanted to the Arizona desert, where she lives with her husband, son, and requisite cat.

Deborah J. Ross writes and edits fantasy and science fiction. Her short fiction has appeared in *F&SF, Asimov's, Star Wars: Tales From Jabba's Palace, Realms of Fantasy, Sword & Sorceress,* and various other publications. Recent books include Lambda Literary Award Finalist Collaborators (as Deborah Wheeler) and The Seven-Petaled Shield, an epic fantasy trilogy.

Cynthia Seelhammer grew up in Minnesota where she taught herself how to ride at age 10 by reading every book about horses that she could find. She lives in Arizona with her writer husband. Cynthia attended the Clarion writers' program in 1992.

PUBLICATIONS

JAMES BALDWIN, "Griffen, the High Flyer," "The Eight-Footed Slipper," "The Horse of Brass," "Al Borak," and "The Winged Horse of the Muses" from *The Wonder-Book of Horses*. New York, The Century Co. Copyright 1895, 1903.

L. FRANK BAUM, "Jack Pumkinhead and the Sawhorse," from *Six Little Wizard Stories of Oz*, Chicago, Reilly and Britton, 1914.

AMBROSE BIERCE, "A Horseman in the Sky," *The Collected Works of Ambrose Bierce*, vol. 2 ("In the Midst of Life") (New York: Neale Publishing Co., 1909). Originally published in *Tales of Soldiers and Civilians*, (San Francisco: E.L.G. Steele, 1891; New York: Lovell, Coryell, 1891; New York: United States Book Co., 1891.)

RENEE CARTER HALL, "Horseman," from *Black Static* #29, April/June 2012. Reprinted by permission of the author.

BETH CATO, "Red Dust and Dancing Horses," from *Stupefying Stories* Issue 1.5. Reprinted by permission of the author.

KATE CHOPIN, "A Horse Story," original manuscript unpublished.

EDMUND DULAC, (ED.), "Ivan and the Chestnut Horse," *Edmund Dulac's Fairy-Book*, New York, George H. Doran Company, 1916.

JACOB AND WILHELM GRIMM, "The Goose Girl," and "The Fox and the Horse," Grimm's Fairy Tales

GEORGE BIRD GRINNELL, "The Dun Horse," from *Pawnee Hero Stories and Folk-Tales*. New York, Forest and Stream Publishing Company, Copyright 1889 by George Bird Grinnell.

WASHINGTON IRVING, "The Devil and Tom Walker," from *Tales of a Traveller*, 1824.

JOSEPH JACOBS, ED., "The Black Horse," from *More Celtic Fairy Tales*, New York: G.P. Putnam's Sons; London: D. Nutt, 1895.

ANDREW LANG, (ED.), "Dapplegrim," from *The Red Fairy Book*, New York, Longmans, Green, and Co. 1890

ANDREW LANG, (ED.), "The Goblin Pony" and "The Magician's Horse," from *The Grey Fairy Book*, New York, Longmans, Green, and Co. 1900.

D.H. LAWRENCE, "The Rocking-Horse Winner," *Harper's Bazaar*, July 1926.

DEBORAH J. ROSS, "The Hero of Abarxia," from *When the Hero Comes Home 2*, Dragon Moon Press, 2013. Reprinted by permission of the author.

CYNTHIA SEELHAMMER, "Gentle Horses," *The Magazine of Fantasy and Science Fiction*, March, 1998. Reprinted by permission of the author.

www.ingramcontent.com/pod-product-compliance
Lightning Source LLC
Chambersburg PA
CBHW020754250626
47155CB00003B/1075